Books by Anina Collins

The Eleventh Hour (Poppy McGuire Mysteries #1)
After Hours (Poppy McGuire Mysteries #2)
Top of the Hour (Poppy McGuire Mysteries #3)

AFTER HOURS

ANINA COLLINS

2016 Eight Feathers Press, LLC

Copyright © 2016 Eight Feathers Press, LLC
Print Edition

Published in the United States
ISBN: 978-0-9972153-2-8

Book Cover design by Natasha Snow Designs
www.natashasnowdesigns.com

After Hours

While life in Sunset Ridge is quaint and charming during the day, what happens after the sun goes down might shock the citizens of this small town. Things are heating up in Poppy McGuire's home town, and it isn't just the July weather.

Poppy and her new partner Alex have their eyes opened to the realities of Sunset Ridge after dark when a traveling salesman is murdered in his room at the Hotel Piermont, a common destination for cheating spouses on the outskirts of town. When they find out what he sells, the mystery gets even more interesting.

Chapter One

M Y CELL PHONE vibrated across my desk in the middle of my weekly meeting with my editor at *The Sunset Ridge Eagle*. I'd made him a very happy boss with my work on the Founders' Day celebration last month, which had gotten the planning committee's coveted seal of approval, and now as I tried to furtively glance toward the message waiting on my cell phone, he began to talk about the same topic he'd latched on to week after week since I began working with Alex.

Me taking over the crime beat feature.

Ever since he got wind of the fact that I'd been a part of cracking the Geneva Woodward case, he'd been all excited about what I could do to make the crime reporting better at *The Eagle*. As if that many people actually read the newspaper or cared about the sundry complaints that constituted most of the Sunset Ridge police department's cases.

It's not that I didn't necessarily want to add on that responsibility at the paper. Like any other writing assignment at *The Eagle*, it would involve reporting, just on the police activity in town every Thursday. I wasn't afraid it would be too much additional effort, but when I thought of my work helping Alex with cases, I felt protective in a way that I couldn't explain.

A big part of me didn't want to share what we did together with the newspaper and its readers. That's why I hadn't agreed to take on the crime beat feature yet, despite my boss's once-a-week pleas.

"I can't think of a better person for this, Poppy. Please say you'll do this. It won't be much more work, and even though it doesn't really involve a pay raise, I think you'd really love reporting on what's going on in the seedy underbelly of this town."

Any attempt at stifling my laughter would fail miserably, so I just let it out right there in front of him and hoped he wouldn't be offended. "Seedy underbelly of Sunset Ridge? Feeling a bit hyperbolic today, Howard?"

He leveled his gaze on me and stabbed his finger in my direction. "You and I know there is some freaky stuff that goes on in this town. Don't deny it. But I'm not even asking you to report on that kind of thing. I just want you to take over the crime feature and include the police blotter each Thursday. All you'll have to do is just jazz it up a little. That's all. Will you do it?"

Glancing over at my phone and knowing it may hold a message from Alex about some new and exciting case, I caved and with a nod agreed to take on the new feature. "Okay. I'll do it."

I'd only seen my editor's face light up once before, and I'd had the busybodies on the planning committee to thank for that. Now as he barely contained his glee, he bounced up and down in his seat and grinned like a kid who'd just had his first taste of cotton candy at a summer carnival.

"This is fabulous! Great! Okay, we'll talk later about

how I'm going to need you to coordinate your two columns, but this is great. Thank you, Poppy."

He bounced out of his chair and stood to leave, but I grabbed onto his wrist to hold him there for just a moment longer so I could make sure I got something out of this new responsibility other than more work and a few pennies.

"Hold on. This new column is going to mean I might not be behind my desk here as often as you're used to. Crime happens outside this office, if you know what I mean. Do I have your word that you're going to be okay with that and not leave nasty sticky notes with frowny faces on my desk calendar passive-aggressively reminding me of things like deadlines?"

In his excitement, he didn't think twice about my request. "Of course. No nastygrams on your desk calendar. I'm just happy to have the person who works directly with the police department writing this feature for the paper. The police blotter has always been so boring, and our subscribers are dying to know more about what happens right outside their doors."

I had a feeling the truth was Howard's bosses and the owners of the newspaper were more the reason behind wanting the crime beat feature beefed up. *The Eagle* may still have been selling copies every day, but with twenty-four hour news stations and the internet, details on just about anything were merely a click or two away. The more exciting crime section of the paper more than likely was intended to entice readers with salacious details instead of real reporting.

I'd avoided agreeing to it for a number of reasons and that one topped the list, but now that I had, if the higher ups thought I'd be writing some glorified gossip column sprinkled with a healthy dose of blood and gore, they were going to be sadly disappointed.

Howard left and I finally could look at the message that had come in during our meeting. I'd seen Alex's name flash across the screen, but that was it, so I was anxious to know what the message said. After nearly three months of rather boring cases involving petty theft and neighbor disputes over property lines, misplaced flower pots, and dogs barking at all hours of the night, I was eager for a real case.

A murder was probably too much to wish for, but a nice B and E could be good. I chuckled at the idea that I now called breaking and entering how Alex referred to it as I swiped my forefinger across the screen to see his text. Just one of the little things I'd picked up from him.

Murder victim found stabbed in his room at Hotel Piermont Room 307. Meet you there.

A.

I knew I shouldn't be so thrilled at the news that someone had been murdered, but for a detective, this was the world series of crime and I got to work alongside the starting pitcher who had already headed out to the mound, so I needed to get myself over to the Hotel Piermont.

Located just outside the main town area of Sunset Ridge, the hotel had a reputation as a common spot for rendezvous between lovers. It wasn't rundown and shabby as much as the kind of place that screamed secret sex. If someone wanted to cheat on their spouse in this town but didn't want to go too far, the Hotel Piermont was their destination.

And with that, our newest case became one hundred times more interesting.

FIVE MINUTES AFTER tearing out of my office at *The Eagle*, I arrived at the Hotel Piermont and parked my car as close as possible beyond the three police cars, the ambulance, and the coroner's vehicle already there. This place wasn't used to all this activity, and parking spots were at a premium after the handful of spaces just outside the building had been taken, so I had to walk nearly a block to reach the scene.

I saw Craig standing outside doing his usual job of keeping nosy people away and doing it well, as always. Since normally he only had to make sure the usual gossips didn't get themselves involved in the all-too-common neighbor disputes that were the usual police cases in town, his excitement at once again working on a case with an actual murder was written all over his face. He grinned at me as I approached the double glass front doors where he'd positioned himself as guard.

"I had a feeling we'd see you here today, Poppy. This one's got juicy details written all over it."

"Craig, I had no idea you loved that kind of thing. Juicy details. I learn something new about you every time I see you."

"Alex asked me to send you up as soon as you got here. They're all up on the third floor. Room 307. We've been here for nearly a half hour, so you might have missed some things."

"Then I guess I better hurry. See you later!" I yelled back at him as I strode through the front doors of the hotel.

The lobby of the Hotel Piermont instantly reminded me of what I imagined Hollywood hotels looked like in the 1920s and 1930s, just without the glitz and glamour. A round royal blue upholstered seat directly in front of the doors with a huge planter in the middle offered tired travelers a place to rest as someone arranged their room. At least that's what it seemed like it would be for, but I couldn't imagine many people who'd driven any real distance ever staying at the Hotel Piermont.

A glass chandelier hung from the ceiling in the center of the lobby, but since nearly half its lights had long ago burned out, it had a creepy, haunted house feel to it that didn't do much to illuminate the area. On the far left, the front desk took up the entire length of the wall, another grand touch that seemed to belong to another time.

Behind the check-in desk were small wooden cubbies with room numbers stuck above them like the type found at home stores to use on mailboxes. Each cubby contained an old-fashioned room key attached to a black plastic fob with the words Hotel Piermont 650 Serpentine Trail Road, Sunset Ridge, MD and a room number written in white. While every other hotel I'd ever visited had changed over to the plastic credit card style room keys, the Hotel Piermont stayed with the old-time style for theirs, which only made the place feel even more like somewhere from another time period.

I saw Derek walking down the worn royal blue carpeted stairs and approached him eager to hear any details he wanted to share. All smiles for me, like usual, before I could get the words out he pointed behind him and said, "Room 307. Your partner is already up there."

"I was going to say good morning, you know, before

I asked anything."

"Well, that's a change. The last time I saw you, I didn't even get a hello or anything," he said in a tone full of skepticism.

That morning I'd overslept and he'd seen me as I hurried to meet Alex for our morning coffee before I had to see my boss. I'd raced right past Derek with barely a wave on my way to our usual table at the back of The Grounds. Being late, I hadn't thought much of it, but now as he stood in front of me, I felt a twinge of regret at how rushed I'd been.

"Sorry about that. I slept through my alarm. I didn't mean to be so rude, though, Derek. You know me too long to think that, right?"

He rolled his eyes and pointed up the stairs. "Room 307, and the next time I see you at The Grounds, I'll take a coffee to make up for this morning. Regular roast, black."

I filed that detail away and patted him on the shoulder as I moved past him on my way to the third floor. "Black it is. I would have thought you were a sugar kind of guy, though. And did I happen to mention how distinguished you look in your chief uniform lately?"

He turned and winked at me as I hit the landing and rounded the corner. "Flirting isn't going to get you out of it, Poppy. Just remember that."

"Got it!" I yelled back as I took the stairs by two to reach the crime scene where the officer standing guard at the door happily let me pass.

I found Alex standing in Room 307 with the coroner discussing the man hunched over the desk on the far wall with a kitchen knife sticking out of his back. The room looked orderly, other than the fact that a dead man was the focal point of it. The bed with its green and yellow geometric print bedspread neatly stretched across it looked as if no one had slept in it recently, and the victim's single piece of luggage sat open and neatly packed on the stand near the closet just inside the door.

All in all, if there wasn't a murder victim sitting there, the entire scene would look perfectly normal, albeit a bit too OCD for my taste. After spending months learning from my partner, though, I knew by the intense expression he wore as his eyes scanned the room that what surrounded the man with the knife in his back was anything but normal.

The coroner, an older man named Donny, smiled at me as he returned to examining the victim. Alex walked over to where I stood in the doorway, and in his usual calm way asked, "What took you so long?"

As I reached into my bag for a pair of gloves, I explained, "My boss. He's a talker, so I couldn't get here any sooner. Sorry."

He smiled and nodded toward the coroner as he flipped through an empty brown wallet. "No problem, but I had to ask Donny to drag his feet since I wanted you to see this before he carted the victim off to the morgue."

"Sorry, Donny. So what do we know?"

Alex thumbed through his little notebook and began reading. "As the victim sat at the desk doing work, the murderer stabbed him in the back with a knife from his room service tray he'd had delivered earlier last night around seven, according to the hotel. He was also stabbed about a dozen times more, all on various locations on his back. He was found by housekeeping at ten this morning when they came by to clean the room and didn't see a Do Not Disturb sign on the door. We've dusted for prints, and I'll be waiting to hear from the lab about them."

"That's a lot of stabbing. Seems like overkill."

Looking up from his notes, he gave me a look that told me my flippant remark wasn't helping. "So what do you think happened to Mr. Canton Walters here?"

I slipped on the same kind of blue latex gloves Alex wore and moved across the room. Looking over the thin man with curly blond hair and a knife in his back, I said the first thing that came to my mind. "I think this guy had at least one enemy who finally took that last step last night. Maybe something he did pushed them over the line. If I had to take a guess, I'd say a female."

"Really? Why?"

I turned back to face Alex and knew he was quizzing me in his own way, so I took the challenge. "Men are more forthright and aggressive. There's something sneaky to stabbing someone in the back as they sit at a desk doing work. That screams a woman to me."

Donny lifted his head at my explanation and gave me a skeptical look. "She'd have to be a pretty strong woman. It takes some power to get a knife of any kind through muscles, and this knife is in there deep."

"Well, I amend my statement then. A big woman. Maybe there's a female weightlifting team staying in the area?"

Alex guided me toward the windows and out of the way of Donny and his men as they prepared to cart the body out. "I've never been to this place until today. You're my resident historian on this town, so what can you tell me about it?"

"Think midnight rendezvous between secret lovers.

Remember Dominick told us that he and Geneva used to meet at a hotel? It's that kind of place. I've only been here once, but I can tell you it looks pretty much the same as when I was here years ago."

"Have you really?" he asked, his dark eyes wide with interest as he stared down at me.

I sidestepped his question, knowing that was his roundabout way of telling me he wanted to know the details of my one time to the Hotel Piermont. Pointing toward the bed, I said, "Either this guy is a total neat freak and makes the bed whenever he leaves it, or this hasn't been slept in."

Donny finished his examination of the man and said, "I'd put the time of death between midnight and four this morning, so he may never have had a chance to go to bed."

I nodded, happy that he'd helped me make my point and added, "He only has one suitcase, and it's filled with neatly folded clothes. Are there any in the closet and dresser, or was he getting ready to leave?"

As Donny moved to let his men take the body, he added, "Oh and about those dozen or so other cuts. I'd venture to guess the killer stabbed him, removed the knife to make the other more superficial cuts, and then stuck it back in the wound that killed him."

Alex raised his eyebrows but said nothing as he jotted something down in his notebook. To me, that definitely sounded like overkill. Why bother to stab him all those other times if they weren't necessary to kill him?

The coroner and his assistants wheeled Canton Walters out of the room, and we searched for any other personal items that might give us a clue as to what was going on when the killer stabbed him. At the closet, Alex announced he found two white dress shirts hung from hangers, along with a black suit, and in the dresser drawers, I found two pairs of underwear and the same number of socks.

Looking over at Alex standing with the dead man's suit in his hand, I said, "I don't think he was planning on leaving just yet. The killer seemed to have different plans, of course."

As I closed the top dresser drawer, I heard him make a noise like something had surprised him and turned to see him holding up something sparkling between his thumb and forefinger. "This was in his suit coat pocket."

He walked toward me, and as he got closer, I saw what he held was a large diamond earring. "I didn't see that his ears were pierced, though, Alex. I would have noticed a rock that size, I think. That's got to be at least a carat."

"More evidence to support your claim that this involved a woman," he said under his breath as he dropped the earring into a clear plastic bag.

I looked around the room for anything else that could tell us what had happened to make someone kill Canton Walters as I made my usual excuses for why I liked to jump to conclusions, which was the complete opposite of how Alex preferred to work.

"I know you don't like when I do things like that, but it's how I am."

"You mean how you throw out unsubstantiated ideas?"

I looked up from searching under the bed and saw him smiling at me. "Yes, that."

"I don't dislike it at all, Poppy. I keep saying you have great instincts. I might not immediately jump to the conclusion that a woman killed Canton, but what you said does have a ring of truth to it, so I'll keep it in mind as we move along in this investigation."

Smiling at how he'd come to accept how I worked, I said, "I'm happy to hear that. I was afraid all my jumping to conclusions muddled your thinking or something like that."

Alex shrugged. "Oh, it used to, but I've gotten used to it."

Running my hand over the carpet beneath the bed, I found nothing, so I stood up and began searching the nightstand while Alex looked over what our victim had been doing when someone jammed a knife between his shoulder blades. The single drawer in the stand next to the full size bed had a copy of the King James Bible and an out-of-date telephone book. I flipped through the pages of both but saw nothing that would indicate our victim had even opened either book during his stay.

"Mr. Walters was filling out expense forms when he was murdered."

I looked up to see Alex leaning over the desk. "Poor working sap. Just trying to do his job and he gets stabbed in the back? Seems pretty unfair."

"It looks like Canton Walters was a traveling salesman, if I'm reading his notes right."

"What did he sell?" I asked as I walked over to take a look at his notes for myself.

Alex lifted the papers to show me. "I have no idea. These forms are generic and have no business name on them to indicate what company he worked for."

I took the papers from his hold and flipped them over. There on the back of the bottom form was a series of numbers. Too many to be someone's phone number,

I instantly saw another clue that a woman had been involved.

"See this?" I asked as I pointed to what had been written on the bottom sheet of paper. "A woman wrote this."

"More proof of your conclusion," he said with a smile. "And why do you think a female wrote those numbers?"

"I'm going to make you a believer in my ideas about handwriting yet. The loops and swirls are quintessentially female. Haven't you ever seen a teenage girl's handwriting? It's like looking at a drawing of a roller coaster. Loopdy-loop and all hearts to dot the I's. Yep, a female wrote these numbers."

He chuckled at my description and shrugged. "I'll have to take your word on this point."

Handing him the papers, I triumphantly announced, "This is a love affair gone bad. That's my theory of the case. Everything points to that."

I didn't really know if that was what had happened, but I liked to see the look on Alex's face when I said those kinds of things not an hour after getting to the scene of the crime. Like always, he shook his head and smiled.

"Do you think we could hold off a little while before deciding what happened? Maybe ask some questions, poke around, and see if anything else comes up? You know, investigate."

I smiled at his making fun of me and nodded my agreement. "Of course, but I just want it known I'm calling this one a love affair gone horribly wrong."

Stuffing the victim's papers into another baggie, he turned toward the door to leave. "I'll be sure to make a note of that. We need to make sure the hotel knows this room is off limits until our investigation is over, and I want to know everything they can tell us about what he was doing here. Ready to get to work?"

"I'm ready. Something tells me this case is going to get down and dirty really quickly. I hope you're prepared for that."

Alex rolled his eyes at me, but I saw he was thinking the same thing I was. Murder at a hook-up hotel? That screamed sex. Maybe my editor was right. Maybe Sunset Ridge did have a seedy underbelly.

Chapter Two

WE HEADED DOWN to the front desk to find the clerk to ask them about Canton Walters' stay at the Piermont. Alex said nothing as we walked down the threadbare carpeted stairs, so I let my mind wander to who our victim may have been meeting with. I didn't recognize him, so I guessed he was likely from out-of-town. He was a traveling salesman, but what was he peddling here in Sunset Ridge? And was he here for any extracurricular activities? Most businessmen wouldn't have stayed in the Hotel Piermont while on a sales trip.

Lost in thought about what our victim had been up to, I didn't hear Alex when he asked me a question, so he nudged my shoulder and said, "Did you hear me? Where were you there?"

I shook my head. "No, sorry. What did you say?"

"I asked you if you'd ever seen our victim before."

Thinking about what he looked like, I couldn't remember ever seeing him in town. "No. Not that he was extraordinary looking so he'd be noticeable, but I can't say I've ever seen him before this morning. Why?"

"Well, I figured since you'd been here to the Hotel Piermont before you might have met him. You know, maybe you passed him in the hall on the way to your room."

Alex's wide grin took the edge off his teasing, but not by much. Irked that he was acting so childish, I put on a fake grimace and said, "Oh, I see. You've chosen to act like a teenage boy today. I'm not sure it's a good look on you, though, partner."

"I have to keep you on your toes. I don't want you to get lax in this partnership."

"I think I miss the old Alex who rarely talked," I joked while I pushed his shoulder.

We reached the first floor and saw an attractive brunette standing behind the counter at the opposite end of the front desk. Alex took his notebook and pen out of his pocket to get ready to ask her questions.

"Why do you get to do the asking? Is it because she's a female? Because I think I could handle it."

Pointing to the silver badge he wore on his shirt, he smiled. "I get to ask her because I'm the cop."

"I keep forgetting that," I said as my shoulders sagged from disappointment that I wouldn't get to interrogate the girl. "I don't know why. You'd think the uniform would be a dead giveaway."

The fact that when I sometimes looked at Alex I saw one of those sexy male strippers who came to bachelorette parties dressed as cops was likely why his new job still hadn't sunk in three months since he started. I could never admit it to another living soul, but there were days that I had a hard time concentrating when he was standing next to me in that uniform looking so incredibly masculine and powerful. I'd never felt anything like that before for any man, so I'd brushed it off as silliness the first few times after he joined the police force, but now months later, I wasn't sure how to handle the reality that

I liked him more than just a partner or a friend.

I felt my cheeks grow warm and knew I was blushing from my thoughts about him, so I turned away and pretended to thumb through some travel brochures that sat on the desk. Thankfully, he didn't appear to notice since he was busy looking over his notes.

"Can I help you, sir?" the young woman asked from the opposite end of the front desk.

"Yes. I'm Officer Alex Montero and this is my partner Poppy McGuire. I need to speak to the desk clerk who was on duty last night. Was that you?"

I watched as she walked toward us with a bounce in her step. Barely in her early twenties, if she was lucky, she had dark brown hair and big blue eyes with eyelashes that were so long and thick they had to fake. Only men had eyelashes like that in real life. She reminded me of a doll I had as a child.

"No, I came on this morning. The night clerk will be back tonight if you want to come back then to talk to them. I don't have the schedule so I don't know who it was, though."

Alex wrote down the details he judged important and after a lull in the conversation, he looked up from his notes and asked, "And your name is?"

"Elizabeth Freely. I work as the desk clerk here during the day."

"What time did you start your shift this morning, Elizabeth?"

"I start every day at seven AM sharp."

Alex continued to write in his little notebook, so I followed up his question with one of my own. "Did you see anything strange when you came to work today?"

He shot me a glance and then returned to writing as

Elizabeth began to explain what she'd seen that morning.

"No. I don't think so, at least. I got here at about quarter to seven and clocked in at seven exactly. They don't like me to begin work early because I was getting overtime for a while and they didn't like that."

"Who are they?"

"The owners and my boss."

Alex stopped writing and set his notebook and pen on the counter. "As you were saying, Elizabeth."

Her big blue eyes showed her confusion for a moment, but then she continued with a rundown of her day so far. "Oh, yeah. I clocked in and then immediately began setting out the continental breakfast. After I set out the coffee, danishes, and muffins over there in the corner of the lobby, I returned to my post and I've been right here ever since."

"And you saw nothing odd?" Alex asked as he turned to look in the direction where the breakfast had been laid out. Seeing nothing there, he looked back at her and asked, "Who cleaned up after breakfast was over?"

Elizabeth looked confused again and then giggled in a way that made me think I might have been too generous to guess she was in her early twenties. "Oh, well, that was me, of course. I'm sorry. I guess I'm just not very good at this, am I?"

I instantly realized the giggle and her response were flirting. She was flirting with Alex. Curious to see his reaction, I turned to look at him and saw him doing exactly what he'd done with Shelley Steadman that day. I didn't think it could bother me more than it had then, but as I stood there feeling like some kind of unwanted third wheel with him and doll-faced Elizabeth, all I wanted to do was smack him and push her face in.

"You're doing fine, Elizabeth," he said in a low voice that told me he thought he had to manipulate this one like he had with Shelley. Personally, I didn't think a girl this young needed that much effort, but who was I to say?

"I wish I could help more…" She leaned forward over the counter and read Alex's name tag pinned to his shirt pocket. "Officer Montero, I really do."

"Well, if you tell me everything you know about Canton Walters, that would be a great help."

Her eyes lit up with excitement. "Give me a second. I just have to go into the office to get that. I'll be right back."

Elizabeth scurried away into the office behind the front desk while Alex returned to writing things in his notebook. Crossing my arms, I stared at him in disgust and waited until he noticed. When he didn't, or intentionally avoided my gaze, I said, "I know you can see me standing here."

As if nothing was wrong, he turned to look at me with a look of innocence I knew was forced. "Something up, Poppy?"

"I think I might need a shot of insulin after that little exchange."

He tried to keep a straight face, but he couldn't, and a slow smile spread across his mouth. "You know how I work. I figured she'd respond better if I acted a little friendlier."

"Trust me. You didn't have to with this one. She's more than eager to please. It's written all over her kewpie doll face."

Alex arched one dark eyebrow. "I'll keep that in mind."

Elizabeth returned with a handful of papers and set them down on the desk. With a quick smile for Alex, she said, "Canton Walters stayed in Room 307 the entire time he was here. He checked in on July 3 and paid for a week in advance in cash. He wasn't scheduled to check out until July 9. You know, I think I remember seeing him this morning at breakfast."

I put my hand down on her stack of papers to stop her. "Are you saying you think you saw him sometime after seven this morning down here in the lobby?"

She blinked a few times like she'd just noticed I was standing there and nodded at me. "Yes."

Alex said nothing, but I saw him write something in his notes and then draw a big question mark next to it. Looking up, he asked her, "Can you tell me where Mr. Walters was from? Did he give an address?"

Shaking her head, she didn't even look down toward the information on the papers in front of her. "No, he didn't."

Before Alex could respond, I quickly asked, "You aren't even going to look at any of those sheets of paper to check?"

Elizabeth looked at me for a moment and then focused on Alex. "I don't have to. We aren't that type of hotel. The people who come here usually aren't interested in giving out too much personal information, if you know what I mean."

By the time she finished, her gaze was firmly on Alex's face, and I had the feeling she was trying to throw a hint out to him. Although my partner was more than adept at using sexuality to get the answers he wanted out of people, he was also able to turn the charm off as easily as he turned it on and even though Elizabeth clearly liked him, he didn't seem to have much interest in her after drawing his question mark in his notes.

"Thank you, Elizabeth. If we need to speak to you again, we can find you here working during the day?" he asked flatly without a hint of what he'd been just a minute ago.

"Yes. I'm here every day but Sunday."

And with just as little emotion as when he asked his last question, he thanked her and turned to walk back up the stairs. Elizabeth looked at me with a thoroughly confused expression as if I could tell her how he'd slipped away so suddenly, but I just gave her a forced smile and hurried away to follow him back upstairs.

I caught up with him just as he hit the second floor. "You know that kind of hot one minute cold the next thing you do could confuse a poor girl like her."

He stopped walking and turned to face me. "So it's a problem when I turn it on, and it's a problem when I turn it off. I don't think you can have it both ways, Poppy."

"It's not a problem for me either way. I'm just saying poor Elizabeth down there thought you two were on the same wavelength and then you went ice cold on her and walked away. That's all. You don't act that way toward me, so it's not an issue for me personally."

"Good. Now what do you say we talk to house-keeping and see if they can tell us anything more about Mr. Walters?"

As we walked down the hallway looking for someone to talk to, I asked, "What do you think of her claim that she saw the victim at breakfast this morning?"

He turned and smiled. "I think she lied. I called Donny on my way up here and he says rigor mortis had begun to set in by the time we got to the victim, so there's no way he could have been able to show up at breakfast after seven."

"The question is why then."

"Exactly. Why would innocent Elizabeth Freely lie to us about seeing a dead man at breakfast?"

I couldn't hold back commenting on how he'd characterized the desk clerk and mumbled under my breath, "Innocent my ass."

He chuckled but said nothing, instead waving at a member of the housekeeping staff at the end of the hallway. She stopped and instantly looked terrified to see a policeman coming toward her.

"Is something wrong, officer?" she asked in a shaky voice.

Alex gently touched her arm to calm her, and that's all it took to bring a smile to her face. "We're just hoping to speak to the housekeepers who handled Room 307."

She pointed toward the ceiling. "We each have our assigned floors, and I only do this one, but there are two of us who handle the third floor. Penny and Marilyn have the top floor. I don't think you'll find them up there right now since it's break time, but I can take you down to the basement where we all take our breaks."

"Thank you. If you'll lead the way, we'll follow you," he said sweetly.

She took us down a back staircase to the basement where five other women dressed in light blue housekeeping uniforms sat around a card table with a single light above their heads and surrounded by concrete walls. Each of them looked terrified when we walked into their break room, but Alex quickly turned on the charm to calm them, although it seemed far more genuine with them than it had with the desk clerk a few minutes earlier.

"Please don't worry. I'm not here to accuse anyone of anything. I'm Officer Alex Montero and this is Poppy and we're investigating the murder in Room 307. We just want to ask some questions about the room and the man who was staying there for the last few days."

A pretty blonde looked up at us and I saw sadness in her eyes. "You mean Mr. Walters? I can't believe anyone would murder him. He was just the sweetest man."

"Did you have occasion to speak to him? What is your name?" Alex asked as he leaned against a stack of boxes full of toilet paper rolls.

"My name is Penny. Penny Sanders. Mr. Walters never refused cleaning each day, was always out of his room by 10 AM when we begin our cleaning, and always left a tip in the room along with a nice note. If only all the people who stayed here were like him."

Remembering the handwriting I'd thought was a female's, I asked, "Did you happen to keep any of those notes, Penny?"

"I did," she said excitedly as she stuffed her hand into the pocket in her maid's uniform. Pulling out a tiny piece of paper folded in half, she held it up for everyone to see. "Here it is! I saved it because it was so nice."

"Can I see that, Penny?" Alex asked and reached over to take it from her.

As she continued talking about how awful it was for someone to hurt such a wonderful man, Alex and I read the note.

Thanks for everything. You're the best!

I looked up at Alex as I pointed at the loops and swirls of the handwriting. "It's the same as the note we found with just numbers. Now I'm sure it's a female who wrote both of them."

An older woman at the end of the table piped up and said, "He wasn't that wonderful. I'm not saying I wished him dead, but he wasn't as nice to me when I had his room."

Looking up from the note, Alex and I focused on the woman and he said, "I thought Penny was his housekeeper."

"She was the last couple days, but for the first two days of his stay, I was the one assigned to Room 307."

"What's your name?" he asked as he got out his notebook and pen again.

"My name is Marilyn Angerson."

As he wrote down her information, I studied this woman and saw how different she was from everyone else sitting around that table. Much older than the rest of the housekeeping staff, she had golden blond hair with grey mixed in that even her hair dye couldn't cover, and she wore her shoulder-length hair in a teased style more popular to a generation or two ago than now. She also had deep lines in her face, especially around her mouth and eyes, all of which told me she was likely in her fifties or even older.

Marilyn also had a different way of approaching people than her co-workers, if the scowl she wore as Alex spoke to her was any indication. I had a feeling no amount of charm would work on her.

"So you didn't find the victim to be as pleasant to

you as Penny says he was with her?" he asked.

She sneered at the question and then at Penny. "No, I did not. In the two days I was assigned his room, he left no tip whatsoever and no cute note thanking me for doing my job."

The rest of the housekeepers erupted into laughter, and a dark haired woman close to where Alex and I stood said, "That's because you're as mean as a hornet. He probably saw you in the hallway when he was leaving one morning and you gave him that look of death you always have on."

The woman next to her chimed in and added, "And you're not very good at your job. I see you outside taking smoke breaks all the time during the day."

Marilyn's mouth dropped open, and then she angrily pushed her chair out from the table and stormed out of the room. The other housekeepers laughed as she left and began talking among themselves about her.

I turned to face Alex, who looked like he couldn't figure out how he'd lost control so quickly. Patting his shoulder, I said, "It's okay. You never had a chance once the first one decided it was hunting season on Marilyn. It's best to just sit back and let it all unfold because if you try to get involved, they'll eat you alive."

He didn't say anything, but instead asked them all for their names before he put his notebook and pen away. "Thank you, ladies. We'll be in touch if we need any more information."

I followed him up to the first floor where he stopped for a moment. Turning toward me, he pointed toward the upper floors. "I think I want to head back up to the room to look at a few things. Do you have to get back to work?"

"That's right! I forgot to tell you. It's looking like I'll be able to spend more time away from my desk from now on. I'll be able to come along for more cases."

His face showed his confusion. "What happened?"

"I'll tell you on the way upstairs. By the way, I'm waiting for you to admit that I was right about a female writing those notes. No self-respecting male would be caught dead writing like that."

We walked up the stairs, and he agreed I was likely correct about that detail. "I'll give you that it's a possibility, but I want to hear about what's changed at your work that means you'll be out more."

As we hit the third floor, I said, "I agreed to take on the crime beat feature each week, so in exchange for me saying yes, I made my boss agree that I'd be able to be out with you more since crime isn't going to be happening in my office. At least I hope not."

Alex seemed surprised at my news. "Really? That's good. Any more money or just more work?"

He'd listened to me complain about how little *The Eagle* paid a number of times before, so he knew more pay would be an incentive for me to take on more responsibilities. "No, but I was happy to get the ability to leave more often so I could join you like this today, so I figure that's a good trade off."

At the doorway to Room 307, he turned to face me wearing a serious expression. "Do they expect you to put details of our investigations in the newspaper?"

I couldn't help but smile. Always so serious when it came to the job, he naturally would ask that. "No, I think they want me to make the police blotter sexier and more interesting. I have no idea how I'm going to do that, though."

That dire look he wore when he was worried faded away. "Oh. Okay."

He stepped into the room, but I stopped him to explain myself. He needed to know, if he didn't know already, that he could trust me. "Hey, I would never share details about the cases we work on. You know that, right?"

"Of course. I was just worried they'd try to force you to do something to keep your job. I don't want to see what we do together endanger your work."

"This is just as much my work as writing my columns for *The Eagle*, Alex."

For a moment, we stood there awkwardly staring at one another, but then he smiled and walked over to the desk Canton Walters had been sitting at when he was murdered. Changing the subject, he slipped on a pair of gloves, took out the papers we'd found there, and lay them on the desk in their original position.

"I wanted to take a better look at the handwriting in these forms and compare it to the two notes we have from him."

I joined him and immediately saw the handwriting on Walters' business forms wasn't the same as the writing on the notes. The numbers and words on the expense sheets showed a male had written them. They had no loops and no swirls like the notes had.

Pointing at the male writing on the top sheet, I said, "See? This is what male handwriting looks like. Nothing fancy, nothing girly. Canton Walters sat here and wrote on these forms, but he didn't write those notes."

Alex nodded but said nothing. Maybe he didn't agree, but he was wrong if he didn't. Those notes were written by a woman, and I was convinced that same woman was likely the person who jammed that knife into his back to kill him. Now the question was why.

What had Canton Walters done to his killer to make them angry enough to stab him in the back?

Chapter Three

THE MORNING BREAKFAST rush had ended and the lunch crowd hadn't arrived yet, so the Madison Diner was almost completely empty when Alex and I arrived at just before noon. Unlike at The Grounds where we had our usual spot, neither of us had spent much time at the most popular diner in Sunset Ridge since becoming partners a few months ago, so as we walked into the main dining room and saw the sign that said Seat Yourselves, we stopped and looked around and then at one another.

"Any particular place you want to sit?" I asked him.

He scanned the diner another time and then pointed toward a booth in the back left of the restaurant. "We should be able to get some privacy back there. I don't want people hearing us talking about the case."

"Lead the way."

I followed him to the most secluded table in the Madison and took a seat with my back to the rest of the room. I hated being in that position, but I imagined it would be awkward if I sat next to Alex on the opposite side of the table. Plus, I hated when couples did that. As if they couldn't be separated by even a table for a meal without missing one another.

"You look uncomfortable, Poppy."

I noticed I'd been fidgeting since I sat down and stopped my legs from moving. "I don't like sitting with my back to an entire restaurant. What if someone came in and I was in danger and couldn't see it because my back was turned?"

He cracked a small smile. "You mean like a ninja? Because other than that, you're safe. I can see the entire restaurant, and I wouldn't let anything happen to you."

"And if a ninja shows up?"

"Then we die together right here in the Madison Diner because I'm good but I'm not sure I'm ninja good."

The server arrived with menus just as I was about to chastise Alex for slacking off on his skills. A short, round woman in a traditional black and white waitress uniform, her white name tag said her name was Dorothy. I lifted my gaze from her name to look at the face of the woman with a name last popular in the 1950s and saw a person who looked no more than forty years old. Fifty tops, but her face wasn't even as wrinkled as Marilyn's from the hotel.

Maybe her parents had been fans of the Wizard of Oz.

When she spoke, a distinctive New England twang came through loud and clear. "What can I get you to drink, hon?"

I doubted the coffee at the Madison would be like the dark roast I liked, so I reconsidered having another cup of caffeine and smiled at her as I said, "I'll have an iced tea."

She nodded but wrote nothing down before turning to look at Alex. "And you?"

"Coffee. Black."

"Right back," she said with a smile like she approved of Alex's beverage choice.

I scanned the laminated cream colored menu for what to eat and noticed how nearly every dish the Madison offered seemed overloaded with cholesterol. The word fresh appeared to be foreign here. I'd been to the diner a few times years ago, but once The Grounds opened, the Madison had little to offer and I'd abandoned it. Now I remembered why.

Peering over the menu at Alex, I asked, "So what's your feeling on The Case of Canton Walters and The Kitchen Knife in the Back?"

He lowered his menu so I could see only his dark eyes and raised his eyebrows. "Is that what we're calling it?"

I may not have been able to see his smile at the name I'd given our newest case, but I heard it in his voice. He definitely was a serious guy, but in the past few months he'd gotten used to my sense of humor and even lightened up a little around me. I liked that. It made him easier to work with and made me feel less like his inferior.

"Like the Sherlock Holmes stories. It's catchy, don't you think?"

He lowered his menu to the table and laughed. "About as catchy as the fried crab cake salad with cole slaw and fries listed under Healthy Choices on the bottom of the menu."

"Don't get that. I'd hate to see you stroke out right here before we find out who killed our victim," I joked.

"No fried crab cake salad for me then. We've narrowed it down to a female, so that eliminates half of the population already."

I sensed he was poking fun at me. He didn't believe anyone had been eliminated. "You doubt my handwriting expertise?"

"Not necessarily. I just don't feel as sure as you do that Walters was killed by a woman."

Dorothy returned with my iced tea and Alex's coffee and took our order, again writing nothing down. Not that I didn't think she could remember a chicken salad sandwich with chips and a pickle for me and a ham sandwich on rye with a pickle but no chips for him, but I always felt more comfortable when servers wrote something down when I ordered.

As Dorothy headed to another table, Alex continued our conversation where we'd left it. "I will admit, though, that I've never seen a man write like you pointed out, but then again, I can't say I've ever put much thought into it."

"That's because as a male you didn't spend hours writing your boyfriend or crush's name in the margin of your notebooks every day of high school. Trust me. I know handwriting, and those two notes were written by a woman."

The steam floated up from his coffee cup, but still he lifted it to his lips to take a drink. Before I could open my mouth to warn him it was still too hot, he burned his tongue and dropped the cup onto the saucer. Coffee splashed everywhere, hitting him down the front of his uniform and me all the way across the table.

"Hang on!" I said as I jumped up to grab napkins from the dispenser sitting on the end of the table. I took a handful and awkwardly hovered my hands over his chest, unsure if my desire to help would be crossing some line. Finally, I just gave them to him to replace the single one he'd saturated already and returned to my seat.

As he dabbed the napkins over his shirt, he said with a hint of embarrassment, "I should have known it was still too hot. My mind must be somewhere else."

I wiped up the spilled coffee from the table and threw away the used napkins in the garbage behind the waitress station before returning to the table. Alex looked upset about the accident, so I tried to lighten his mood by joking. "You know this wouldn't happen if you used milk. It cools it down."

Despite himself, he smiled and nodded. "I can see that, but I wanted my coffee black."

Feeling good about taking his mind off the coffee mess, I asked, "So other than the female who wrote those notes, do we know anything else?"

He started to remind me about Elizabeth Freely's lie concerning seeing Canton at breakfast that morning when someone yelled my name. I turned to see Bethany making a beeline toward us, her wide eyes and huge smile showing how thrilled she was to see me.

Or Alex. I wasn't sure.

"Hey! What are you doing here?" she asked before turning to offer her hand to Alex. "Hi, I'm Bethany. I work with Poppy over at *The Eagle*."

He shook her hand and introduced himself like he always did with people he didn't feel he had to manipulate or cajole into giving him information. His voice was deep and steady and indicated no excitement, and he said no more than he had to.

Not that this deterred Bethany. I knew her far too well to expect that. She appreciated a good looking man too much to let him get away with just telling her his name and then ending the conversation. She'd had to wait all these months to finally get her chance, and she wasn't going to let it pass.

Flashing him another pretty smile, she asked, "How do you like it here in Sunset Ridge?"

Alex politely told her he enjoyed his adopted hometown but said nothing more. He was pleasant and civil, as he always was with people he didn't know.

And still she continued talking. "I bet it's boring for someone who's spent time in a great city like Baltimore, but we have some things here that might interest someone like you."

I wasn't sure if he'd caught the meaning behind her words, but I knew what Bethany hitting on someone sounded like loud and clear. I'd seen it many times for myself.

For his part, Alex appeared oblivious to her attempts to make him like her and merely smiled and then said, "Poppy has never mentioned you, Bethany. Do you write for the paper too?"

Unfazed by his disinterest, she looked over at me and poked me gently on the shoulder. "No way. I couldn't do that kind of thing, right, Poppy?"

I waved off her false modesty as she continued, now looking back at Alex, "I work in advertising, and I can tell you it's no easy job to get people to want to advertise in a newspaper these days."

Alex didn't seem to have anything to say to that, so I quickly jumped in and said, "It's got to be easier now that the paper is going entirely online too."

"Thank God, right? *The Sunset Ridge Eagle* finally jumps into the twenty-first century. Well, I'm just here to pick up some lunch for the department since we have our monthly sales meeting and it's going to be a doozy. It was great to meet you, Alex. Maybe I'll have the pleasure again."

She extended her hand once more and he shook it for the second time. "It was nice to meet you, Bethany."

She flitted away to pick up the lunch order she'd come for, and without missing a beat, he returned to where we'd been before she came over to the table. "We need to find out what that desk clerk at the Hotel Piermont is hiding since we can be sure she didn't see our victim at breakfast this morning. Maybe she's your female with the fancy handwriting."

For a moment, I sat a bit stunned that Bethany hadn't seemed to make much of an impression on him. Men loved Bethany. She was blond, good looking with a great body, and full of energy, which seemed to be part of her brand of magnetism. I found her exhausting at times, but I'd never seen men feel that about her.

Alex appeared to think nothing of her, though, strangely enough. Unsure if I should say something, I chose to leave the topic of Bethany to him. If he wanted to talk about her, so be it. Until then, I wasn't sure what to say, so I'd say nothing.

"Elizabeth Freely is definitely hiding something. I agree."

"I think after lunch I want to find out where Canton Walters was from, so if you want you can see what you can find out about Elizabeth Freely. I'm a little surprised you don't know her. I thought you knew everyone in this town."

"Not everyone," I said with a smile, knowing he was teasing me about being a small town local yokel.

"Well, then you can dig up whatever dirt there is on

her and I'll find out about our victim."

Dorothy arrived with our lunches and effectively put an end to our conversation for a while. As we ate, the diner filled up around us until it was standing room only by the time we finished our meals. I turned around after taking my last bite of my chicken salad sandwich and was surprised to find nearly all of Sunset Ridge behind me.

"See?" I asked as I pointed to the people who'd come in after us. "This is what I'm talking about. I never even saw them before I turned around."

In his usual calm way, Alex shrugged. "No ninjas, though, so you're safe."

"I guess. So I'll be looking for clues to show Elizabeth knew Canton Walters and might have killed him. Nice way to spend an afternoon."

The pleasant expression slid from Alex's face. "No, I want you to simply find out about her. If you go looking for something to connect her to this case, you'll end up twisting the evidence to fit your theory. You're a fan of Sherlock Holmes. He always cautioned against doing that."

"I know. You're right. I'll keep an open mind and find out whatever I can about our desk clerk."

He pushed his chair back from the table and threw a twenty down next to his napkin. "Good. We'll figure out what's useful and what isn't once you find out about her. I need to get back to the station, but call me and let me know what you find out."

"Okay. I'll make sure to get your change for you too."

Flashing me a smile, he said, "No need. This was my treat. See you later, Poppy."

After he left, I sat there with my back to the rest of the patrons of the Madison Diner and couldn't help but think the whole thing was a metaphor for my life in Sunset Ridge. Just like in the restaurant, I knew all the people around me in town were there, but I did next to nothing to engage with them other than superficial chatter as we passed on the street or stood in line for coffee each day. I didn't know when I'd become this person turned away from all those around her, but other than Alex and Derek, and my father and Bethany, I really spent time with no one else.

Like a train jumping onto a different track, just the thought of Bethany made me wonder if Alex had liked her as much as she clearly had liked him. There was no denying he was good looking, and as much as I rarely thought about it, he was single.

And Bethany had liked him since she first mentioned seeing him a couple months ago. At the time, I knew she had just broken up with Rex and had begun dating someone new, so I hadn't given the possibility of her and Alex ever getting together another thought, but now that she was single again, I had a feeling she would be setting her sights on Sunset Ridge's newest bachelor.

It was more like a sinking feeling.

Why should their dating one another bother me? As my stomach slowly twisted into knots, I silently admitted more than a little jealousy at the idea. Alex and I had been working side-by-side for months and not once had I had even the tiniest inkling that he felt anything for me other than friendship. Yes, it was true by his own admission that he never spent any time with anyone but me, male or female. And it was also true that I'd never shown him that I considered him as anyone but a male friend and work partner.

I had my reasons for not letting myself think of him as anything but those roles in my life. They may have been ridiculous excuses, but regardless, I'd never given him any indication that I liked him more than a friend.

Now as the pain in my gut grew over the possibility that he and Bethany might get together, I regretted not showing him how I really felt.

The problem was I didn't know. Alex had everything I ever wanted in a man, but after a handful of unsuccessful relationships going all the way back to college, I'd basically given up on finding someone. And after being cheated on by my fiancé and publicly humiliated, I wasn't exactly the most trusting soul when it came to men.

And then there was my father. When my mother died, I accepted the reality that I'd have to live in this small town so my father wasn't alone.

Even if it meant I was.

At first I spent a lot of time denying that reality, telling myself that there were more important things in life than getting married and having children. Lots of people didn't live happily ever after, and if I was one of them, then that's the way it had to be. My father needed me.

Then slowly the desire to be with someone who cared for me made me venture out into the dating world. Sometimes it was through blind dates. Other times it was through reconnecting with friends from college. I'd even tried online dating for a while. A few relationships came out of them over the years, but they all ended because I couldn't leave Sunset Ridge.

Not yet.

My father still needed me. He said he was perfectly fine and happy living his life, but I knew better. I saw the sadness in his faded blue eyes every time a major holiday came around and every May when my mother's birthday came up on the calendar. He put on a brave front, but I knew.

Slowly but surely over time, it had become an accepted fact that I was Poppy McGuire, the single girl and daughter of Joe who owned the bar everyone knew of. The town busybodies thought of me that way, as did even friends like Bethany. She never came right out and called me that, but I saw the way she reacted to that time I didn't know if Alex's asking me to dinner at Diamanti's was a date or not that she had mentally tagged me as that girl who was always single.

I felt a tap on my shoulder and looked up to see Dorothy staring down at me. "You looked like you were a million miles away, hon. Do you need anything else today?"

Handing her the check and Alex's twenty, I pushed my thoughts about him and Bethany to the back of my mind and smiled. "No, thank you. Keep the change."

Dorothy returned my smile and patted me on the shoulder again. "Don't worry so much. No matter what's on your mind, it'll all work out for the best."

As she walked away, I wondered if that was true, and if it was, what was the best?

I HEADED OVER to my office at *The Eagle* to begin my search for information on Elizabeth Freely and hoped Bethany's meeting would run all afternoon so I wouldn't have to see her. As I passed the conference room, I heard the head of the advertising department bellow at his staff about them not meeting quarterly projections and threatening to keep them in that room until they all came up with ideas on how to fix their shortcomings.

Maybe I'd get my wish and not have to face Bethany and what would likely be far too many questions about my partner.

Sitting down in front of my laptop, I began my search for any and all information on the Hotel Piermont daytime desk clerk. I found out that Elizabeth Freely had been born in Virginia twenty-three years ago to John and Caroline Freely. She graduated high school after being a cheerleader for the football team for all four years and attended the University of Maryland. I found no evidence of her ever graduating from college, and according to everything I found on social media, she ended up in Sunset Ridge, and like most residents in their twenties, she hated how boring the town was and couldn't wait for the chance to move.

I looked through her posts to find out her likes and dislikes, other than the small town she felt trapped in, and found very little to indicate what she did in her spare time. My gut told me Elizabeth had to be more than just the cute cat memes she posted and games she played online, but there was no evidence of that.

After the basic internet search, I wanted to do a more detailed online database search available to me since I worked for the newspaper, but just as I began, I heard a group of people walk past my door grumbling and knew the advertising meeting had ended all too soon. I didn't want to be caught in my office, so I quickly closed my laptop and grabbed my bag, but it was too late.

As I turned around in my chair to leave the office, there stood Bethany in my doorway looking like someone had killed off her favorite relative. The dejected look on her face told me the meeting had been even worse than what I'd overheard.

"Hey, I was just heading out. Tough meeting?" I asked, faking cheerfulness the best I could and hoping she couldn't see how much I didn't want to be there with her at that moment.

"It was awful. We all got our asses chewed out, so it wasn't just me, but it was still terrible having to listen to Reynolds tell us we all failed last quarter."

"Sounds pretty bad. I'm sorry."

Instantly, her expression changed to one of happiness. "Well, that's not what I stopped in to talk about. I was so happy to finally meet that friend of yours, Poppy. He's a little slice of heaven right here on earth, you know that?"

I wasn't sure I'd ever thought of Alex in those exact terms, but I knew what she meant. Unsure of how to answer, I nodded and forced a smile.

"Did he say anything about me after I left?"

Bethany's eyes had a hopeful look in them that I hated seeing, especially since he hadn't mentioned her even once after she walked away. After the tongue lashing she'd just taken from her boss, though, I didn't want to add to her terrible day.

So I told a little white lie.

"It got so busy in there we could barely hear each other across the table, so we didn't say much about anything. I'm sure he thought you were very nice."

I stood from my chair to leave, sure I didn't want to continue this conversation anymore. Bethany didn't seem to pick up on the sign, though, and said, "He's still single, right? You know him better than anyone else in town since you're best friends, so I figured I should ask you if there's anything I should know. You know, before I go ahead with anything."

My mouth dropped open for a moment as my brain processed her words. *Go ahead with anything.* What did that mean?

I needed to get out of there. Forcing yet another smile, I said, "I think he's single, yeah, but I really don't know much more than that. I have to leave now to do some work he asked me to do, but I'll talk to you later, okay?"

She said something about definitely talking more about him as I brushed past her on my way out, but I didn't hear what because all I could think of were those words *go ahead with anything* as they echoed in my head.

Go ahead with anything.

Bethany planned to ask Alex out on a date, and there was nothing I could do about it because he and I were just friends. Correction. Best friends.

I'd officially been best friend zoned.

Chapter Four

"HOW DOES A trip to Virginia sound?" I heard Alex ask in my ear as I hurried down Main Street to get away from *The Sunset Ridge Eagle* offices.

Stopping dead in the middle of the sidewalk at the entrance of Stildon Park, I created a bit of a traffic jam between two moms with strollers and a little boy on a scooter who all crashed into one another when I stopped walking. The mothers glared at me like I'd broken some well-known adult female rule, so I quickly stepped out of the way as I apologized.

"Sorry. So sorry. I didn't mean to cause a pileup there."

"Poppy, what are you talking about? Did you just get into an accident?" Alex asked in a worried voice. "Where are you?"

"Relax. I'm fine. No accident. Just a little crash between two strollers and a scooter because I was so surprised to hear you ask if I wanted to go to Virginia."

"What are you talking about?"

His worry had morphed into confusion mixed with irritation. Very much a friend response that I instantly hated. "Nothing. So when are we leaving for our road trip and where are we going in Virginia?"

"Right outside of Falls Church. I'll pick you up. Where are you?"

Stuck in the friend zone.

That's what I wanted to say since my conversation with Bethany wouldn't leave my mind, but instead I just said, "Wait for me at the station. I'll be there in a minute or two, okay?"

I didn't give him a chance to answer since it seemed pointless and hurried across the street to the Sunset Ridge police station. Derek sat in his new chief office staring at his laptop, so I poked my head in and said hello.

"Hey you! How's the chief of police doing?"

He looked up from whatever was so interesting on the screen and smiled. "He's pretty good. How's my favorite investigative reporter?"

I sighed as I realized I hadn't told him what happened. "I lost that job, so I guess you can't call me that anymore."

"What happened?" he asked as he folded his arms behind his head.

"Missed too many deadlines. I did get a new assignment at *The Eagle*, though. Did Alex tell you? You're looking at the new crime beat feature reporter."

"No, he didn't. Congratulations, Poppy!" he said with a big smile I knew was genuine.

For whatever else he was, Derek was exactly that. Genuine. And good looking. Interesting that I had yet another attractive male friend I had never been with. This was beginning to be a pattern, and I didn't like it.

"Hey, Derek. What do you think of Bethany?"

He slid his arms from behind his head and sat straighter in his chair. "Why are you asking?"

"I don't know. I was just curious."

"I don't think anything of her. Am I supposed to?"

"No. I was just wondering. I have to go find Alex, so I'll see you later."

As I headed down the hall to Alex's office, I wondered why Derek didn't think anything of Bethany. He was single, like her, and he was probably the most eligible bachelor in Sunset Ridge. In addition, Derek had dated most of the available women in town, so why not her?

Lost in thought, I ran into Alex, or more correctly, I ran straight into his chest as he was coming out of his office. My second traffic pileup of the day left my newest victim stunned, and I quickly backed away to a more appropriate distance from him about an arm's length away.

"Hey, I was just looking for you. Ready to go?"

"Yeah. I didn't get a chance to explain before, but we're going to Canton Walter's house right outside of Falls Church."

As we walked out to one of the squad cars, I asked, "Why would a traveling salesman stay here when he lived only about an hour away?"

Alex opened the driver's side door and tapped on the roof of the car. "That's what I wondered. I'm hoping someone at his house can shine a little light on our victim because so far we don't have much."

"You know what I forgot to tell you before that I think I noticed but you didn't?" I asked as I climbed into the passenger seat next to him.

He raised his eyebrows like I'd offended him, but I knew better. Alex wasn't that prickly about things, especially my figuring things out before him.

"What's that?"

"What didn't you see in that hotel room that virtually everyone has and a traveling salesman would definitely have?"

Starting the car, he took his phone out of his pocket and set it down in the console between us. Smiling, he answered, "A cell phone."

"You did notice, didn't you?" I asked, crestfallen that I hadn't picked up on something first for once.

As we hit the road, he nodded and smiled once more. "I did. I was just waiting for you to mention it."

I slumped back against the seat in defeat. "I hate it when you use that 'patience, grasshopper' tone, you know that?"

He stopped the car a minute later at the last red light before leaving Sunset Ridge and looked over at me as I stewed over still not being as good at this detective thing as he was. I was naturally competitive, but working with Alex brought out my hyper-competitiveness for some reason. It probably wasn't healthy for our partner relationship, but I really wanted to learn from him and prove that I had those great instincts he so often complimented me on.

"Poppy, I knew you noticed there was no cell phone in that room."

"I know. I just want to show you that those great instincts you say I have are really there. That's all."

As usual, he said nothing more, but as we left town, I knew how I was feeling wasn't just because I hadn't beat him to the punch with the phone. I didn't want to think about what was really wrong, though.

WE PULLED UP to the front of Canton Walter's pleasant suburban home, and I wondered how he'd gone from being someone who lived in that red brick house with a good sized yard and well-tended flowerbeds on both sides of the front porch to the man I'd seen slumped over that desk with a knife sticking out of his back in the questionable Hotel Piermont.

"His wife's name is Rose. I spoke to her earlier. I got the feeling she wasn't exactly surprised by her husband's death," Alex said as we got out of the car.

"The first crack in the perfect life of a suburbanite façade," I thought out loud. "Well, not all married people are happy, or maybe it was just shock at the news."

We walked up the white concrete sidewalk flanked by a perfectly manicured lawn too green and lush to be natural and rang the doorbell. Canton Walters' house reminded me of one that might be found in Sunset Ridge, but as I'd learned all too well in the past few months, what could be seen from the street often obscured lives far less perfect.

Alex stood silently waiting for someone to answer, but I knew by the pensive look on his face his lack of interest in speaking meant he was watching and thinking. Of all his traits, I had to admit the ability to simply stand quietly no matter what was happening around him was the one I may have admired the most. Never much for silence, I was his polar opposite, and finally after about three minutes, I had to say something or go crazy staring at the Walters' dark blue front door.

"Maybe she's out. I bet there are things that have to be taken care of when your husband dies. I know when my mother died, my father and I—"

He cut me off with a look more serious than I'd ever seen from him and said sharply, "I know what has to be done when someone you love dies."

I didn't know if I should apologize, so I closed my mouth after it dropped in surprise at how he'd snapped at me and looked away as he banged on the door one more time. He'd never spoken one word about his wife's death to me, and if what he'd just said was any indication of how he felt about it, I wasn't sure I wanted him to.

Finally, after more than five minutes of our standing on that porch in silence, the door opened. A plain woman in her early thirties stood in front of us with a look I recognized immediately. The look of loss. I'd seen it on my father ever since that day my mother died, and sometimes when I looked in the mirror, I saw it in my own reflection.

"Who are you?" she asked sadly.

"Mrs. Walters, I'm Alex Montero from the Sunset Ridge Police and this is Poppy McGuire. We're sorry for your loss. I was hoping you'd be able to speak to us to help us figure out who did this to your husband."

She hung her head and nodded as she stepped back and opened the door to let us in. We entered a house that looked as solidly middle class on the inside as it did on the outside. Mrs. Walters escorted us into a living room to the right of the front door, and as we walked in, I noticed wood framed pictures of Canton Walters, his wife, and their three children above a blue patterned sofa.

She pointed toward them as she offered us a seat. "Those are our children, Canton Junior, Michael, and Emma."

Alex gave them a cursory glance as he sat down, but I took a longer look and saw all three children had their father's curly blond hair and almost angelic face, even the baby girl who couldn't have been older than a few months in the picture. It seemed that none of their mother's traits had transferred to them.

I sat and realized this was the first time I'd ever been with Alex when he had to speak to the wife or husband of a murder victim. Unsure how he'd handle it, I decided this would be a good time for me to begin practicing silence and let him do all the talking.

"Mrs. Walters—"

She raised her hand to stop him and smiled. "Please, call me Rose."

"Rose, thank you for agreeing to speak to us. When we talked on the phone, you said your husband was a salesman. Can you tell me what he sold?"

Her cheeks grew pink, which made her blue eyes even bluer, and then a look of discomfort settled into her face. "Marital aids."

Now I was definitely happy to let Alex handle this visit with her.

He lifted his gaze from his notebook and repeated what she'd just said in a voice that sounded as awkward as she looked. "Marital aids?"

Rose Walters took a deep breath in and exhaled slowly before she answered. "Mr. Montero, my husband was a good man. He supported his family the best he could. I could only work part time once Emma came along last year. He was a high school biology teacher and a very good one, but his pay wasn't enough. So he took on a second job selling for Naughty and Spice Toys."

I'd heard of the sexy toy company once or twice in college. Their representatives held parties much like makeup or candle parties, and groups of women got together to drink wine and giggle about sex toys like vibrators.

"So that's why he was in Maryland this past week?"

"Yes. When he began making more from selling for the company than he made in two years teaching, we agreed he should leave his day job and go where the money was."

She sniffled a tear away and sighed. "If I'd known it would all end like this, I would have never told him I was okay with him leaving his teaching job."

Still sounding uncomfortable, Alex asked, "What did he do to sell the products?"

I lowered my head to stare down at my legs and pressed my lips together so I wouldn't begin laughing. Had he just asked our victim what he did to sell sex toys to groups of drunk women? He surely had never experienced a Naughty and Spice party or he would have never asked such an indelicate question.

"What are you implying?" Rose snapped.

I quickly felt Alex's control over the situation begin to slip away, so I looked up and gave her my best sympathetic smile as I explained why he didn't seem to have a clue at the moment.

"Rose, please excuse my partner. As you can see by the confused look on his face, he's a typical bachelor who has no idea about parties women have when they want to buy makeup, kitchen containers, candles, or sex toys. But I know, so please understand he meant no harm. He just doesn't know."

Her eyes studied me for a long moment like she was

trying to figure out if I was someone she could trust, and then she nodded and smiled at the two of us. "I'm sorry. I shouldn't have snapped like that. I know a lot of people didn't respect Canton for what he did for a living, and I thought you were one of those people."

"Thank you for understanding. He's such a typical guy that he just doesn't know."

I elbowed Alex in the side and turned toward him hoping he understood the look I was giving him meant back off from asking any more questions about what our victim did at his job. For his part, he seemed confused about what had happened but understood the look I shot him and returned to asking other questions we needed answered.

"When did you last hear from your husband, Rose?"

"The night before last. He called me to tell me he had to stay over in Maryland because it was late and he didn't feel right about driving. He said he'd only be gone one night, so I didn't think much of it."

Instantly, my mind kicked into high gear. Why would he have felt uncomfortable driving on a Tuesday night? The weather that night had been gorgeous. Clear skies, lots of stars and a full moon shining lots of light, and not a drop of rain to be found. And why had Canton lied to his wife about only being gone for one night when he'd been at the Hotel Piermont for days before?

"Did he give you a sense of why he didn't feel right about driving the hour or so back home?" Alex asked.

I heard the indictment from one man about another in Alex's voice and hoped Rose didn't hear it too. I didn't want to have to explain to her again how he was perfectly clueless, especially since I couldn't account for his clumsiness with her. He was never this way when he questioned people, and this was the widow of a murder victim, for God's sake. Of all people, he should know how delicately he should be approaching her.

But Rose didn't seem to pick up on his tone and simply answered, "At first I thought he sounded strange, like he had the flu or something, but I think he had stopped at a bar for a drink or two and didn't want to risk getting a DUI. He wouldn't have been able to make any money if he couldn't drive, you see."

"I understand. So when he didn't arrive home, did you try to call him?" Alex asked, his voice ever-so-slightly less accusing.

"I took the children to my mother's to celebrate the Fourth of July holiday, so I didn't return until this morning. I'd just gotten home when you called to tell me the news."

"Is your mother's house close?"

Rose began to cry and covered her face with her hands. "Just a few miles north in Wolf Trap. I just can't believe this happened. All he wanted to do was make an honest living. Why would anyone kill him?"

Still fixated on her calling him, he asked again, "So you didn't try to call him when you got home and didn't find him here?"

She lifted her face and wiped her tear-stained cheeks. "Yes, I did, but I got no answer. I trusted him, so I didn't really worry, but then you called and I knew why he hadn't answered."

Rose started to sob again, so I nudged Alex and looked toward the door. "We're so sorry for your loss," I said as I gently patted her arm. "Thank you for your time. We can see ourselves out."

She nodded as she continued to cry, and we left even as I practically had to pull Alex out of the house. When we got to the car, I saw he still had no idea of what had happened in there.

Closing the door, I turned toward him in the front seat and grabbed his arm to stop him from starting the car. "Hold on. What was going on with you in there? You aren't that clueless, so what gives?"

He looked at me and gave me one of those sly smiles that often made me want to shake him. "I'm happy to know you don't think I'm a thoughtless idiot, Poppy. I'd hoped you thought more of me."

Frustrated, I slumped back against the seat. "Alex, please tell me you didn't think it was okay to practically accuse the victim of sleeping with other women as you talked to his widow? That's all I want to know."

"I asked her that question to see if she thought he was sleeping with other women. You're the one who said from the very beginning of this case that you thought a woman was involved."

"Oh. Sorry," I mumbled. "I guess I should have trusted you."

Alex started the car and drove away from Canton Walters' nice suburban house. "I will admit one thing, though. You didn't lie to her when you said I have no idea what happens at those parties. I just found it unlikely that a guy selling sex toys to a bunch of women wouldn't get hit on, so I asked her to find out what he did."

Driving down the highway toward Sunset Ridge, I thought about what he said. "You know what? I've been to parties like those. Not Naughty and Spice parties, but similar ones, and I can tell you women get a little wild at them. The combination of alcohol and sex toys makes for a pretty rowdy time. I'm having a hard time imagining our victim not getting hit on a lot at them. He was a good looking guy. Not my type, but I can see lots of women liking him. That blond sort of surfer guy look with a touch of innocence works for some women."

Alex chuckled and passed a truck before turning to look at me. "I don't think I would have described Canton Walters like that in a million years."

"You're not a woman. We see things differently. That's what makes us such good partners. Dark and light. Yin and yang. You know, opposites."

"I don't know if we're dark and light, but I'll agree to the opposites. So Yin, what did we learn from Rose?"

"We learned our victim was lying to his wife. He wasn't home all that time and then gone for one night, so if she knew what he did for a living, why would he lie?"

Pursing his lips, Alex shook his head. "I have no idea. We need to get the details about his cell. I want to see if she actually called him when she said she did."

"Do you think we should consider her a suspect?"

With a smile, he said, "Definitely. The spouse is always the first one to look at when someone is murdered, if just to cross her off the list. For now, she may not be a formal suspect yet, but I'm not ruling her out, by any means."

I thought about Rose saying she was at her mother's for the past week and said, "Imagine having a mother-in-law who lived in a place called Wolf Trap."

Alex smiled. "If this was a novel, I'd say that would be a huge clue that one of those women did something to him. Do me favor and look to see how far that town is from Sunset Ridge and then how far it's from their house."

I took out my cell phone and in seconds I had my answer. "It's less than fifteen minutes from their house. It's about forty-five miles from Sunset Ridge and just under ten from where they live."

"Certainly not far enough to make it impossible for her to get up to Sunset Ridge, kill her cheating husband, and then get back to her mother's."

"So you agree a woman is involved?" I asked excitedly, happy to think he was coming around to my idea, as hasty as it may have been.

"I never thought you were wrong, Poppy. I think you've been right about the handwriting from the beginning. We just need to find out whose handwriting that is since it isn't Rose Walters."

Now he'd amazed me. How did he know that? "How can you say that? Did you slip a letter of hers in your pocket as we were leaving?"

He shot me a sideways glance. "Who writes letters anymore, Poppy? I didn't steal anything. I just happened to notice she had written a few things down on a piece of paper that was sitting on the coffee table. The handwriting on our notes is definitely not Rose Walters'."

Unable to hold in my disappointment at missing a detail right in front of my eyes, I smacked my leg in frustration. "Damn it! I didn't even see that paper."

"That's because you were too busy looking at the pictures of their kids."

I heard the same indicting tone in his voice when he said that as I'd heard when he was talking to Rose, and I turned toward him to argue my point, but I didn't have one. He was right. I'd missed getting a glimpse at her handwriting because I had been more interested in looking at their three children.

"If it makes you feel any better, I wouldn't have known to pay attention to the writing on that piece of paper if it weren't for you and your knowledge of handwriting. That says something."

"I guess. I'm just disgusted with myself. For months I've been following you around like a puppy, and what have I learned? Not much, it seems."

Alex stopped the car at a red light and turned to look at me. "Don't be so hard on yourself. Remember Yin and Yang? Maybe I'm good at the little details and you're good at instinct."

He turned away to drive again and I mumbled that he might be right. I just wished I would get better at the details part too.

Chapter Five

THE NEXT DAY while I sat at my kitchen table drinking a cup of iced coffee I'd brewed myself, I thought about the possibility of Canton Walters hosting sex toys parties and remaining a committed married man. I didn't need a lot of caffeine to figure out the odds of that happening were thin, at best. Added to that the female's handwriting that wasn't his wife's on those notes in his room at a hotel notorious for on-the-side rendezvous, and those odds shrank even more.

I checked my phone for the fifth time that hour, but still there was no text back from Alex. I hadn't heard from him since we returned from our little road trip the day before, and he'd never gotten back to me about meeting at The Grounds that morning either. So I'd stayed home and christened my new iced coffee maker my father had given me for my birthday a few weeks earlier.

Taking a sip of the refreshing drink, I had to admit it was good and it did exactly what I needed my caffeine to do on a hot July morning. Cool me off while waking me up. The temperature had settled into the mid-seventies the night before, so by the time the sun was up for a mere two hours, the mercury had climbed to nearly eighty. As the guy on the radio had lamely joked, it was going to be a scorcher out there today.

At a few minutes after nine, I found the number for the Naughty and Spice Toy Company on their very colorful website and figured I'd try to find out what they knew of our victim. The worst they could tell me was nothing, so I had nothing to lose.

A young woman with a far sexier voice than I expected answered the phone and happily introduced the company with the words, "Welcome to Naughty and Spice. We make sex fun! My name is Candy. What can I do for you today?"

Caught off guard, particularly with her emphasis on the word *you* in her greeting, I fumbled my words and finally stuttered out, "I…I'm…I was hoping to speak to someone about one of your party reps?"

"It's my pleasure to connect you to one of our Naughty and Spice counselors. Please hold."

I wasn't sure, but I didn't think I'd ever heard anyone tell me to hold on in such a sexual way. Candy certainly did seem to enjoy her job.

"Hello, my name is Audrey. You'd like to speak to someone about one of our party givers?"

Givers? Was everything with this company all sex?

Recovered from my earlier awkwardness, I answered, "Yes, Audrey. My name is Poppy McGuire and I'm calling about one of your reps. I mean party givers. His name is Canton Walters."

"Pardon me? I don't understand."

I stood up and walked over toward the kitchen door. Sometimes my cell phone lost all its bars when I stood in certain spots in the room. Once I reached the outside wall of the kitchen, I repeated, "My name is Poppy

McGuire and I'm calling about one of your party givers named Canton Walters."

For a long moment, all I heard was silence from Audrey and then she said, "There must be some mistake. We don't have anyone by that name on our party giver roster."

"How can you be sure? I didn't even give you his location where he holds parties. He's from the Virginia and Maryland region."

"See, there's the thing. I don't need his location because at Naughty and Spice, we don't have any male party givers. Our company is almost completely female driven, and every one of our party givers is female and even the supervisors and managers are female in our company. The only male involved in Naughty and Spice is our president and CEO, Charles Axelrod."

"Really? That's your company's CEO's name?" I asked as I struggled to stifle a laugh.

Audrey didn't seem to understand my amusement with Mr. Axelrod's name as the CEO of a sex toy company. "Yes, but he wouldn't have anything to do with our party givers. I'm sorry, but if you've been told that a male is giving parties for Naughty and Spice, then you've been misled. It's company policy that all party givers are female. No exceptions."

"Thank you for your help. I appreciate it."

And just like Candy before her, Audrey said in a sultry voice that must have been a requirement of employment, "It's my pleasure. Goodbye."

Well, that was interesting. Canton Walters wasn't a Naughty and Spice sales rep at all. So what was he doing in Sunset Ridge?

On a hunch, I called the Naughty and Spice number

again and this time a woman named Kimberly answered with her same sexy speech. When she finished, I asked, "Can you give me the names of party givers in the Sunset Ridge, Maryland area? I'm looking to attend a party, but I don't know anyone who hosts them."

"My pleasure. Hold one moment, please."

I did as she asked and a few seconds later she returned to tell me the two party givers in my area were Delilah Roberts and Elizabeth Freely. I thanked her for the very interesting information and then called Alex to give him the news.

He answered on the first ring and said, "Hey, Poppy. What's up?"

"Where have you been? I texted you about coffee and never heard back, so I was forced to brew my own. Thankfully, my father got me a new iced coffee maker, so I wasn't stuck sans caffeine. I've got news."

Skipping right over my initial question, he answered, "Really? What did you find out?"

"Canton Walters wasn't working for the Naughty and Spice Toy Company. Never had and never could since they only have female party givers."

"Interesting. So what was our victim doing the whole time he said he was working for them and how was he making money?"

I heard the excitement in Alex's voice that I felt too. Now this case was about to get really interesting.

"And I found out something else. The two party givers in the Sunset Ridge area are Delilah Roberts and Elizabeth Freely. Delilah is known around town as the happily married wife of Dr. Alan Roberts, the town chiropractor. He's a bit older than she is, but there's never been any sense or gossip that they're anything but a happy couple. And you know Elizabeth Freely already, our favorite desk clerk who sees dead men at the continental breakfast."

"You've been busy this morning, Poppy."

"Unlike someone else who seems to be slacking off, unless you have some big news to tell me."

He hesitated for a moment, but then said, "No, nothing to tell. I think we need to go speak to Elizabeth at the Hotel Piermont again. It's daytime, so she should be behind the desk. Can you be ready in ten minutes?"

Still in my tank top and shorts I'd thrown on after my shower and without a stitch of makeup on my face, I said yes anyway and hurried upstairs to get ready. Interrogating our first official suspect was more important than looking my best, and anyway, I'd washed up so it wasn't like I was a complete mess.

ALEX SAID LITTLE on the short drive to the Hotel Piermont, but something seemed off about him. I didn't get the sense that he was ever the type to talk about what was on his mind when it came to personal things, so I let it go, but I couldn't shake the feeling that he didn't seem the same as usual.

We got to the hotel but found someone different manning the desk. An older woman who reminded me of the housekeeper nobody liked stood in an oversized yellow t-shirt leaning over the desk, her large chest resting on the countertop. She wore a little too much makeup, which made her look cheap.

As we walked toward where she stood, she practically grunted, "Can I help you?"

Alex introduced us and said in an authoritative voice

I'd rarely heard come out of his mouth, "We're looking for Elizabeth Freely. Isn't she working today?

The new, far less pleasant desk clerk stood up straight and folded her arms across her enormous chest. "She was supposed to, but they called me in to fill in for her."

He looked at me, and I saw he shared my distaste for this woman. "Where does she live? I need her address."

The woman looked up Elizabeth's address and gave it to him. Without saying another word to her, Alex gave me a tiny smile and then turned on his heels and walked out the front door. I followed him to the car and got in before giving any comment on the new Hotel Piermont clerk.

"She's a real beauty, isn't she?"

He winked at me. "I'm sure she does wonders for business, but then again, I get the feeling the people who check in there aren't really interested in who's giving them the key to their rooms."

We drove the half mile or so to Elizabeth's apartment on Carson Street in the far western section of town. As he parked the car, he noticed the difference in this part of Sunset Ridge from the rest of town.

"Not exactly like Victorian Row," he commented, referring to the far statelier homes like those the wealthier people of Sunset Ridge owned.

I looked around at the far less opulent single and double block homes that made up Carson Street and this part of the town and agreed. There were no wrought iron fences or big yards here. We walked to the dingy white house at the address the desk clerk had given him and saw it had been divided into three apartments, each with its own entrance. Elizabeth's was on the second floor in the back.

"This used to be a nicer section of town when I was young. It never had the homes the mayor and the Woodward family lived in, but it wasn't like this. Then the Treemont Farm went out of business, and it slowly became like it is now. A lot of the people who lived here used to work on the farm, but when it closed down, they couldn't afford their homes anymore and landlords took them over. So what used to be one house is now three or even four apartments like the house she lives in."

Alex listened to my mini history lesson and nodded. "It happens everywhere. Baltimore has gone through the same thing, just on a much larger scale."

I spied the stairs to Elizabeth's apartment and pointed toward them. "Yeah, but the difference is there's always a chance for new businesses to come to a bigger city. Here in Sunset Ridge, that's probably not going to happen. The Treemont Farm has been out of business for over a decade, and nobody's expecting it to reopen, so things will only get worse, not better."

We walked around the back of the house and up the rickety wood stairs to apartment 2B. The door was open, and merely standing there I felt the stifling heat come from inside the apartment. Elizabeth wore a black tank top and jean short shorts and sat on an old brown couch watching television in front of a fan blowing directly on her. Alex rapped his knuckles on the screen door, instantly getting her attention.

Wiping the sweat from her hairline, she stood from the couch and walked toward us with a big smile. "Officer Montero, isn't it? What brings you to me today?"

With every word, I couldn't help but think that

Elizabeth would be perfect for the customer service job at Naughty and Spice. She had the same sultry way of talking as Candy and Audrey had.

"We'd like to speak to you about the Canton Walters case. May we come in?"

Elizabeth stopped in front of the screen door and slowly slid her hand down the front of her neck until her fingertips reached the swell of her breasts bulging out of her tank top. She still hadn't looked at me once, focusing exclusively on Alex in his police officer uniform, and asked, "Don't you need a warrant or something if you want to come in to someone's house?"

With an all-too-sexy grin, Alex said, "I just want to talk to you and ask you some questions, Elizabeth. I don't need a warrant for that."

And the voice full of syrupy charm was back.

It had the exact desired effect on her, and with no more thought, she opened the door for us to come in. I guess I should have been pleased, but it almost felt like it was too easy for him. She offered us a place on her couch next to her, but the mere idea of sitting that close to anyone in the heat that had taken over that apartment made me refuse. I expected Alex to take her up on her offer, if only to have a chance to watch her closely as he questioned her, but he surprised me by taking a position just inside the door.

"What can I do for you today?" Elizabeth asked looking up at him as she reclined against the back of the couch.

Alex took out his notepad and pen and flipped through it until he found a blank page. The entire motion seemed to take much longer than it usually did, and I had the sense he was intentionally dragging it out to throw her off balance.

Then he looked directly at her and said, "We've found out that Canton Walters was a sales rep for Naughty and Spice Sex Toy Company. We've also found out you too host parties for the company. This seems like a strange coincidence, so I'm wondering if you had ever seen him at one of those parties."

She shook her head and flashed him a toothy grin. "Nope. I didn't even know he worked for Naughty and Spice. That's wild. I thought all their party givers were female. I think I remember hearing it was a company policy."

"So it's merely happpenstance that a man who was murdered at the place you work at was also associated with another place you work at? That seems like an incredible coincidence, don't you think, Elizabeth?"

Coming out of my mouth, those questions would have resulted in her throwing me out of her house, but the way he said it didn't seem to bother her in the least. Her smile never faded and she shook her head.

"I'm not sure what to say to that, Officer Montero, but I didn't know the guy. You can ask my manager, Giselle Martin, if she knows anything about him. She's the person who gets me all of my stock. I can give you her number, if you'd like. She can tell you all about how good I am at the sex toy business."

For the first time since we'd arrived, Elizabeth looked over at me standing next to Alex. "Have you ever been to a party, Poppy?"

"No, I don't think I have."

"It's a lot of fun! Women these days are liberated, and they want to have fun in the bedroom. Would you like to see some of the most popular products? You two could have a very good time with them."

Even without seeing my face, I knew my cheeks turned bright red at her offer. I merely shook my head and corrected her faulty assumption that Alex and I were a couple. "We aren't together. Thanks, though."

Her eyes grew wide in surprise. "Really? I would have bet money you two were."

I didn't bother to ask why she was acting like a dog in heat every time Alex was around if she thought we were together, and Alex quickly changed the subject back to questioning her about Canton Walters.

"Where were you the night Mr. Walters was murdered, Elizabeth?"

She sat straight up and thought about the question for a minute. "I was right here in my apartment all night."

"Were you alone?" he asked, all the charm gone from his voice now.

"Unfortunately, for one of the few times recently, yes. I decided to stay home that night and take it easy. I've been going out a lot with my friends to a club a few towns over, but I didn't feel like drinking, so I sat in front of my handy dandy fan here and just let the air blow all over my body."

"So you were home all night alone and didn't leave here until the next day when you went to work at the Hotel Piermont where we saw you that morning?"

Nodding, she said, "Sounds about right."

Alex flipped the pages of his notepad until he reached the notes from our first discussion with her. "Do you still think you saw Mr. Walters at breakfast that morning?"

For the first time since he began questioning her,

Elizabeth Freely didn't seem as confident as she had before. She looked away, avoiding our gazes, and shrugged. "I don't know. I thought I did. I really did. Now I'm not sure since I guess he was dead before I even got to work that morning."

"Okay, thank you, Elizabeth. If we have any more questions, I'll let you know. Have a good day."

His implied threat that he didn't believe the answers she'd given him clearly frightened her, and she quickly said, "Okay. I didn't tell you anything that wasn't one hundred percent true, though. I'll be here or at the hotel if you need to talk to me again, though."

Although he didn't respond to her and simply walked out, I hung back and tried to make her feel less like he'd just put her on warning that he thought she was guilty. "Thank you, Elizabeth. Try to stay cool."

She relaxed and sat back against the couch to enjoy the full effect of the fan again. "I really did think you two were a couple, you know? I've got a pretty good sixth sense about things like this. You sure I'm wrong?"

"Yep. Stay cool."

I caught up with Alex who had gotten down to the bottom level apartment below Elizabeth's and was already speaking to her downstairs neighbor through the screen in her front door. The woman told him she didn't know if Elizabeth had left at any time that night of Canton Walters' murder because she had been away at the beach until that very morning.

As we walked around the house to knock on the other main floor apartment's door, he asked, "Did I do something wrong?"

Confused, I shook my head. "No. Why?"

He stopped at the second apartment and before he

knocked on the door, he smiled. "I figured since you stayed back to talk to her you must have been apologizing for something you thought I did wrong."

I didn't know if he was toying with me or not, so I took a step forward and stood toe-to-toe with him. He towered over me by more than half a foot, but it didn't matter. I craned my neck and said, "Did you do something wrong? I'm the student here, so if you did, it would help me to learn."

Alex stared down at me for a few seconds and shook his head. "You're a funny one, Poppy. No, I don't think I did anything wrong up there."

"I'm getting used to that smarmy thing you do with certain women, if that's what you're referring to."

"Good. Maybe now you've come around to the way I do things."

His concern that I thought he'd done something wrong made me chuckle, and I stepped around him to knock on the apartment's door. "Let's not go that far."

The second downstairs neighbor couldn't say whether Elizabeth had been home all night either, so we asked around her neighborhood and found no one who could say one way or another if they saw her during the time Canton Walters was murdered.

We walked back to the car, and when he started it to leave, I pointed him in the direction of Sunset Ridge's extremely popular chiropractor's home back near the Victorian houses. "Onward to Delilah Roberts, or are we leaving that until tomorrow?"

"No time like the present. We've got our second suspect, so maybe we can get a third. What are the chances Elizabeth and Delilah are friends because of their connection with Naughty and Spice?"

I thought about the possibility for a moment and decided against it. "Slim, fat, and none. They may both like sex toys, but they're worlds apart. My guess is they aren't close at all."

With a grin, he said, "Good. I prefer talking to suspects when they haven't been given a warning I'm coming."

Chapter Six

Dr. Alan Roberts and his wife Delilah lived at 933 Richmond Lane, deep in the heart of what Alex sarcastically called Victorian Row. As the most popular doctor in town, Roberts' waiting room at his chiropractic office on Madison Street was always full. I'd gone to him a few times a couple years ago when my lower back had started giving me problems. His combination of cracking me in all the right places and giving me exercises to do each night worked like a charm, so I hadn't been back since.

This is all I really knew about Roberts, but I assumed that wasn't what Alex had meant when he asked about him, so I tried to remember any impression the good doctor had given me on those few office visits as we walked down the sidewalk to the couple's slate blue and white painted Victorian house.

"He's older than his wife. I remember that being the topic of conversation for the gossips in town when they married about five years ago. The busybodies were sure she was a gold-digger, and I distinctly remember hearing the First Lady claim that Delilah would leave him before they hit the wood anniversary. I think it bothered them that even though she and her husband had money, they kept to themselves and didn't associate with the upper crust of Sunset Ridge."

"The wood anniversary? What's that?" Alex asked in a way that told me he knew nothing of the traditional anniversary gift list the old women in town knew by heart.

"Wood's the fifth, I believe. Paper's the first, cotton's the second, and then the big ones are silver for the twenty-fifth and gold for the fiftieth anniversary."

He chuckled and shook his head. "You seem to know a lot about anniversary gifts for a single woman."

I didn't appreciate the verbal swipe at my bachelorette status and pushed on his arm. "Hello? Society page writer. And for your information, any well-read person knows at least the silver and gold anniversaries. You're just a Philistine."

Alex climbed the front steps to the Roberts' grand Victorian wrap-around porch that surrounded the front half of the home and turned to look down at me still standing on the sidewalk. I truly enjoyed how comfortable we'd gotten with each other in the past few months, and now as I looked him, I worried that would all go away if Bethany began dating him. It was stupid and petty of me, but I didn't want to lose what he and I had between us.

With a smile, he asked, "You coming, or is this merely a job for a Philistine?"

He rang the doorbell as I walked up the stairs, and by the time I joined him on the welcome mat, the massive blue painted wood door had opened and Delilah Roberts stood staring out at us with a look of worry etched into her classically beautiful features.

"Is there something wrong, officer?"

"I'm Officer Montero and this is Poppy McGuire. We're investigating the murder of Canton Walters, and we'd like to speak to you about it. May we come in?"

"Yes, of course." She stepped back to let us enter her foyer and continued, "I read about it in the newspaper. So awful."

Delilah closed the door behind me and walked quickly to catch up to Alex, who had already made his way into her living room. As she passed me, I watched her. She truly was beautiful. Long blond hair framed her oval shaped face perfectly, giving her a youthful, fresh look, and her wide green eyes were dark and intense. Added to that was a body any twenty-year-old would kill to have, and the combination was near perfection.

But she looked different from other women who possessed beauty like hers. Something in the way her perfectly shaped mouth turned down at the corners unless she was smiling told me she had more unhappiness than those who hadn't been blessed with all her physical gifts.

She was stunning, though, so naturally, I fully expected Alex to turn on that charm of his to get what he wanted to know out of her.

"Officer Montero, I'm not sure what I would know about that unfortunate man's death," she said softly as she offered the two of us a seat in the wingback chairs that faced the sofa. "I'm sure I didn't know him."

"Please feel free to call me Alex. May I call you Delilah?"

The formality that had seemed so thoroughly a part of her before that moment instantly melted away, and she smiled at him as she took her place on the sofa opposite us. "Yes, please do. Thank you, Alex."

Turning to look at me, she said, "And I know you, Poppy. You've written very graciously about a number of my dinner parties I've held for my husband."

"Thank you, Delilah. It's always nice to know the subjects of your work appreciate what you wrote. The ladies who share things with me always tell me that your dinners are the living end."

She demurely dipped her head, as if to bow to me, and I had to admit I couldn't imagine this woman plunging a knife into anyone's back, least of all Canton Walters' as he sat in a room at the less-than-reputable Hotel Piermont. She just didn't fit the image of the killer I'd created in my mind.

"Now Delilah, you say you're sure you didn't know him. Would you look at this picture and tell me if you're still sure you didn't?"

Alex put his notepad and pen down on the table and held up a picture of Canton Walters his wife had given us to help with the investigation since showing people a picture of a dead man didn't seem like it would work with the likes of Delilah Roberts. She leaned forward to take the picture from his hold and stared down at it for a long time before reaching back across the coffee table to give it to him again.

"No, I'm sorry. I don't know this man," she said quietly.

Alex placed the picture in his pocket and picked up his pad and pen again as he leaned back in his chair. Now I was sure he'd turn on that charm.

"We've been told you were a party giver for Naughty and Spice Sex Toys. Is that true?"

At first she simply nodded as she averted our glances, but then she answered, "Yes."

"We've also been told that man, Canton Walters, was also employed by the Naughty and Spice Company. Do you know anything about that?"

Still unable to face us, she shook her head. "No. I don't know anything about that."

"So you've never met Canton Walters and never seen him before I handed you that picture a few moments ago?" Alex asked with a sharpness to his voice that surprised me. Of all the women I'd seen him question, other than Canton's wife, Delilah was by far the most beautiful and deserving of his charm act. Far lesser women had gotten far sweeter treatment from him.

"No," she answered in a tiny, shaky voice.

Whatever Alex thought he was doing, it wasn't working, so I jumped in. If we ever wanted to hear anything other than the word no for an answer, a new tactic was in order.

"Delilah, you don't have to be embarrassed about being a Naughty and Spice party giver. Alex doesn't know anything about it, and I'm like any other woman. I like a good time as much as the rest. So please don't think we're judging you for hosting those parties. It's just a chance for some ladies to drink some wine and have a few laughs, right?"

For the first time since Alex began questioning her, Delilah turned to face us and a gentle smile crept onto her face. "We just like to have a good time sometimes. We don't hurt anyone with the parties. It's just married women like myself getting together like you said. For a few laughs."

Out of the corner of my eye, I saw Alex open his mouth to ask her more questions, so I gently put my hand on his knee to stop him and continued with my far less confrontational approach. This was one time a woman's touch was definitely in order.

"Exactly. It's just harmless fun. We talked to Elizabeth Freely, the other woman who gives Naughty and Spice parties in this area, and she said the same thing. Do you know her?"

Those green eyes of Delilah's grew wide, and she shook her head. "No, I don't. I have to admit I don't really associate with anyone else who holds parties for them. I just have them every so often for my friends."

I believed her on that. She and Elizabeth were just as I'd suspected—separated by far too many social levels to be friends.

"I'm sorry I wasn't more forthcoming. I'm just a little embarrassed about the parties. My husband has never liked them. He says it's not proper for a doctor's wife to sell things like that. He doesn't understand how boring life is now that I don't work anymore, and the parties are just silly fun to break up the monotony of life sometimes."

The loneliness in her voice was impossible to miss, and I saw Alex jot something down in his notepad as she spoke. Oddly enough, I understood what she meant. I may not have been married and a stay-at-home wife, but life in Sunset Ridge could get tedious for anyone. That she had everything her heart could desire when it came to possessions didn't mean she didn't feel that same boredom and crave some distraction from the proper life she was expected to lead.

"We need to find someone who knew Canton. He didn't deserve to be left for dead in that hotel room as he filled out expense forms. That's not right, is it?" I asked softly.

Tears welled in Delilah's eyes. "No, it's not. I hope you find the person who did this to that poor man who deserved so much better. I truly do."

"Delilah! Where are you?" a male voice boomed from the back of the house. In seconds, the man appeared in the doorway, and I recognized him as Dr. Alan Roberts.

Ten years older than his beautiful wife, his grey hair and deep crow's feet around his pale blue eyes made him look more like fifteen or twenty years older than her. Tall and wiry, he had a flinty look about him that made him look angrier than when I'd gone to see him just a few years ago.

He walked directly into the room to stand behind his wife on the sofa and asked, "What's going on here?"

She looked back at him and forced a smile. "This is Officer Montero and Poppy McGuire. They needed some information about my parties because that man who was murdered was involved with the company too."

Alan Roberts squeezed his wife's shoulder until she winced and then slowly released his hold on her. "I can't imagine why. There's nothing illegal about them."

Alex spoke up and directed his question at Delilah. "So you have never seen our victim before, not even on the street?"

The doctor came around the sofa and sat beside his wife. Taking her hand in his, he answered for her. "My wife would no more know a murder victim than I would, as I'm sure she's told you already."

"I'd like to hear it from her, Dr. Roberts," Alex said sharply.

"You'll hear it from me since I'm her husband. I

don't appreciate you coming into my home and accusing her of something."

"No one's accusing anyone of anything, Dr. Roberts. I just asked her if she knew Canton Walters."

The animosity in the room bristled around us, and I saw the fear in Delilah's eyes. The question was, though, what was she afraid of? Her husband or something we might find to connect her to the murder?

"Were you home all Tuesday night?" Alex asked, clearly directing his question to Delilah once again.

"Of course she was home all night!" Alan Roberts bellowed. "What are you saying?"

"I have to ask these questions, sir."

I sensed the dire need for something to diffuse the situation, so I put on my sweetest smile and asked Dr. Roberts, "Do you remember me? You helped me with my back problems a few years ago, and you were just a godsend. I don't know if I ever thanked you for that, but I just wanted to say the exercises you gave me to do still help to this day."

Alan Roberts snapped his head to look at me, and for a moment, he looked like he wanted to leap over the coffee table and drag both Alex and me out of his house. After a few seconds ticked by, though, his expression softened a little.

"It's always nice for a doctor to hear he was successful in helping a patient. Thank you."

It wasn't exactly détente, but at least I'd been able to get him to calm down for a few minutes. I looked over at Alex and saw in his eyes he was expecting more fireworks from the doctor.

"Delilah, I'm going to need a list of all the guests who've attended your Naughty and Spice parties."

No sooner had the words come out of Alex's mouth, Dr. Roberts leaped to his feet, and pointing his finger at him, barked, "She isn't responsible for doing your work for you! Find out who those people were on your own!"

Gently, Delilah tugged at her husband's hand and stared up at him with a plaintive look like she was begging him to stop yelling. "It's okay, honey. I don't mind. I really don't."

He looked back at her and shook his head. "I don't like it. It's not right."

"Dr. Roberts, I'm afraid that if your wife doesn't give me a list of those names, I'll have to go public with the whole connection between our murder victim and your wife's Naughty and Spice parties."

Alex's implicit threat to announce to everyone in town about Delilah Roberts' sex toy parties wasn't lost on the doctor. Although his face was still full of rage, he nodded his agreement to his wife giving Alex what he'd asked for and sat down next to her.

"Fine. She'll give you what you want. Is it possible that this won't have to go public if she does?"

In a rare moment of kindness toward the doctor, Alex agreed to do whatever he could to keep the list and Delilah's parties a private matter. She thanked him, and then she and her husband walked into the next room and closed the door behind them.

Leaning over to whisper to Alex, I said, "I don't think the good doctor approves of his wife's sex toy parties."

Alex grinned and shook his head. "I don't think he does. Not surprising, I guess. Look at this house. He's created a certain kind of life for himself, and her dabbling in sex toys embarrasses him. You can see it every time he refers to them."

I looked around the room where we sat and knew Alex was right. Fine artwork hung on the walls, and expensive furniture filled the room. An expensive Persian area rug covered real cherry wood floors that had obviously been completely refinished recently. Everything in the room screamed wealth and status, and a wife who held sex toy parties didn't fit there.

"He has a beautiful young woman for a wife, and all he can worry about is how it looks that she likes sexy stuff? You think he'd be thankful since that's the only way anyone would ever think of him as anything but a tight ass."

Alex's eyebrows shot up. "You seem to like Delilah Roberts."

"I understand her. She just wants to have a little fun and she's married to a stick-in-the-mud and lives in a town full of judgmental people who look down their noses at anything involving sex."

The look he gave me made me feel exposed, so I hurriedly joked, "Or maybe I just don't have many friends and I'm hoping to find a new one."

Dr. Roberts and Delilah returned, and she handed Alex a list of people who she remembered had attended any of her parties since she began giving them. The two of us read down the list, and I noticed a few familiar names, but absent were Elizabeth Freely and Canton Walters. I looked up to see if Alex planned to ask any more questions and saw him smiling.

He stood and thanked both of them before we left. Delilah walked us to the front door, and just as I was about to follow Alex out onto the porch, she caught my hand in hers and squeezed it. "I truly hope you find the person who did this."

"We will. Take care, okay? And don't stop having fun for anyone."

Tears filled her eyes again, but she forced a smile. "Thank you."

I JOINED ALEX on the sidewalk as Delilah closed the front door behind me. Nudging my shoulder, he said, "It looks like you may have made that friend."

Looking back toward the house, I said, "I think she's even lonelier than I thought."

As we walked back to the car, he handed me the list Delilah wrote out for him. "But is she a killer is what I want to know."

Seated in the car, I looked over the list of names and still couldn't imagine her as a murderer. "I don't think so."

Alex started the engine and tapped on the piece of paper in my hand. "Notice anything about the handwriting?"

I'd noticed immediately when he showed me the list the first time that Delilah's handwriting wasn't the same as the one on the notes we'd found in Canton's hotel room. Some small part of me liked that she hadn't been the woman to write them. I wanted to see her happy, and if she'd been involved with Canton, she certainly couldn't be happy now that he was dead.

"Of course I did. I was just waiting for you to say something about it. A good teacher lets the student learn at his own pace."

I looked over at him as he drove toward my house and saw a smile break out on his face. At a stop sign, he turned his head and asked, "Is that a critique of my teaching ability?"

"Not at all. I'm just glad you've come around to my thinking on the handwriting. I have to know, though. Is that why you asked for the list since we could have gotten the names from the Naughty and Spice people just as easily. You might even have liked calling their customer service department."

He stopped the car in front of my house. "Yeah. It seemed like the easiest way to get her handwriting to see if she was the female who wrote those notes."

I thought about Delilah Roberts and the sad look in her eyes as she closed the door behind us. "Do you consider her a suspect, Alex? I just can't see it."

For a moment, he sat silently before he said, "I'm not sure, but I'm not discounting the idea that either of the Roberts were involved in Canton Walters' death. For now, they'll stay in my mind as possibilities, even though I know you don't want her to be our killer."

"I don't. She just looks like she doesn't need any more unhappiness."

"It's not good to get personally involved like that when you're on a case, Poppy. It makes it hard to be objective and see evidence for what it is."

He was right. I knew that, but it didn't change the fact that I really didn't want to see Delilah Roberts be our murderer.

"I know, but I'm the Yin to your Yang, so think of it as a different perspective. I promise I won't let it impede my job. By the way, I'm glad you didn't use that technique you use on other women on Delilah. You didn't need to, but I thought you might do it anyway."

"I haven't thanked you for butting in when you did.

See? Those instincts I'm always talking about told you I needed to take a different tactic with her, but I didn't see it. Thankfully, you did. We make a good team."

"Absolutely. Yin and Yang."

I opened the car door and moved to get out, but Alex touched my arm and stopped me. Turning to face him, I saw his expression had changed to a serious look.

"Is something wrong, Alex?"

He didn't say anything for a long moment and then just smiled. "No. Forget it. I'll see you tomorrow, okay?"

I sensed he had something he wanted to tell me, but whatever it was, he wasn't ready yet. I understood. I wasn't ready either.

Chapter Seven

M<small>Y EDITOR AT</small> *The Eagle* sat beside my desk chatting about the million and a half freaky things he was sure were transpiring at that very moment around Sunset Ridge, but all I could think of was what Alex had tried to tell me when I got out of the car the day before. He obviously had something on his mind, and I wondered if he was wrestling with the same ideas I was about him.

"Poppy, did you hear a thing I said?"

I looked at Howard and realized I had missed whatever he thought was so important. Quickly, I came up with an excuse. "No, I'm sorry. I had a hard time sleeping last night. You know, since it's so hot? I apologize."

Without missing a beat, he continued. "I was telling you about this one time when I was at Diamanti's just minding my own business and the former mayor and his wife came in and I was sure they'd been up to no good. It was written all over their faces!"

I didn't doubt it, but there was no way I wanted to get into a conversation about all the things the former First Couple had done during the mayor's time in office. Changing the subject, I asked, "So did you decide on a schedule for when you'd like my articles submitted each week?"

"Yeah, yeah, but do you think I was right? Something tells me that Mayor Girard and his wife have been guilty of some kind of malfeasance in their time. I know if you found out from working with the police you probably can't tell me, but can you at least say if I'm on the right track?"

My editor had a way of blinking his dark eyes really fast when he got excited, and at that moment as he stared at me waiting with bated breath for my answer, he looked like an owl on speed with how fast he was blinking at me. Afraid he might stroke out if I didn't give him something, I smiled and shrugged before I said, "You're right I can't, but if you promise not to do anything with the information, I can tell you you're not wrong."

In a flash, he went from looking like a spastic owl to acting like some kind of crazy donkey right there in my office. Jumping up, he stomped his feet and clapped as he guffawed so loudly I thought he might frighten the person in the next office.

"Shhhh! You can't tell anyone, remember?"

The one thing I could count on was that my editor wouldn't write a single word about even that practically meaningless tidbit. Once he moved into his job as overseer, as he saw his position, he had no interest whatsoever in writing another word for *The Eagle*. No, he'd likely just gossip among his friends, all of whom lived outside of town, about how ridiculous this place was and how much better they all were than the provincial rubes who lived here.

"Okay, okay. I won't. I'll get you that schedule later

today. Be checking your email because it will be there."

I turned back toward my laptop and hoped he got the hint. "Okay, Howard. I'll keep an eye out for it."

He left my office mumbling about how he knew he was right about the Girards. He wasn't that far off at all. Malfeasance did apply rather well to them.

Hoping for a few moments to myself to think about Alex and if I should be the one to start the conversation about how we felt, assuming we felt anything, I was sorely disappointed less than five minutes after my editor left when Bethany poked her head in through my almost closed door.

"Hey, do you have time to talk?"

Whether or not I had time to talk, I didn't want to talk about what I suspected she did want to talk about. I wanted to be a good friend. I really did. Bethany and I had grown quite close in the years we'd working together at the paper, and I considered her a close friend.

The problem was I got sick to my stomach every time the thought of that close friend dating Alex even briefly crossed my mind.

So pushing all that nausea and misplaced resentment down, I turned around and gave her my most sincere friend smile. "Sure! Come on in."

She plopped down in the seat next to my desk and leaned forward toward me as I braced myself for what might come out of her mouth. Bethany had never been one for subtlety or easing into a situation, so I expected the questions about Alex to come fast and furious.

But to my surprise, she didn't ask about him right off. Instead, she whispered, "Hey, what happened with that guy at the Hotel Piermont? You know what people tend to go there for, so was it a rendezvous gone bad?

Maybe a threesome someone decided they didn't want?"

I couldn't help but laugh. I'd been so keyed up about having to talk to her that it was more a release of nervous energy than an expression of some amusement. I did have to admit she might not be that wrong about what had happened at the Hotel Piermont.

"I don't know. We haven't found out what he was doing there. Did you know him?"

She reached over and picked up the newspaper with Canton Walters' picture on the front page. "Let me look again. I didn't recognize him the first time I saw it, though."

After studying the picture for a few seconds, she shook her head and tossed the paper back on my desk. "He doesn't ring any bells for me. He looks young, but then again, that might be the blond curly hair. That always seems to make guys look younger, don't you think?"

"I guess. He was in his early thirties, I think. He was the father of three children."

Bethany's expression changed from interested to sad. "Oh, I'm sorry to hear that. No matter what he was up to at that hotel, he didn't deserve to get stabbed in the back over it."

"Hey, have you ever been to a Naughty and Spice Toy party? He may have been associated with the company."

Her smile returned and she nodded. "Not one for Naughty and Spice, but I've been to a party like that. The one I went to was more a lingerie type of party, but there were toys there too. You went with me. Don't you remember? My friend Erica had it right before she got married."

I thought back to the party she referred to. Her friend was getting married a few weeks later and then she and her husband were set to move to Europe, or maybe it was South America. I wasn't sure, but the memory of that night and all those drunken giggling women talking about how much their boyfriends would love the lingerie being offered was as clear as day.

"That's right. Whatever happened to your friend and her husband?"

Bethany picked up a paper clip from my desk and chucked it into the container for them. "Divorced. She caught him cheating on her with their Brazilian maid. She lives in Boston now."

South America it was. "Sorry to hear that. I can't believe I didn't remember that party when this whole Naughty and Spice thing came up in this case."

"Speaking of this case…"

Before she went any further since I knew she wouldn't be as easy to discourage as my editor, I held up my hand and stopped her. "I can't talk about it. You know that."

She rolled her eyes and snorted in disgust. "I don't give a damn about the case, Poppy. My interests are focused on that delicious partner of yours."

And there it began. There was no way I could just rebuff her on that topic, but there was no way I wanted to encourage her either. I wasn't sure what my expression was saying, but inside everything in my body was screaming, "No!"

"I don't know a lot about him, Bethany. I'm not sure how much help I can be."

A lame response, but when I couldn't tell the truth, lame was often my fall back.

"I saw him at Diamanti's last week sitting all alone and couldn't believe nobody in this town had scooped him up yet. I mean, look around. He's the hottest guy in Sunset Ridge. I was on a blind date my friend Carey had convinced me to go on, and he was way better than the guy I was stuck with the whole night."

Desperate to deflect the conversation from its current topic, I chose to ask a question usually out of character for me, but desperate times called for desperate measures.

"Did you sleep with him?"

"Yes, and it wasn't anything to write home about. Perfectly pedestrian like he had read a book once on how to have sex and that's all he knew."

"Sorry. It sounds awful."

"You see that twisted face you have on right now? I think that's what I looked like from the minute he opened his mouth to when he left my place a few hours later. He was just no good. Definitely attractive, you know, but even good looking has to have something else to work with."

I fixed my expression, which was more a reflection of how much I hated even thinking of Bethany with Alex, and pasted a smile on my face. "The life of a single girl."

She sat back in her chair and folded her arms across her chest. "Speaking of that, why aren't you two together? He's good looking. You're cute as a button. You obviously have the same interests. So what's up?"

Just as much as I didn't want to talk about Alex with her, I didn't want to explain why someone I admired and cared for wasn't the man I was dating. I didn't know why. Well, that wasn't true. I knew why I hadn't told him how I felt. Why he hadn't said anything to me was a different matter. Maybe he didn't feel anything and that's why he hadn't said anything.

"We're just not that way. That's all."

Screwing her face into a look of distaste, she repeated what I'd said. "That's all. Hmmm. Seems strange to me. Is it that he has bad habits or problems I'm not seeing?"

I considered mentioning how I thought he was still in love with his wife who'd been dead for five years and how I had the feeling ever since her death he'd hidden himself away from the world—the land of the living, as he referred to it—but I didn't say anything about either one. Somehow, it felt like betraying him by saying those things, like telling Bethany about them would make me no better than the busybodies in town.

"I really don't know. We're not that close."

I didn't really consider that a lie, to be honest. While Alex and I spent hours together each day, in truth, he'd never shared much about his personal life with me, even though I had the feeling he knew a lot about mine. We just didn't talk about non-work issues much.

Or at all.

Bethany sat up straight in her seat and shook her head. "How can you two not be that close? You're together every day working on some case or another. You meet him every morning for coffee, and he saved your life when Dominick Hampton was planning on killing you. Those kinds of things usually make two people pretty close."

The way she listed those things made me feel inadequate as I sat there unable to explain to her why we weren't that close. I'd always been like this, though. When other females would have had a man wrapped around their pinky finger, if I was with him, he and I would still be arm's length away and I'd be left wondering why he wasn't wrapped around my finger. Or any other part of my body.

I didn't want to think about it anymore.

"We're friendly. That's it. I can't explain it. That's just how we are. I respect him, and he respects me. I like tagging along on cases because I think he's a great detective and want to learn as much as I can from him."

"And what does he think of you?"

"I don't know. You'd have to ask him that question."

That I had good instincts. That I saw things differently than he did. That I was a small town hick who liked to play detective with him because I had nothing better to do. That I was a single woman who'd been crowned an old maid by the busybodies of Sunset Ridge.

"So I'm going to stop beating around the bush and just come out with it. Do you have feelings for him, Poppy?"

Sure my expression was betraying the truth I so desperately wanted to hide at that moment, I said in as casual a voice as I could muster, "I don't feel that way about him."

"You mean you've never considered the idea of the two of you becoming more than just two people who work on cases together?" she asked in complete disbelief.

Swallowing hard, I shook my head and said in a way even I had to admit wasn't convincing, "No. Not at all."

"Well, I think you're crazy, but if you aren't going to go after him, I am. I mean, unless you have a problem with me doing that. I don't want this to come between us, Poppy. You're one of my best friends in this town, and no man is worth ruining a good friendship."

There was my chance to stop everything she had planned with him. All I had to do was say the word and she'd put the brakes on going after him. Whatever he and I felt could blossom into something naturally, or it could never occur, but her dating him wouldn't affect it one way or another.

All I had to do was say what was on my mind. But I couldn't. I didn't know why, but when I opened my mouth to speak, I didn't tell her the truth—that I didn't want her to have anything to do with him.

No, when I opened my mouth, the exact opposite came out. "I don't dictate his social life, so go ahead. Don't let me stand in your way."

Visibly excited, she jumped up and gave me a tiny hug. "Thanks! I think I will. And don't worry. Nothing that happens between us will change anything you guys do during work hours."

And with that she left my office, her goal accomplished. Already things were changing. Us? Nothing that happens between us? So now they were already an us, an us separated from me.

As I sat there staring blankly at my laptop screen, jealousy swirled around inside me like some poison infecting my brain and my heart. Thoughts of how Bethany had never had a successful relationship crept into my mind, and as soon as I pushed those away, other negative thoughts about her marched in to take their place.

How every serious relationship of hers had been superficial and meaningless in the end. How she didn't so much care about men as much as liked what she could get from them.

In just a few minutes, I'd made myself miserable, first from the reality that she was about to ask out the one man I liked in all of Sunset Ridge and then from how terrible I felt after thinking such awful things about her.

Consigned to the fact that I must be the world's worst friend, I shut my laptop and sat back in my chair to close my eyes. I didn't want to be jealous. I knew it was entirely my own fault that I hadn't told her how I really felt about her dating him and had basically given her the green light to do whatever she wanted. I'd had my chance and didn't take it.

My office began to feel like the walls were closing in around me, so I grabbed my purse and got out of there. I didn't know where I was going, so I let my feet just take me wherever. As long as I wasn't sitting in my office stewing in my own jealous misery, that's all that mattered.

Taking out my phone, I scrolled through my calls to find Alex's number and put the phone to my ear as it began to ring. He answered quickly, as he usually did.

"What's up, Poppy?" he asked like he was happy to hear from me.

"I was wondering if you found out anything more about the case."

"Not really. I've been swamped with paperwork Derek dumped on me as soon as I came in today, and there's been one problem after another about something the garbage men did on their route this morning. Just when I think I might be able to get some work done, I get another call about it."

"Oh."

What I really wanted to say was I'd give anything to

go on another road trip to get out of this town for at least a few hours. At that moment, I'd have taken a quick coffee break at The Grounds with the two of us at our usual table in the back of the shop.

"You okay? You don't sound right."

Again, fate dropped the chance for me to say what I wanted to right into my lap. All I had to do was take it. But once again, I couldn't find the words needed to say what was on my mind.

So instead I did what I always did. "I'm good. You know how it is. The heat and the humidity gets to you after a while. I'll be fine."

"You sure? It sounds like you have something on your mind."

A thousand ideas ran through my head, most of them about him, but for whatever reason, I didn't say anything about them. "Just thinking about our case. I'm on my way home to get a big glass of iced tea and relax."

"No iced coffee for my favorite caffeine addict?" he asked, teasing me like he usually did about how much coffee I drank each day.

"Not today," I said as I crossed Main Street to get to Barn Street where my house was. "I guess I'm going to go now. I'll talk to you later, and if I come up with anything about the case, I'll let you know."

"Okay. Sounds good. If I don't talk to you tonight, I'll see you tomorrow morning like usual at The Grounds, right? Around eight sound good?"

"Yep. I'll be there."

"Good. Talk to you later, Poppy."

I pressed END and stuffed my phone into my bag as regret threatened to choke me. Why hadn't I told him what was on my mind? I had the chance to let him know

I liked him as more than a friend and work partner, and I didn't take it. Missing one chance could be excused, but missing a second one?

Now whatever happened, I had no one but myself to blame.

Chapter Eight

THE CROWD AT The Grounds seemed to grow exponentially every time I looked up from checking my phone to see what time it was. Tossing it into my purse, I returned to staring at the front door of the shop. Alex was already ten minutes late, something very unlike him. As I watched for him through the steam drifting up from our coffees, I wondered what could make him so late.

Or who.

A spike of jealousy exploded inside me. I didn't want to think of who could be the reason he was late. What. Best to stick with what could be the reason he was late. Maybe there was an accident he stopped to handle since he was a police officer for the town. Or maybe Derek had waylaid him as he made his way to our usual morning coffee meeting. Our new police chief loved nothing more lately, it seemed, than to pile more work on his newest hire, and I had never met a man who loved to talk more than Derek Hampton. The phrase talk a blue streak never applied to anyone better.

There could be a million reasons why he was late. None of them necessarily included a certain person. Absolutely.

I looked up after I'd almost convinced myself Bethany had nothing to do with his being late and saw him walking toward me dressed not in his uniform but in jeans and a black t-shirt. A black t-shirt that showcased his incredibly muscular arms and chest. Pushing through a small group of people who'd taken up residence blocking his seat, he finally reached our table and sat down.

"Sorry I'm late. I just got off."

"Got off? What does that mean?"

He took a sip of coffee, and as my question sank in, a look of confusion came over his face. "What do you mean what does that mean? I just got off my shift. I had to work the overnight, so I just got out. I didn't think about what time I'd have to work yesterday when I was talking to you. What's up with you lately? You're acting really strange."

I hadn't realized my behavior had moved into the bizarre, but he did have a point. I couldn't explain yesterday or why I'd practically freaked out over him saying he'd just gotten off either. God, I was turning into a real fool! Even if he had just come straight to The Grounds after a night of sleeping with Bethany, he'd never tell me and certainly never say he'd just gotten off.

Clearly, I was losing my mind.

Focusing his dark brown eyes on me, he leaned forward and asked, "Are you okay, Poppy? What's going on?"

"Nothing," I answered with a smile as I took a sip of my coffee. "I'm great."

"You sure?"

"Yeah. I'm okay."

Satisfied with my answer, Alex looked around the

restaurant teeming with customers and mumbled, "This place is mobbed today. You'd think in the middle of July people wouldn't want coffee so much."

"Maybe they're getting iced coffee. It's all the rage," I said, not even sure he was talking to me or if he was just thinking aloud.

He shrugged like he didn't care one way or another. "Maybe. I'll take my coffee hot and strong no matter what time of year."

"I started drinking iced coffee recently. It's not that bad, actually. It just takes a little getting used to."

Good God, we had officially descended into the world of banalities. I had become the intensely boring, stereotypical Sunset Ridge resident. How much longer before I moved from meaningless chatter about coffee temperatures to gossiping about what other people were doing with their lives and how I felt about those choices?

Alex smiled and lifted his cup in the air as if to toast to something. "By the way, thanks for getting mine this morning."

"You're welcome."

We'd never had truly scintillating conversations, to be honest, but somehow we'd gotten to a point where everything we said verged on the mundane. I needed to change this quickly.

"So where are we on the Canton Walters case? Did you find out anything new since the last time we talked?" I asked, eager to get back on track with our work in the hopes that I could put my silly issues to the side for at least a day.

He opened his mouth to tell me something, but I didn't hear a word because just as he began to speak I saw Bethany come through the front door and head right toward us. She knew full well we had coffee every morning in this very spot because I'd told her myself more than once, and she'd obviously decided a captive audience of Alex was her best chance to make her move. With every high-heeled step she took, I resented her intrusion even more.

From the looks of things, she'd pulled out all the stops that morning as she stood in front of the mirror planning out how she'd begin her seduction of my partner. Dressed in a green sundress that left little to the imagination, she looked sexy and cool all at the same time. As I studied her face, I saw she'd gone the whole nine yards with her makeup too.

Were those false eyelashes on her eyes? Was she wearing eye shadow? She never wore anything but a quick swipe of mascara during the day. Well, at least not when she was going to work at *The Eagle*. She'd once commented on how little effort she put into getting ready for work because nobody appealing worked with us at the paper. I'd teased her that Prince Charming might someday come through the front door and then what would she do. Clearly, this morning was an altogether different affair.

"Poppy! Good morning!" she chirped at me when she was about six feet away from our table.

There was one time when I was in high school and I liked a boy who was a year ahead of me. I was sure he'd never noticed me staring at him with that dreamy look girls get when they see someone they like, but one day at lunch he must have since he walked up to me and asked me out to that Friday's dance. For a few minutes as I stood there talking to him, it felt like the world around us faded away until it was just the two of us. I'd never forget that feeling of being so entirely immersed in the way someone made me feel for the rest of my life.

At that moment as Bethany came toward where I sat with Alex, I had the same feeling, but this time, it was like the rest of the world had simply moved off to the sides of the coffee shop to watch on the sidelines as she made her move and I did absolutely nothing to stop her. I imagined onlookers staring as the scene unfolded and wondering why I was so lame.

I saw Alex look around to see who had said my name and then he turned back to look at me as he took a drink of his coffee. "Looks like we're going to be three this morning."

"Yeah. Looks like it," I said in what could only be described as a grumble.

Bethany stole a chair from a nearby table and pulled it up to ours to sit with us. Giving me her best smile, she said, "Funny seeing you here. I have just a few minutes before I have to get to the office, but I wanted to come over and say hi."

I wanted to be polite as much as I wanted to chop off my right arm and beat myself with it, but I didn't have a choice. Even that teenage girl in the high school lunchroom would have known she had to be polite, and I wasn't a teenage girl anymore. I was a grown woman who had done nothing to stop what was about to happen, so I had no choice but to accept it.

"Bethany, you remember my partner, Alex Montero. Alex, this is Bethany Lewis. She works at *The Eagle* with me."

I wasn't sure how that sounded to the two of them, but with each word all I heard was the sound of the end. The end of my friendship with Alex and maybe even the end of my working with him. The end of everything I'd come to love about every day.

The end.

They shook hands, and I saw in Bethany's eyes as she looked at him that he was everything she'd built him up to be. For his part, Alex seemed more polite than smitten. At least there was that consolation.

"What are you two up to today?" she asked. "You're not dressed in your uniform, Alex, so do you have the day off?"

I watched as he explained how he'd just finished the overnight shift and now he and I were going to work on a case we were involved in, and I had to admit he didn't seem to be bowled over with interest in her. I wanted to think that maybe his head wouldn't be turned by her, but I knew better. He was a red-blooded American male, after all, and a beautiful woman sat next to him practically drooling over him. Why wouldn't he want that?

Unsure whether I was driven to be helpful or petty, I blurted out, "Bethany works in the advertising department at *The Eagle*. It's her job to get people to pay money for ads in our little newspaper."

Somewhere not so deep inside I wanted him to look at her and think she was boring because she worked in advertising. Until recently, I'd never seen her job as anything close to dull since she often got to leave town and travel around Maryland to meet with potential clients. In fact, I'd often envied how her job allowed her to meet so many new people. Now, though, whatever jealous demon lurked inside me had taken over and I wanted her to appear so much less than the pretty young woman sitting too close to him.

Always the gentleman, he politely listened to her as she explained her job responsibilities a bit too excitedly for me. They talked a little more about his job as a police officer, and then it was time for her to go, thankfully. I forced myself to be nicer than I wanted to be and smiled as she told me she'd see me at work, wishing her a good day as she left.

Her interruption of our morning coffee irked me. It was childish and petty and I had no one but myself to blame, but it annoyed me nonetheless. This was something Alex and I did every morning, just the two of us at our table with only two chairs, and she'd barged in and disturbed it.

"She seems nice," he said in a casual voice as he lifted his coffee cup to his mouth to take a drink.

"Yeah. She's nice."

What else does someone say in that position? The jealous demon screamed inside my head to tell him something bad about Bethany, but I couldn't. I wasn't that kind of person. Or at least I didn't want to be.

"Are you two close?" he asked, his tone far more pointed now. He wanted to know more about her.

My heart sank, and I swallowed hard. "I've known her for a few years. You know, co-workers."

"Interesting."

No, it isn't interesting. She isn't interesting. She goes through men like I go through tissues when I have a runny nose. She isn't serious about anything, like you are, Alex. You have nothing in common. Why can't you see that?

"I guess," was all I could say, my brain and my heart engaging in a full-scale tug of war as I watched him as he became interested in her.

And then he said the very words that made me feel

like a knife slicing right through me.

"Is she single?"

Nodding as my heartbeat pounded in my ears, I answered truthfully, knowing I'd be sealing the deal without even making her do any more work. "Yes."

I excused myself to go to the counter as I couldn't think of any other way to avoid showing Alex how disappointed I was. I willed myself to be okay as I stood in line, and when Jennie asked me what I wanted, I had to hold myself back from telling the truth, instead just asking for a cherry danish. When you're down, comfort food helped.

I was going to need a lot more than that to find any comfort in the fact that the man I cared for was now going to be dating Bethany.

Taking a deep breath, I returned to the table and hoped more than anything that we could talk about poor Canton Walters and his untimely death. Even our boring conversation about different ways of drinking coffee would be better than Alex's not-so-sly questions about Bethany and her availability.

"So where are we on this case?" I asked, deciding that if I was going to have to live with Alex liking Bethany that at least I'd do it on my terms. And that meant not thinking about it unless I absolutely had to.

For a second, he looked at me like I'd interrupted him during some important explanation, but then he nodded and began talking about the case, thankfully. "Right. I talked to the night desk clerk at the Hotel Piermont when I had some time on my shift last night."

"What did he have to say?"

Alex opened his notebook and flipped through a few pages before he got to the one with the information he was looking for. "Joseph Steadman." Looking up at me, he said, "That's the night clerk's name. I asked him if he remembered the last time he saw Canton Walters before his death. He said he didn't see him at all the night of the murder."

"There have to be emergency exits on every floor, right? Maybe if when he left his room to go out, he left by one of them."

Alex nodded again. "I thought that too, but I asked the clerk and he said that if anyone tried to open any of the emergency doors on any of the floors, an alarm would sound. I checked and he was telling the truth. He's sure no alarm went off that night, so if Canton left the hotel, he would have had to go past the front desk and he would have seen him."

"Are we sure this Joseph Steadman, night desk clerk, isn't someone we should consider a suspect? Is there any reason not to believe him?"

Smiling, Alex pointed his finger at me. "Exactly what I thought, so I checked with the owner. He has cameras on the desk and in the back office, and he says Joseph Steadman didn't even take a bathroom break on his entire eight hour shift. He was either out at the front desk or in the office for no more than a minute or so."

"Do the cameras show who came in and out during the night?"

"Nope. They're focused on the owner getting to watch his employees, not the guests. Seems he's had some problems with some of his recent hires. He installed the cameras about six months ago."

"Okay, so Canton decided to make it a night in. Did the desk clerk remember anyone coming to visit him?"

"Not according to Steadman. Only three people

came in after midnight. Two wanted a room and one was already staying at the hotel for the past two days, according to him." Alex flipped a page in his notepad and tapped his finger on the names. "Josh Meyers and Britany Jones were the couple who wanted the room."

Chuckling at dear Britany's name, I said, "Now there's a fake name if I've ever heard one. Sounds like someone didn't want anyone to know she was there."

Alex smiled but didn't say anything about Britany, likely some poor guy's cheating wife. "The third person who came in but who was already staying there was named Cecil Simon."

"Really? You don't think that sounds like a made-up name too?"

"Yes, but it's not like the Hotel Piermont requires ID to get a room. It's not exactly that kind of place. Steadman says Mr. Simon checked in two days before the murder and was a perfect guest. He never called down to the front desk, and he didn't even ask for extra towels, which from what he said seems to be a common request for their guests."

I didn't want to think about why people needed extra towels at the Hotel Piermont. If I did, I'd start to think like my editor and all sorts of freaky deaky ideas would be popping up in my brain.

"Did you get to talk to Mr. Cecil Simon while you were at the hotel last night?"

Alex frowned and shook his head. "No. Unfortunately, he checked out just hours before our victim was found by housekeeping that morning."

"That's interesting, don't you think?"

"I agree, but we have nothing to go on concerning Mr. Simon. The desk clerk said he'd never seen him before at the hotel or anywhere else, for that matter."

I took a bite of my danish and thought about our hotel guest who had coincidentally left the scene of the crime in time to have murdered Canton Walters, calmly check out of the hotel, and walk away scot-free.

"What did he look like?"

Alex read directly from his notebook. "Tall, dark hair, average build. That's about all Joseph Steadman remembered."

He looked up at me and twisted his face into an expression of frustration. I knew how he felt. That wasn't exactly much to go on.

"You just described half the average American males in this country. That narrows it down."

"Even worse, the desk clerk isn't exactly a big guy, so when he says someone is tall, it may not be what you or I think is tall."

"Well, this is certainly a conundrum then because we now have a possible suspect we may never be able to find. And even if we find him, if our mystery hotel guest Mr. Simon was just in the same place at the same time as a murderer, we're left with the fact that if no one came in, then how did Canton end up with a kitchen knife in his back? Assuming we don't think it's any of the cleaning staff, which I don't think we do, then we're looking at someone else who works at the hotel, right?"

Marking a star next to Mr. Simon's name, Alex nodded his agreement of my assessment of the case as it stood at that moment. "A ghost for a suspect or one of the Hotel Piermont's employees, but we can't forget the grieving widow and the Roberts."

Choosing to ignore them, I decided that had to mean an employee other than the housekeeping and janitorial staff, which we'd thoroughly checked. All signs pointed to Elizabeth Freely since she had something in common with Canton Walters and had the opportunity because she could easily get in and out of the hotel without even garnering a second glance.

And then Alex ruined my perfect murder scenario.

"I know who you're thinking, and I'm not saying Elizabeth isn't our killer, but Delilah Roberts sent over another list of all the people who've ever attended one of her Naughty and Spice parties. I guess she forgot some people the first time. She's had four parties in the last two years, and the list of people numbered a little over fifteen. I checked out every person but one, and they all have alibis for the night Walters was murdered."

"You certainly were busy last night. Who is this person?" I wondered, curious to know if I knew the name.

"Mary Jessick. She lives at 1525 Sanderson Street."

I tried to remember when I'd heard Mary's name before. It sounded so familiar, but in a town like Sunset Ridge, names often began to run into one another. So many families intermarried that sometimes when I thought I knew someone, it turned out that I'd confused them with their sister or brother who'd married into a family with that name.

"You look like that name rings a bell, Poppy."

I put the last forkful of danish into my mouth and enjoyed the taste of the canned cherry filling on my tongue. I knew that name, but from where?

"Old high school friend? Fellow cheerleader at the bottom of the pyramid?" Alex joked as I tried to jog my memory.

"For your information, I was a cheerleader, thank

you, but I don't remember any Mary Jessick on any squad I was on."

One of his slow grins spread across his face, like what I'd said amused him. "I can see you as a cheerleader. You've got that fresh faced, girl-next-door look about you."

Feeling particularly defensive after all that had happened that morning, I folded my arms across my chest and asked, "Is there a problem with that? Does that make me less than other people?"

"No. Why?" Clearly taken aback by my outburst and the scowl I didn't plan on removing from my face any time soon, he continued, "Poppy, I didn't mean anything by that. I bet you were cute as a cheerleader."

Cute? I was cute as a cheerleader? I knew he wasn't trying to stick his foot into his mouth, but with each syllable he uttered, I felt worse.

As my frustration mounted, I suddenly remembered where I knew Mary Jessick's name from. "I'm going to let that cute comment pass because I know this Mary Jessick person. I mentioned her in an article I wrote a while back."

"On the society page?"

"Yes. Mary Jessick is Dr. Roberts' former sister-in-law. She was married to his brother until his death a few years ago. While she was out shopping for his birthday gift with her sister-in-law, he died sitting in a chair watching television. His passing left her a very comfortable young lady."

Alex's eyes lit up with interest. "This town just gets more and more interesting every day. Let's go pay Mary a visit and see if she's connected to yet another man's death."

Chapter Nine

THE ROBIN'S EGG blue house at 1525 Sanderson Street reminded me of a cottage on a small lake my father used to rent for a week each summer when I was a little girl. Quaint and compact, it always had more than enough room for my father, my mother, and me, even though each time my mother saw it for the first time of the season she'd remark how it wasn't going to be big enough for all of us. My father would smile and take her hand in his, never saying anything about her complaint but promising she'd love it.

She always did, and at the end of each week, she'd regret having to leave to return to civilization, as she called it.

Now that I was an adult, I knew her fake complaining each summer was just her way of teasing my father. That's the kind of love they had. Gentle and free to let each of them be the person they wanted to be.

That cottage had been brown instead of the pale blue Mary's house had been painted, but it had the same tiny look to it. I expected to be surprised when we got inside, just like I was every summer when we arrived at the lake house.

Alex nudged my arm with his elbow, shaking me out

of my memories of summers long past. "It doesn't look like she's here. Want me to just ring the bell and you stay in the car?"

He was right. The front door was closed, and all the windows were too. But that didn't mean I wanted to sit in the car like an invalid.

"Why would I want to stay here? It's a beautiful day out."

"I figured you might want to stay and enjoy the air conditioning. I was just trying to be nice."

I looked into his eyes and saw something unfamiliar in them. Pity? Regret? What was it, and why did he feel that when he looked at me?

"I'm fine, Alex. I can walk the ninety feet to her front door. Why are you acting like this?"

He turned the car off and opened his door. "Like what? A gentleman?"

"Like I'm some sickly thing you don't want to tire out. I'm fine. Stop acting so weird."

Mumbling something as he slammed the door shut, he came around the front of the car still muttering. I had no idea what had gotten into him, but I wanted it to stop. The lame conversation problem back at the coffee shop was bad enough. I didn't want us to move into the realm of him thinking I was some pathetic soul he had to worry about all the time.

"I don't know what you said there under your breath, but I don't need you acting like I'm not someone who can handle herself."

Alex stopped dead and turned to face me with an expression of frustration. "I was saying that I don't know what's gotten into you today. First you jump on me as soon as I sit down at the table over at The Grounds and then you act strange over the tiniest things. Since you won't tell me what's wrong, what do you expect me to do? I've known you for three months, Poppy. I know when you're not okay. Remember when you got sick right after the Geneva Woodward case? I sensed you weren't okay without you even telling me. That's what partners do, but since you won't tell me what's wrong, I assumed you were coming down with something again. That's all I was doing in the car."

His outburst surprised me, and I wanted to hide away after hearing how awful I'd made him feel. Hanging my head, I stared down at my newly painted pink nails peeking out of my white sandals and tried to find the words to explain to him what was wrong.

None of them came to me, though, so instead I said the only thing a good partner should. "I'm sorry. I didn't realize I was making things so difficult on you."

He softly touched my arm and then cupped my shoulder with his palm. I didn't want to look up because he was so close right there in front of me, but I did and I saw real concern in his brown eyes. I didn't like him looking at me like that. I wasn't some sad girl he needed to feel bad for.

"It's okay. I just wish you'd tell me what's wrong, Poppy. We're partners. Whatever affects you, affects me."

His plea washed over me, filling my head with possibilities that maybe I could tell him what was really wrong with me. The right words that had eluded me for days suddenly came to me there as we stood on the sidewalk in front of Mary Jessick's tiny cottage house, but then the reality I hadn't considered before struck me like a bolt of lightning.

What if I did tell him I didn't want him to see Bethany because I cared for him, and what if he said he cared for me and we began dating only to find that it didn't work out? Everything we did together now as partners would be lost. I loved working on cases with him and knew with each one I learned more than I ever could on my own. He noticed details I never thought of before, and I wanted to continue to improve my investigating skills with him. I didn't want to risk losing everything we had already for the chance that we might be good together romantically too.

It was just too big a gamble.

And knowing that put everything I'd been going through into perspective. I smiled up at him and for the first time in too long, I told him the truth. "I'm fine, Alex. I got a little turned around about something a few days ago, but I think I figured it out now."

When he smiled back at me, it went all the way up to his eyes, and the concern that had filled them disappeared. "Okay. I'm happy to hear that. It's my job to make sure whatever's turning you around knows you have someone watching out for you. Don't ever forget that. That's what partners do for each other."

"Thanks, I won't. Let's go see if Mary can help us figure out who killed our victim. I'm starting to bake in the sun standing out here on the sidewalk like this."

We walked up to her front door, and as Alex knocked on the old wood screen door, I enjoyed the shade her little front porch afforded us. While I cooled down a few degrees, I thought about the revelation that had come over me out there on the sidewalk and liked the choice I'd made. I still didn't like the idea of his dating Bethany, but I would need to accept that. Alex was my partner, and if he was happy, then I should be happy for him.

"I don't think she's home. Let's go around back and see if anyone answers there," he said as he walked down the front porch stairs.

We made it halfway around the house when a deep, gravelly voice called out, "You can knock all you want. She's not home."

Looking behind us in the direction where the words had come from, I saw a heavy elderly lady with short grey hair standing on the sidewalk in what I was sure was the biggest tank top dress I'd ever seen. Bright yellow with gigantic red flowers, it hung loosely around her hefty body. Her arms were crossed over her chest, and she had a look on her face that told me Mary hadn't lucked out in the neighbor department when she moved to this house.

Alex spoke up and said, "We're looking for Mary Jessick. Do you know where we can find her, ma'am?"

The woman's right hip shot out and she snapped, "I know who you're looking for. I'm surprised you brought a female with you, though. Won't your girlfriend there mind you spending time with Mary right in front of her?"

He and I looked at each other, partly confused about what she meant about our potential suspect and party confused as to why people more and more seemed to assume we were together as anything more than work partners.

I smiled at the elderly woman and yelled out to her, "It's not like that, but thank you for letting us know she's not home."

She flashed me an unconvincing smile that said she

didn't believe me on the girlfriend part or the part about me being thankful for her help and turned to walk away. Alex quickly asked, "Do you know what time she gets home from work?"

Spinning around quite fast for someone so heavy, she waddled toward us with a determined look that showed she had something more to say. I wasn't sure I wanted to hear it, though, but Alex seemed acutely interested in what this woman might tell us and walked up to meet her halfway. Sure whatever she might say would be snarky, I double timed my steps and caught up to him just as he reached her.

"Who are you? What do you want with Mary?" she asked with eyes narrowed to slits in her pudgy face.

He flashed her his badge and one of his most sincere smiles. "I'm Officer Alex Montero from the Sunset Ridge Police, ma'am. What's your name?"

"Eudora Stark. Mrs. Eudora Stark. It's about time you came here since I've called no less than six times."

"We're just looking for Mary to speak to her."

Mrs. Stark pointed her chubby index finger in my direction and ignoring his statement asked, "Who's she?"

Alex began to explain how I was his partner, but I knew what would work much better on this woman. Thrusting my hand forward to shake hers, I introduced myself. "I'm Poppy McGuire from *The Sunset Eagle*, Mrs. Stark. How are you today?"

Her demeanor instantaneously changed. Gone was the snarky tone and nasty look, replaced by a smile and a handshake that enveloped my much smaller hand in hers.

"*The Sunset Eagle* newspaper? I knew I recognized you

from somewhere. You write the society column each week. I read it all the time. Did I hear you were taking over the police blotter feature too? Is that why you're with the officer?"

News certainly traveled fast, but that never surprised me in my hometown. What did was that my editor had already begun flapping his gums about my new assignment even before I'd handed in my first column.

"I'm so happy to hear you read it. In today's world with computers and hundreds of channels on TV, it's hard to keep people interested in the newspaper, especially the society column. I'm so flattered whenever I have the chance to meet a reader."

I wasn't lying about any of what I said to Mrs. Stark. Most days, I didn't understand how *The Sunset Eagle* still continued to operate considering anyone with a computer could find out news one hundred times faster with a few website clicks, but then I remembered the basic truth that small town people like her enjoyed the local feeling of their town's newspaper more than anything else, and this was doubly true with elderly folks.

"I never miss reading *The Eagle*!" she said as she clutched my wrist in her chubby hand.

She gazed into my eyes like I was some kind of movie star and she was entranced by meeting someone famous, but Alex interrupted her adoration of me in his attempt to get our visit back on its original track.

"Do you know what time Mary usually gets home, Mrs. Stark?"

I smiled and nodded as she continued to stare up at me, and she reluctantly looked over at him after a few moments. "I usually see her back by six at night. She's a young widow, you know. I think that's why she acts the way she does."

My ears perked up at her characterization of Mary in such a provocative way, and Alex jumped on her statement.

"Like what? How does she act?"

A deep frown settled into her doughy features, making the creases next to her nose and mouth even more pronounced and dragging the skin around her eyes down with them. "She sees too many men. You won't be including any of this in your column, will you? I'd hate to have this get out."

"No, no," I reassured her. "This is entirely between us, Mrs. Stark."

Happy to know the entire town wouldn't hear about what she thought of Mary, she continued. "I know you young girls these days don't do things like we used to back when I was young, but there can be too many men. A lady has to be careful with these things."

My curiosity spiked, and I asked, "How many?"

"Two different ones just this week." Mrs. Stark leaned forward toward me and said in a much quieter voice, "They both came over the same night."

I looked over at Alex standing to my right whose knowing grin nearly made me chuckle right there in front of this elderly woman who clearly didn't approve of whatever Mary was doing with her male visitors. There really was no point in trying to explain to her that they may have been just friends. Someone like Mrs. Stark wasn't going to believe that anyway.

Changing the topic, Alex asked, "What did you call the police about all those times?"

"Mary has recently had people over who park with two wheels on the sidewalk and make my dog Muffy bark at all hours of the day and night."

Alex asked, "How many people and when?"

Mrs. Stark scrunched up her face as she thought about the details and then said, "Three nights in the past week Muffy was up barking in the middle of the night. I go to bed early, and I'm sound asleep with her in her little doggy bed next to mine by ten o'clock. When she hears a car outside, she wakes up and runs to the window. I know it's Mary's house because Muffy is pointing that way when she barks. I don't know how many people because it was dark, but I know I saw Mary on two of those nights get out of the car at that ungodly hour in the middle of the night."

I knew he'd heard the same thing I'd heard—that Mary had come home late a couple nights in the past week. But had she been out the night of Canton Walters' murder?

"Do you remember if one of those nights was Tuesday, Mrs. Stark?" he asked with excitement in his voice.

She nodded and continued to frown. "Yes, it was. Muffy was especially perturbed that night because Mary and some man made all kinds of noise when they got out of the car. I had to rock her to sleep and it took nearly an hour to calm her down!"

"Do you remember anything else about that night, Mrs. Stark?" I asked, hoping she was as nosy as I thought she might be and maybe watched out that bedroom window of hers for a while after Mary and her male friend arrived.

"It was late and Muffy was upset is pretty much all I remember."

"What about what the man looked like?"

"He had blond hair and it looked a mess when he stepped out of the car. That boy needed a haircut. What kind of girl would date someone who didn't even bother to do his hair for their date?"

Taking the picture of Canton Walters out of his pocket, he held it up for Mrs. Stark to look at. "Was this the man you saw getting out of the car that night?"

She took the picture from his hold and examined it. "It could be. I never saw him in the light, but it could be the same person. All I can say is the man I saw needed a haircut."

As Alex wrote down the details from Mrs. Stark's complaining, he asked, "Do you remember anything else from that night? Anything that seemed odd or out of the ordinary?"

She handed him the picture again and shook her head. "You mean other than what I already told you? I don't think so. I've never seen him again here with her, and since that night, it's been pretty quiet around Mary's house."

"Okay, thank you, Mrs. Stark. You've been very helpful."

She beamed at Alex's compliment and once again grabbed my arm. "It was so nice to meet you, Poppy McGuire. I'm going to tell all my friends I got to meet a real reporter from *The Sunset Eagle*."

"You are so sweet. Thank you. And thank you for helping us today. You've been so good to tell us what you saw. Have a wonderful day, okay?"

"Oh, you too!"

She walked backwards toward her house next door wearing a smile from ear-to-ear as she waved goodbye to us. I wasn't as big a deal as she'd made me, but I had to admit it felt nice knowing someone enjoyed my work that much that meeting me meant something to her.

Mrs. Stark had affected Alex in a different way, and I turned to see him circling Mary's name in his tablet. Looking up, he said, "I think that woman may have been one of the last people to see our victim alive that night. I'll be interested in hearing what Mary Jessick has to say when we come back tonight at six."

We walked toward the car as that thought settled into my brain. I didn't know Mary, but I had to wonder what had happened between when she and Canton came here and when he ended up with a knife in his back in his hotel room nearly a mile away.

"But didn't the night clerk say he didn't see Canton Walters leave the hotel that night?" I asked. "How could he have been here waking up Muffy and Mrs. Stark without that clerk noticing he'd left and then returned again?"

Alex stopped at the car and leaned back against the hood. Crossing his arms, he knitted his brows at the seemingly inconsistent facts from the two witnesses. "I don't know. Maybe he wasn't paying as close attention as he wanted me to believe. Something tells me nothing gets by old Mrs. Stark there."

"Don't forget Muffy too."

"How could I?" he said with a chuckle. "I bet she and her owner have gotten a show a time or two living here next to Mary."

"That sounds pretty provincial, Officer Montero. Aren't women allowed to enjoy the opposite sex like men are?"

Clearly surprised that I'd taken offense at his comment about Mary, Alex held up his hands in faux surrender. "Whoa. That's not what I was saying at all. It just seems like Mary had a good time. You know, with the sex toy parties and guys at her house in the middle of the night."

"I attended one of those parties once."

I didn't know why I blurted that out, but I didn't regret it. I personally had no problem with Mary living life the way she wanted to either. If she wanted to spend time with different men, who was I or anyone else to tell her it was wrong?

Alex raised one eyebrow and then gave me a tiny smile that was definitely sexier than it should have been as we stood there on the street in the middle of the day, but he didn't respond to my confession. All the better. I barely remembered anything other than women giggling at sexy lingerie that night, so if he asked me any questions about it, I wouldn't have been able to answer them anyway. I hadn't intended to make a big deal out of going to one, so his usual stoic response was appreciated.

"You really understood how to deal with her back there. I was impressed. I wouldn't have known to handle her that way."

For a moment, I stood confused by his changing the topic. When I recovered, I waved off his compliment. "It was nothing. I know *The Eagle*'s demographics, and the biggest segment of our readership is older people, especially older women."

"She really liked you, Poppy. I think you have a fan."

"It's been known to happen, every blue moon or so," I joked, trying to seem humble even as I thought it was nice to have someone out there I knew enjoyed my columns.

"I knew I wasn't the only one."

He moved to walk around the car to leave, but I had to ask if he'd actually become a fan of my writing for the paper. "You've read my columns and like them? I never pictured you as a guy who reads a small town newspaper."

Shaking his head, he gave me another sexy smile like he had when I told him I'd been to one of those parties and opened the driver's side door to get in. "No. I've never read even one of them."

I slid into the passenger seat wishing that simple sentence didn't make me as happy as it did.

Chapter Ten

A T EXACTLY SIX o'clock, Alex and I knocked on
Mary Jessick's front door and found her home, just
as Mrs. Stark had told us she would be. A young and
attractive woman with long black hair that fell almost to
her waist and dark brown eyes, Mary struck me as
exotic, yet in some way naïve looking.

She stared out in fear at Alex's badge pressed against
her screen door as he announced in an authoritative
voice who we were. "I'm Officer Montero and this is
Poppy McGuire. We'd like to speak to you about a
murder investigation we're conducting."

I expected her to immediately tell us she didn't know
the victim since it was likely she'd either seen something
in the newspaper about Canton Walters' death at the
Hotel Piermont or heard people talking about it around
town. Sunset Ridge wasn't exactly the kind of place
where you could avoid hearing local gossip, even if you
tried. I knew that all too well.

But she didn't. Instead, she opened the door and
said, "Please come in. I was so sorry to hear about that
poor man's death."

She led us to her kitchen, a tiny room off the modest
living room where we'd entered the house. We sat down

in dark wood chairs at a matching round table and saw how nervous Mary was. Whether she was unnerved by a policeman in her home or something far more serious that would indicate some part in our case, it was clear by how her hands shook as she sat down with us that something was upsetting her.

"I don't know what I can do to help," she began but then stopped and pressed her lips together. I wasn't sure what Alex thought, but she looked plenty guilty about something to me.

"We know from Delilah Roberts that you were one of the people who attended her Naughty and Spice parties. Is that true?" Alex asked.

"Yes. Yes, yes I did," she stammered out before looking away toward where her hands sat in her lap.

"Were you at the most recent party she held last month?" he asked in a matter-of-fact tone I knew he was using to try to calm her down.

"No. Well, yes. I got there late, but I was there. For a little while, at least."

"Can you tell us what transpired at that party, Miss Jessick?"

Mary's cheeks turned bright red, and she kept her gaze pinned on her lap. "Oh, I…nothing really happened. You know how those things go."

I looked over at Alex and gave him a nod to let him know I understood what was going on. Mary was embarrassed talking about a sex toy party with him. He smiled and nodded, giving me the sign that told me I could take over the questioning. With my head, I motioned for him to get up from the table and walk over to the window. He'd still be able to hear what she said since the room was barely big enough to hold the table, refrigerator, and stove, so it wouldn't be like he was leaving the questioning entirely.

He slid his chair back from the kitchen table and moved away, and I saw Mary's body language instantly relax. Leaning forward toward her, I offered my hand. "It's okay. There's nothing to be scared of."

She pressed her hand into mine and squeezed as she raised her eyes to look at me. "I'm a little embarrassed is all. All my neighbors think I'm some town slut, and now the police are in my house asking me about a sex toy party. I'm really not like that at all."

I smiled, hoping to make her feel better. "It's okay. Really. My partner intimidates everyone, so don't worry. Do you know the first time I met him he barely spoke four words to me, and then the next time we met he aimed a gun at my head?"

Mary's eyes grew as wide as saucers. "He did? Really? Why?"

"I was sort of trespassing on his property, so he probably had every right to, but I know how scary he can be. You don't have to be frightened, though. We're just here asking questions about a case we're trying to solve. You see, that man at the hotel, Canton Walters, was murdered and we need to find out who did it."

A frown marred her beautiful face and she shook her head. "I know all too well about murder in Sunset Ridge."

"What do you mean?" I asked and then looked over toward Alex, who raised his eyebrows in surprise. Even I hadn't expected her to be that forthcoming after a few nice words.

"My husband was murdered, Miss McGuire. Five years ago, I came home to find him dead and even though no one on the police wanted to listen to me, I know someone murdered him."

"How? I thought he died of a heart attack."

"My husband was older than I was, but he wasn't that old. A heart attack in a man who wasn't even forty? I don't know how they did it, but whoever killed him found a way."

"Why would someone kill him?"

Mary hung her head. "It doesn't matter now. The police never believed me, and even the autopsy didn't show anything, but I know in my gut he was murdered."

I looked over at Alex, who stood writing feverishly in his notepad. He lifted his gaze from the details he'd just put down and mouthed that he had no idea about her husband or his death.

"I'm sorry, Mary. I didn't know this about your husband."

Lifting her head, she forced a smile. "It's okay. I miss him, but I've accepted what happened. That's why I want to help to find this man's murderer, but I don't know what I can do."

"Just tell me anything you can about the parties at Delilah Roberts' house."

"It's really not as bad as everyone thinks. Delilah is alone most days since Alan spends all day and even some nights at his office. She understands that he's dedicated to his practice, and all she ever asks of him is to let her have parties every so often. We don't do anything terrible at them, Miss McGuire."

I patted her hand and smiled. "Oh, I know. I've been to one once. It was fun."

"They are. We get together to drink some wine and giggle at sexy toys and things we can wear when we're with our boyfriends and husbands."

She looked over at Alex and blushed. "You know what I mean."

"Not really. Men prefer to get together and watch sports," he said with a chuckle. "It usually involves beer."

Mary turned her head toward me and said, "Well, I bet your girlfriend understands, right? You know what I mean, don't you? It's fun to get together with the girls and laugh and drink wine. Nobody gets hurt and Delilah makes a little money on the side."

I didn't bother to once again explain to another person that Alex and I weren't a couple and stayed on the topic at hand. "I completely understand wanting to enjoy yourself with the girls. My friends and I get together for a few drinks every so often, and it's always great fun. So nothing out of the ordinary ever happened at one of the parties?"

Looking away, Mary thought about what I'd asked. "My brother-in-law has never liked Delilah having them. I can tell you that."

Her admission didn't surprise me in the least. Dr. Roberts was a man who thought women should behave demurely, and his wife having friends over to drink and look at the sex toys she sells wasn't modest in the least.

"Did he tell her not to have the parties anymore?"

Hesitating, she thought about what she wanted to say for a moment and then answered, "I don't know, but I can tell you he didn't like her having them. At her third one earlier this year, he came in while the party was in full swing and pulled her into the kitchen right in front of all of us. They had a big fight. I heard a little of it when I was walking past on my way to the bathroom."

"What was it about?" I asked as Alex inched himself closer to where we sat.

"He threatened to throw everyone out of his house and her too. His house. That's what he said to her. After all that she's done to make such a lovely home for him, and he threw it in her face like that. That's why she started having the parties. She wanted to contribute something to their home other than cooking and cleaning. She's told me so many times that she wants to be more than just a doctor's wife who stays at home all day making sure the rugs are vacuumed and her husband's dinner is served whenever he gets home."

"Did he follow through on his threat to throw everyone out that night?"

Shaking her head, Mary sighed. "No. They fought for about fifteen minutes in the kitchen, and then Delilah returned to all of us in the living room looking like she always did. Her makeup was perfect, but I know he made her cry when they were fighting. She would never let anyone see her as anything less than that perfect face because she knows Alan wants her to look like that. She never said anything to any of us about what he said, and when I asked her about it after everyone had left, she made excuses for him like she always did. He works hard. He's just shy about things. All reasons why he could bully her."

I had to admit I felt sorry for Delilah Roberts. I couldn't imagine every day of my life being dedicated to cleaning a house that could be taken away from me on a whim if my husband chose to. My streak of independence ran deep, probably because I'd been single for so long, so the mere thought of someone threatening to throw my friends out or telling me what I could or couldn't do was completely foreign to me.

"She continues to have the parties, though," Alex said as he stepped closer to the table. "Her husband must have come around to being okay with them."

Mary looked up at him and shook her head. "No. He still doesn't like them. I don't know how she keeps having them, but I can't see Alan ever being okay with them. They aren't his style. He couldn't find fun if it was sitting on top of him."

"Can you tell us if you've ever seen this man?" Alex asked as he took out the picture of Canton Walters. Placing it in front of Mary, he added, "Anything you can remember."

She stared down at the picture, and I thought I saw a look of sadness cross her face. But it was momentary, and after it passed, she pushed Canton's picture away. "I don't think I've ever seen this man."

"Are you sure?" Alex pressed, surely seeing the same look on her face that I saw.

She shyly smiled and said, "There were only women at the parties, Officer Montero."

"That's not exactly true, now is it, Mary? Dr. Roberts was there at least for one party since they had that fight in the kitchen you told us about."

I'd been Alex's partner long enough to know when he thought someone was lying. I could always hear it in the way he said things like he'd just done with Mary. There was a lilt to his voice that told anyone who was listening carefully enough that he didn't entirely believe what they were saying. It wasn't a threatening or menacing tone, but there was something about how his words came out that made it clear he wasn't going to just walk away before asking more questions.

She looked at me with a fearful expression, which told me she knew more about Canton Walters than she had let on. I gave her hand a supportive squeeze to let her know she needed to tell us what she knew.

"Let me look at that picture again."

Pulling it toward her across the table, she held it in her hands and looked down at it. That same sad look came over her face again, and she traced the outside of the picture with her fingertips like it meant something to her.

I looked up at Alex to see him giving me a look that said he expected we were about to find out something important from her. I hoped he was right. Our investigation hadn't made it very far yet, and Mary providing an important clue would give us something to go on.

She swiveled her head left and right to look up at Alex and then at me. "You know, there was a male dancer at one of her parties, the second party last year. He might have been that man."

"A male dancer? That might be a reason why her husband doesn't like these parties," I wondered aloud.

"I don't think so. He never knew about that. Alan was out of town at a conference for that party, and even though Delilah didn't really want to have a dancer there, her friends hired him to come. She'd never do that on her own. For all the awful things Alan does, she wouldn't disrespect him like that in his own home. That was her friends, not her."

Mary obviously cared for her sister-in-law and friend, as evidenced by her defense of her every time we'd said something even slightly against Delilah. Alan was another story, though. She clearly didn't like him. I found that interesting since I remembered hearing around town that her brother-in-law had been devastated at the loss of his brother when he died and they'd turned to each other for comfort. The busybodies of Sunset Ridge had even wondered if in all the time they spent together whether he'd cheated on his wife with his brother's widow.

Alex handed Mary a sheet of paper from his notepad his pen and said, "Mary, please write your phone number down for me so I can get in touch with you if we have any more questions."

"Okay. I hope I was able to help in some way. I would never want anyone to feel the way I did after my husband's death. Some things shouldn't remain a mystery."

She wrote her number as Alex had ordered her to and handed him back the paper and pen. As he held it so I could see what she'd written, I noticed she printed instead of using cursive writing, even for her name.

Alex folded the piece of paper and stuck it into his pocket. With a smile, he said, "Thank you. One last question. Where were you Tuesday night after midnight?"

"Tuesday after midnight I was at Poppy's father's bar until around one in the morning and then I came home and went to bed."

"Your neighbor next door, Mrs. Stark, told us she saw you come home late with a man that night. When she looked at the picture I showed you, she said she thought it could have been that man with you when you got out of the car."

All the blood drained from Mary's face until she was pale as a ghost, and her hands began to shake as they had when we first arrived. Clearing her throat, she looked Alex square in the eyes and said, "My neighbor thinks she sees a lot of things because she wants to see them. She thinks I should live as the mourning widow for the rest of my life wearing black and a veil like some medieval nun, and because I refuse to, she spends her days judging me like many people do in this town. You can ask Poppy's father where I was from ten to one in the morning. He saw me and I remember him saying hi when I went to the bar for a drink at one point in the night. As for getting out of a car on Tuesday night with some man, that never happened. I walked home from McGuire's because I hadn't taken my car since I knew I wanted to have a few drinks."

"Okay, thank you again, Mary. I'll be in contact if we need anything more."

She stood from the table to show us to the door, and as I followed Alex outside, she tapped me on the shoulder. I turned to see she had something on her mind and she said, "Don't believe everything you hear, even from the most respectable people in this town. Even those with spotless reputations have skeletons in their closets."

I smiled and nodded, agreeing with every word she said more than she could ever know. By the time I caught up with my partner, he was already behind the wheel and ready to drive away. I climbed into the car and enjoyed the cold air blowing from the vents since just going from Mary's house to the car had made me break out into a sweat.

"What's her address again?"

Turning to look at her house, I watched her close the door and then said, "1525. Why?"

"Look at this."

Alex handed me his notebook and the loose sheet of paper with her phone number. In his notes, he'd circled a number. 15253348256.

"What's this number?" I asked.

"That's the number we found on that sheet of paper in Canton Walters' hotel room. Look at her phone number."

I stared down at his notepad and then at the sheet Mary had written her number on and then back at the notepad. "It's a combination of those two numbers."

Unsure if I wanted to hear his answer, I asked, "Do you think we have our third suspect?"

"Third or fourth. I haven't decided which of the Roberts is more on my list, so I've got them both on it. I have a feeling the next time I speak to Mary, we'll be sitting at the station instead of in her kitchen."

I thought about beautiful Mary with her long black hair and big brown eyes and couldn't imagine her jamming that knife into Canton Walters' back. I did have to admit there certainly was something off about her story, and I had the feeling she had spent time with our victim, but killing him?

No. I just couldn't see it.

Alex was a different story, of course. He saw guilt in people I couldn't.

"Thanks for letting me take the lead in there. I know you probably didn't understand why she'd be uncomfortable talking about Delilah's sex toy parties in front of you, but I figured if she thought she could talk freely around another woman, she might open up."

A smirk came across his face that seemed strange, but then he said, "I trust you, Poppy. I don't understand a grown woman being embarrassed about doing anything in the twenty-first century, but I'm not from this town, so maybe that's why. You always go with your gut when it comes to the people here, and I respect that. I've been telling you since the day we began as partners that I believe in your instincts. They're good, so I follow them."

He didn't say it, but I'd been acting like I didn't believe in him as much. The problem was I didn't know how to tell him I really did trust him.

"I'll find out from my father what time Mary got to the bar, who she spent time with there, and what time she left when I go over there tonight."

"Okay. By the way, there's one thing I can't figure out. Why is Mary's last name not Roberts if she was married to Alan Roberts' brother?"

"If I remember correctly, Jessick is her maiden name," I explained as I pulled my seatbelt across me. "I guess she decided to go back to that name after he died."

Alex made a humming noise but said nothing as he started the car. To me, the far more interesting thing about Mary was that she clearly thought there was something nefarious about her husband's death. I didn't remember hearing anything about that, though. It had always been said he died of a heart attack.

"What did you think of what she said about her husband, Alex? Do you think it's possible he was murdered?"

He put the car in drive and as we pulled away from her house, he said, "Anything's possible, I guess. It isn't impossible for a man in his late thirties to die of a heart attack, though. I'll look into it on my next shift. What was his name?"

I had to go back deep into my memory for that, but as we turned the corner onto my street, I remembered. "His name was Jacob. Jacob Roberts."

"Okay, I'll take a look and see what I can find."

He stopped in front of my house and I opened the door to step back into the scorching heat. "Tomorrow at our usual time?"

"Sure, but who knows? Maybe I'll stop in at McGuire's tonight. Nothing like an ice cold beer on a hot summer night, and I can see if you father remembers anything about what Mary was doing on Tuesday night."

"You don't trust me to get the details, Officer Montero?" I joked as I swung my legs to get out.

He leaned over against the passenger seat and smiled up at me. "Okay, then maybe I'll just stop in for the cold beer and good company."

Chapter Eleven

MCGUIRE'S HAD A few regulars at the bar, but for a Friday night it was pretty dead. My father stood next to a table in the back talking to Albert Lightenton, his barber for life, as he called him. He'd cut my father's hair for nearly forty years, which according to my father was the longest he'd ever stayed loyal to any person other than my mother. As a result, Andrew never paid for any drinks at the bar. It seemed like a fair trade-off.

My father's ability to find joy in what everyone else saw as the mundane had always amazed me. He wasn't just a glass half-full kind of guy. Staying positive was one thing, but my father went way past that. His feelings toward his barber were a prime example of this. As far as I was concerned, it was just a haircut, but for him it was much more. It was part of a relationship he prized, so he tended to it by showing Andrew his appreciation whenever he came into McGuire's.

I was more like my mother, though. For all her crusading, she had a hard time seeing greatness in the everyday. I, too, had that problem. I wanted to be more like my father and have reason to smile all the time, but too much weighed on my mind too often, and I knew firsthand too many people weren't as good as my father claimed. For me, others weren't possible relationships just waiting to be formed but suspicions waiting to be uncovered.

Albert waved to me as I stood behind the bar, and as I waved back, I wished I could be the kind of person who could be open. I truly did. That wasn't who I was, though. I didn't attract people into my life because in my heart I believed there was evil in the world and I didn't exclude many people from the list of who might be the ones to bring that evil into my life.

Alex was one of those people I did exclude, though. While I still hadn't figured him out, I knew I liked being around him. What had begun as admiration for his investigative abilities had morphed into much more for me, but now that I'd decided not to risk our friendship for anything more, I had to find someplace to push all the feelings I had for him. My brain had gotten on board with this, but my heart didn't want to join the friend party. No, my heart was still trying to convince me not to listen to reason. Each time I told myself it wasn't worth the risk, that heart of mine insisted on reminding me that all work and no play made Poppy a very boring woman.

I'd listened to my heart in the past with disastrous results, but still it had the power to make me reconsider my rational choices, and when it came to Alex, my heart seemed ready to work overtime to make me go back on my decision to keep our relationship strictly friendly partners.

"Is this your fourth job, Poppy?"

Roused from my thoughts, I looked up and saw Alex taking a seat right in front of me. My entirely illogical heart skipped a beat at seeing him there. "Fourth?"

"You work with me, at *The Eagle*, at your online job, and here. Four."

"Oh, yeah. Don't you remember? I lost my job online after our first case together, so I'm down to three. Well, two and a half since working here really isn't a job."

"That's right. I do remember. They lost a good person. Two and a half is still a lot, though."

I smiled at his compliment. "Do you want that ice cold beer you mentioned this afternoon or your favorite?"

He thought for a moment and said, "It's cooled down a little since then, so I'll go with the scotch."

Placing his favorite scotch neat in front of him on the bar, I waved my hand as he moved to get his wallet out. "No charge. My treat."

"Are we celebrating something?" he asked with a quizzical look.

"No. Just my treat."

Alex lifted his glass in thanks and took a drink as I studied him in a way I'd never done before. Dressed in a dark blue button down shirt and jeans, he looked bigger. Since we'd started working together just about three months ago, he'd filled out from what he'd been in the spring. Maybe he'd begun working out.

"I thought you were going to tell me your father remembered something about Mary being here on Tuesday night that's going to break our case wide open."

Popping the top on a beer, I took a drink and shook my head. "Sorry, no. I asked him and he said he remembers seeing Mary around midnight, but he doesn't remember seeing her after that because the bar filled up and it was busy."

He took a deep breath in, as if to prepare himself for something, and said, "Then I think she's moving up our suspect list to number one."

I knew he was right to think that. Her neighbor had seen her with a man who she thought could be Canton Walters, and she'd admitted that he might have danced at one of the parties she attended. And then there was the strange detail of her address and phone number on that piece of paper we found in his hotel room that likely meant he knew her.

But I still couldn't see her as the killer.

"You look like you don't agree, Poppy. Do you know something I should know?"

I took another drink of my beer and rested my elbows on the bar. Leaning toward him, I said, "I can't explain it, but I just can't picture her killing anyone, much less driving a kitchen knife into someone's back."

"Hell hath no fury...what is it again?" he asked with a chuckle.

"Hell hath no fury like a woman scorned. I get it, but I can't even imagine her scorned and killing someone. And who's to say Canton scorned her? Why would he? She's beautiful and wealthy."

"She is, but that doesn't mean every man in the world is going to want her. What if she wanted him for more than a mere affair with a married man and he told her no? They fight, she grabs the knife, and it's lights out for poor Canton."

I tried to imagine Mary being that scorned woman, but it didn't work. "I don't think so, Alex. There's one big problem with her being the killer. I don't think she could physically do it."

"That I don't know, but I could find out. In the

meantime, until I get some evidence that contradicts Mary being our killer, she's on the top of my list of suspects."

"Are you expecting to get some of that evidence any time soon?" I asked, curious to know what he hadn't told me about.

"I am. I'm waiting on the list of calls in and out of the Hotel Piermont on the night of the murder. When we see those, we might have a much clearer idea of what happened."

"When do you think that will come?"

Two men came through the door and sat at the opposite end of the bar, so I put my hand up and said, "Wait a second. I don't want to miss anything, so hang on until I get back from taking care of these people."

I hurried to where they sat and took their orders for two beers on tap. Eager to hear when we might have a real break in our case, I set their drinks down in front of them and raced back to where Alex sat.

"Okay, shoot."

"You're really excited about this, aren't you?" he asked with a smile.

"I'm a huge fan of research. You like dealing with people, but I like this kind of thing."

Alex tipped his glass to get the last of his drink and put the empty down on the bar. As I poured him a second, he explained, "People are more interesting. It can be a challenge to figure out what they really mean when they're telling you what they want to believe is the truth. Or what they want you to believe is the truth."

"See, that's my problem with people. That last part trips me up. Phone records don't lie. They are what they are. I like that."

He raised his glass to make a toast, and I raised my drink. Clinking his glass against my beer bottle, he smiled broadly. "To opposites as partners. Yin and yang."

I took a swig of my beer and agreed. We were opposites. Maybe that was why we worked so well together. Whatever it was, I was glad I'd listened to my head instead of following my heart.

And then the one thing my heart feared the most walked through the door to my father's bar and sat down next to him.

Wearing an even tinier sundress than she had on the last time she interrupted the two of us as we talked about work, Bethany leaned forward on the bar so I almost got a show and said, "Poppy, I didn't think you'd be working tonight. When I called Alex and he said he was coming here tonight, I figured I'd pop in and say hi."

I wasn't sure what I was supposed to say to that. She'd basically just announced that she had expected to have him all to herself, even though he hadn't officially asked her to meet him. Stifling the snarky side of my personality, I tried to remain pleasant as I plastered a smile onto my face.

"Yep, I'm here. You know me. Work, work, work. What can I get you?"

"I think I'll do something fruity tonight. How about an orange creamsicle?" she asked with a giggle.

"Orange creamsicle. Okay."

Out of the corner of my eye, I saw Alex watching me and a disturbing idea popped into my head. Had he intentionally encouraged Bethany to come to my father's bar knowing full well I'd be here so he could see my reaction to his dating her?

No. Don't think that way, Poppy. He's given you no indication he knew she was coming here, and how about you remember you decided you didn't want to risk your friendship and working relationship for anything else? And even more, Bethany is your friend, or at least you thought she was until recently. Try remembering that.

As all that rambled around my brain, I made her fruity drink and tried not to let myself be miserable. With my best attempt at a genuine smile, I placed it front of her and finished it off with a rim of whipped cream.

"Viola! That'll be six-fifty."

For a long second, it seemed like the world switched into slow motion. Bethany looked at me and then Alex before slowly opening her purse to get her money, and Alex stared at me like he was surprised I was charging her when I hadn't charged him for his drink.

Some relationships I prized and rewarded and others I didn't so much. If it was petty to charge her, then so be it. She was going to get a far bigger reward than just a few measly bucks.

Alex reached across the bar and ran his fingertip over my cheek, making my body instantly come alive. Surprised, I just stood there as he pulled his hand away with a dollop of whipped cream on his finger.

With that sexy grin he wore sometimes, he said, "You got a little whipped cream on your face when you made that drink."

The blood rushed to my face so I felt like I had a fever of a hundred and five, and then he stuck his finger in his mouth to suck the whipped cream off it and I was sure I'd blacked out and my fantasies had taken over my brain.

Bethany made a joke about me being sloppy or something, but I wasn't listening because my brain and my heart had begun their newest tug-of-war and all I heard in my ears was a single, deafening thought.

Had I made a mistake by not telling him how I felt?

Excusing myself, I made a beeline to the bathroom to rinse off the remaining stickiness from the whipped cream on my cheek. By the time I closed the door behind me, my heart had won the war and as I stared into the mirror to make sure I'd removed the last of Bethany's drink from my face, I thought I knew what I had to do.

Now all I had to do was figure out how.

I returned to my place behind the bar to find the two of them deep in conversation about some club in Baltimore they both had in common. I stood there watching Bethany rave about how much fun she'd had the last time she'd been there and when I turned to see Alex's reaction, my heart sank.

He talked about the place with an excitement he'd never expressed with me. His laughter, his voice never sounded that way when we spoke about anything. For the first time, I realized I knew little about Alex other than his work. He'd never told me anything about his life before he came to Sunset Ridge, and I had to admit a painful truth.

All I understood of him was the one part everyone got to see. Bethany, on the other hand, teased out of him in a matter of minutes what no one in town had found out about Alex Montero. Not even me.

"Poppy, Bethany and I are talking about this place back in Baltimore. It's called Under Tenth. Have you ever been there?"

"No. I can't say I have."

I wanted to be able to talk about it like Bethany did, but I couldn't. I'd never been to Under Tenth or anywhere else, it seemed.

"Poppy doesn't do that club scene, do you, Poppy?" Bethany said with a chuckle.

Nothing about what she said was untrue, but it didn't matter. I felt out of place in my own father's bar, like I was intruding on the two of them instead of her intruding on us.

Who was I kidding? There was no us. I was someone he let tag around with him because I helped get the locals to talk. That's all there was to us. He was Officer Alex Montero, retired Baltimore detective who had agreed to join the Sunset Ridge police force because he was bored hiding out in his house, and I was Poppy McGuire, town nobody the busybodies mentioned in whispered tones only to express pity that in my early thirties I was still unmarried.

"I can understand why you wouldn't," Alex said in response to Bethany's claim that I didn't go out to clubs. "I'm not a fan of them either."

Whatever he was trying to do with that, all it succeeded in making me feel was that he pitied me too.

"We should go there tonight!" Bethany excitedly announced as she grabbed onto his arm. "It would be fun."

Alex looked down at where she'd latched onto him and then up at me. "It could be fun. What do you say?"

I'd never felt more like a third-wheel in my life. Forcing a smile, I declined his offer, hating how out of place I felt at that moment.

"I think I have to work tonight."

Before he could say anything else, I walked down to the other end of the bar to get those customers two more beers. I stayed down there for a few minutes pretending like I had to clean beneath the bar because I didn't want to go back and hear him say they were going to that club. It should have meant nothing to me. I'd come to peace with the fact that I liked us being friends.

Until I saw how easily Bethany had peeled back layers that I hadn't touched in three months of speaking every day with him.

I felt a hand brush my shoulder and turned to see my father at my side. "Everything okay up here? I was back talking to Andrew for a long time. That's what happens when we get talking about forty years of history."

"Can you take over the bar for me, Dad? I know I'm supposed to be helping, but it's not too busy yet. I just need to go into the back for a little bit."

He glanced down toward the other end of the bar where Alex and Bethany sat and then at me. "Sure. Take all the time you need."

I swallowed hard and kissed him on the cheek. "Thanks, Dad. I just need a few minutes."

Without looking back toward them, I headed into the stock room and closed the door behind me. I didn't know why I wanted to hide out. It was foolish. A grown woman hiding out among kegs and cases of liquor.

Burying my head in my hands, I tried not to feel what I was feeling. Just hours earlier I'd convinced myself to forget all this silliness and now it was back with a vengeance. What was wrong with me?

I heard the door open and didn't even lift my head.

If it was my father, then he'd see me like I was and understand. If it was anyone else, they'd see me and leave immediately since it was a rare person who invited someone else's misery into their world.

"You get the same look on your face when you're down that your mother used to get."

I looked up at him standing there and nodded. In my mind's eye, I could see that mix of sadness and disappointment on my mother's face that she let the world see so rarely. She preferred to put on a good face no matter what life threw at her, but on those occasions when the world got too much for her, she would let how she really felt come out for those who knew her best.

He sat down in front of me on a case of vodka and looked at me like he was worried about me. "What's wrong, honey?"

"Nothing. I'm fine. I think the heat might have gotten to me today. Maybe heat stroke. I just needed a cool place to sit."

That last part was clearly a lie since the bar was a very chilly temperature somewhere in the mid-sixties. I wasn't a very good liar when it came right down to it. Not that I wanted to lie to him. I just didn't want to talk about anything.

"I can understand that. Today was a scorcher. At least you and Alex got to drive around in air conditioning. I saw you two, I suspect heading toward Mary Jessick's earlier today. You didn't see me, though, but you two looked like you were deep in conversation."

"Sorry. I didn't see you."

"Alex is a good person. I like him."

I knew what my father was doing, but I didn't want to play this game with him. I didn't really have a choice, though.

"He is. He's a great detective."

"Are you enjoying working with him?"

"I am. I'm learning so much from watching him unravel clues and solve cases. I don't do much to help him, but he's really teaching me a lot."

My father smiled and took my hand in his to give it a gentle squeeze. "Don't discount yourself like that, Poppy. I'm sure he has his strengths, but you bring a lot of great things to the table too. His job would be much harder without you."

I took a deep breath and let it out slowly, wishing everything I was feeling would leave with it. "I'm not sure about that, Dad, but thanks."

"Do you think he'd get the people in this town to talk to him without your help?"

"He's a cop now, Dad. They have to talk to him. It isn't like when we were working on our first case anymore."

Accepting the truth of what I'd said, he nodded and smiled. "Okay, maybe that's true, but you know details about this town he'll never know because you know these people. You've lived around them all your life."

All my life. There in those three words was the reality of all I was.

I'd never really gone anywhere or done much of anything, except for four years of college, and then after I was right back in Sunset Ridge. No clubs in Baltimore. No traveling around the state meeting with potential clients. Just back and forth from my house on Barn Street to my job at *The Eagle* on Main Street and then down to the opposite end of Main Street to this very bar before going back to my house.

"I guess."

"You know, when you were in third grade you wanted to be like that Tamblin girl. Do you remember that? She had short hair and played baseball, and you wanted to be just like her."

"Yeah, I remember. I begged Mom to cut my hair just like Jessica's, and then when she did, I hated it."

"You hated playing baseball too, if I recall correctly."

"It's not like that, Dad," I said, hoping he wasn't about to launch into a discussion about how I was just as beautiful as Bethany. I so didn't need to hear that with the way I was feeling.

"I think it is, honey. You admire how he does the job so much that you don't see how valuable you are. Every time I speak to him he tells me how helpful you've been since that very first case."

"Oh, I thought…" I stopped myself. "You know, ever since Mom died, I've wanted to solve things. I don't know if it's because I feel like I wish I could have figured out what was wrong with her before it was too late or something else. That's why I took that job at that website, even though I never really wanted to spend my time helping others invade people's private lives. I know everyone probably thinks I have no business trying to help the police solve crimes, but I want to because I feel like it's a calling I've never really listened to before."

"I know, but I think you put less value on your abilities to figure things out than you do on his."

"Alex is so much smarter about people than I am. I wish I was more like him with that. He says so little and never jumps to conclusions like I do. He's all mind and I'm all gut, but I'd rather be like him."

Bringing my hand to his lips, my father kissed my fingers like he used to when I was a little girl. "That's why you make such a good team. You're different but in ways that work together. Not everyone can be Sherlock Holmes, Poppy. But sometimes the greatest detective finds useful ideas from Watson."

I hung my head at his description of me as the hapless sidekick of the world's most famous detective. "I don't want to be Watson. All he does is fumble around with every case. He'd be lost without Holmes."

My father stood from his perch on the case of booze and kissed the top of my head. "I love you no matter which one you are, Poppy. Promise me you won't stay too long in here, okay?"

I saw the concern in his eyes and didn't want him to worry, so I pretended our talk had made me feel better. "I'll be out in a little while."

"What do you want me to tell Alex and Bethany if they ask where you went off to?"

Doubting they'd even still be out at the bar, I smiled and said, "Just tell them I'm not feeling well. Thanks, Dad."

"Will do, honey."

He left me sitting there wishing I was anyone but Poppy McGuire and Alex's version of a hapless sidekick. Or even worse, someone who'd never been to some club in Baltimore or anywhere else, for that matter.

Chapter Twelve

G REY SKIES GREETED me when I awoke, a truly symbolic continuation of the night before as far as I was concerned. By the time I came out of the stockroom at McGuire's, Alex and Bethany were gone, but he'd left me a note saying he'd see me at eight at The Grounds like always and he hoped I was feeling better soon. On the bottom, right before his name, he wrote, "If you need anything, call me."

I could have been on fire and I wouldn't have called him. Who wants to be the person to interrupt a date or…

Rolling over, I buried my head in the pillow and told myself I didn't want to think about what else I might be interrupting. Better to remain as ignorant as possible in situations like this. I wasn't sure it was bliss, but it sure as hell was better than knowing what happened between him and Bethany after they left the bar.

My alarm did its morning job, and when I grabbed the phone to turn it off, I saw a message from him. He'd sent it at right after one in the morning.

Hope you're feeling better. Let me know if you can't make it to breakfast and I'll deliver.

So he was up and likely alone at one. Interesting. Maybe she left early or maybe they didn't do anything after leaving McGuire's. Or maybe...

Enough with the maybes, Poppy! Stop thinking about this! You're obsessing, sister, and that's never good. They're together now. Accept it. Put on your big girl panties and deal with it. Alex is with Bethany. It's time to buck up and move on.

After I'd given myself the pep talk I would have done for any of my friends in the same position, I texted Alex to let him know I wasn't at death's doorstep just yet. Part of me felt guilty for letting him think I was truly sick and not just miserable, but then again, he was the reason I felt miserable, so there it was.

I'll be at The Grounds at eight. See you there!

My text sounded far more chipper than I actually felt, but maybe by the time I got there and downed some caffeine I'd start to come around to some happiness again. If only I could find the strength or ambition to get out of bed.

The phone vibrated against my nightstand, and I looked over to see a text from him. Swiping the screen, I saw his message and smiled.

Good. I was worried about you last night. We have work to do on this case and I need you at your best. See you in a few.

Why did he have to be like that? What couldn't he be gruff and unfeeling? Then I'd be able to tell myself he wasn't someone I should care about anyway, but this guy was exactly the type of man women wanted.

Smart, sexy, sweet.

I covered my eyes with my arm and willed away all those thoughts of how wonderful Alex was. He wasn't mine to be wonderful with, and that was the reality I needed to wrap my brain around ASAP or I was going to be spending an awful lot of time in the stockroom of my father's bar feeling like some stupid, lovesick girl.

With some newfound, albeit temporary, strength, I rolled out of bed to start my day. A nice hot shower, my hair pulled up into a ponytail because of the heat, and a light covering of makeup later, I left my house ready to work this seemingly unsolvable case with my partner.

Alex waited for me at our table in the back of The Grounds. Saturday mornings were typically a mob scene at the coffee shop, but for some reason this morning the crowds had cleared out already, leaving just us and two teenage girls who sat on the other side of the restaurant. Dressed in his blue police uniform, he looked very official as he sat drinking his coffee. And very stereotypical.

"You don't think this is sort of a cliché? You know, a cop sitting here in a coffee shop drinking coffee? I think all you're missing is the doughnut," I teased as I sat down in the seat that made me face away from the rest of the patrons.

He smiled, either amused or annoyed by my jabs. "I see you're feeling better this morning."

I looked around, uncomfortable in my seat. "I don't like sitting like this. I can't see anything behind me. How do you sit like this all the time? I feel like someone's going to come up behind me and do something."

Shrugging, he said, "I sit there because you usually sit over here. I have the same feeling every time I'm over there. I have to fight the urge to turn around constantly."

"Then why didn't you tell me you wanted to switch seats?" I asked as I read the writing on my coffee cup. Two sugars and three creams. Just how I liked it.

"Because you like sitting here."

Damn, why did he have to be so wonderful? Why couldn't he do something terrible to make me hate him at least a little bit?

Before I told him something I'd regret, I switched the topic to our case. "So where are we on the murder of Canton Walters?"

Alex looked confused by my quick change, but it didn't take him long to recover and turn all business. "As of this morning, nowhere yet. We've got a few good suspects and no real leads to connect any of them to the murder of Walters. No matter how I read it, we're no closer than we were when we started."

I understood his frustration. At every turn with this case, we learned something new only to find out it didn't get us any further toward figuring out who had actually buried that knife in Canton Walters' back or why.

"Why don't we go over everything, just the two of us talking over some coffee? Maybe we missed something along the way."

He didn't seem terribly interested in my suggestion, but even as his expression told me he didn't want to rehash what we knew so far, he nodded. "Okay. I guess it couldn't hurt."

"Good. Let's look at each suspect for motive, means, and opportunity. Who's first?"

Alex opened up his notepad and flipped to the page where the investigation began. "Elizabeth Freely."

"Our favorite hotel desk clerk from the wrong side of

the tracks," I said as I lifted my cup to take a sip of coffee.

"We have no motive for her yet. She and Walters at first seemed to be associated with the Naughty and Spice Sex Toy Company, but the problem with that is he wasn't employed by them since they have no male party givers. We have no evidence to show she even knew him. Means is weak, at best. I have no doubt Miss Freely could hold her own with most men, but kill one? I don't know. And with a knife? Again, weak. As for opportunity, that's a little stronger. As an employee of the Hotel Piermont, she'd be able to get in and out and would know where the cameras are."

"Okay, well Elizabeth isn't our strongest suspect. Who's next?"

Flipping a few more pages in his notebook, he looked up and smiled. "The lovely couple, Dr. and Mrs. Roberts."

I still couldn't imagine Delilah Roberts killing anything. She likely couldn't kill a spider or a fly without feeling bad.

"Do you still think Delilah should be a suspect? I just don't see it, Alex."

"I agree, but my gut tells me she's involved with this somehow. Maybe she and Canton were lovers after she met him at one of her parties when he was the male dancer her friends hired. She wanted to leave her husband and run away with her dancer boyfriend, but he couldn't get away because he has a wife and three kids at home. They fight and she stabs him."

"As he sits at his desk filling out expense reports?" I asked, in effect ruining his perfect set-up for the murder.

"It's not one hundred percent. I'll admit that."

"So how did she get into that hotel? She doesn't have the opportunity with the night desk clerk at the hotel there all night."

Alex sat back in his chair and let his shoulders sag. "Okay, how about her husband, Mr. Personality? Say he found out about an affair his wife was having with our victim. There's motive. I have no doubt he'd be able to stab our victim. That's only leaves opportunity."

"Which gets us to the same place as his wife. How did he get past that night clerk? And once again, who stabs a guy while he's doing paperwork?"

"Maybe he made friends with him and lulled him into a false sense of security so Walters would let him into his hotel room."

"That sounds a little thin, Alex."

He blew the air out of his lungs slowly and nodded. "I know. That's why this case is frustrating me. None of these people seem to have been able to do it, except for the one who could, but he couldn't have."

"That only leaves Mary," I said even as I silently discounted the possibility of her being able to kill anyone.

"Mary Jessick, the beautiful young widow of a husband she claims was murdered. Mary Jessick, the only one we can put together with our victim the night he died. Remember our witness, Mrs. Stark."

I tapped on his notebook and corrected him. "She said Mrs. Stark was wrong. She says she wasn't with him or any man on Tuesday, and until around midnight we know from my father that she wasn't with anyone and that Canton Walters never came into the bar that night."

"I know. I know. You don't think she should be a

suspect. The problem is that she has more connections to our victim than anyone else. Mrs. Stark identified the man getting out of the car with her as him. Are you saying she was wrong on the day and the man she saw?"

"I don't know. I just know that I can't see Mary killing anyone. Call it a gut feeling. You know, those great instincts you think I have? Well, they tell me she didn't do it."

"Well, my gut tells me she's hiding something and when I have enough to bring her in for questioning, she's going to have to explain how she knew our victim better than she saw him once at a party. I might be able to believe that nosy neighbor of hers made a mistake on when she saw her with Walters, but I don't buy she made a mistake when she identified him as likely the man she was with."

"It seems our guts are at odds," I joked, hoping to break some of the tension that had crept into our conversation. I knew Alex believed in what I thought, but this case seemed to be making him edgier than I'd ever seen him.

He sighed and took a drink of his coffee. "I trust your gut as much as I trust mine, Poppy. I just wish what we're thinking would finally make sense."

"What if we took another run at the night desk clerk this afternoon when he starts his shift? Maybe we can see if he remembers anything more than when you talked to him last time?"

"It's worth a try. I'll swing by and pick you up after I get off. I should be there right after four."

"Okay. Sounds good."

Suddenly, now that we'd finished talking about work, we didn't seem to have anything more to say to one another. The fact that I knew next to nothing about who he was other than as an officer who I investigated crimes with bothered me. I wanted to be able to say I knew the person I called my partner.

"Alex, what do you do when you aren't working?"

Not my smoothest line, but in my attempt to not get too personal, I went for the whole nine yards. His expression told me I'd surprised him with my out of the blue question.

He thought about it for a moment, and then said, "I watch a lot of sports. Summer it's baseball. That's what I was doing when I texted you last night."

"Since when are baseball games on at one in the morning?"

"The Orioles-Jays game ran into extra innings. It took them seventeen innings to get a winner."

"Oh." Then I remembered my father mentioning about the All-Star Game. "Isn't it the All-Star break in the season now?"

"Next week. Why do you sound like you don't believe me?"

So much for catching him in a lie. I didn't even know why I thought he'd lie to me. He'd never shown me he had before.

"Is something wrong, Poppy? You've never asked me about anything but work," he said as he looked at me with concern in his dark brown eyes that felt like they were staring right through me to see my real motives for my strange question.

Affecting my most casual tone, I smiled and said, "No. I was just wondering. I guess I realized last night when you guys were talking about that club that I knew very little about you other than as the person I work with on cases."

"Ah. I never much liked that club, you know that? Too loud for my taste. I prefer something more intimate so I can at least talk to the person I'm with."

I knew exactly what he meant. Big groups of noisy people had never been my thing, even in college. I'd always been more of a one-on-one kind of person. I liked hearing he didn't enjoy the club scene like I knew Bethany did.

"You aren't missing anything by never going there, Poppy. Trust me."

"Oh, it's okay. I'm not into that kind of thing anyway."

We sat there at our usual table at The Grounds not saying a thing after that, but that was okay too. I may not have known much about Alex outside of work, but what I did know I liked.

When we finished our morning coffees, we left to go about our days. I walked home as it began to drizzle and forced myself to think about our case instead of what happened between Alex and Bethany that had him alone watching baseball at one in the morning.

It was strange, but I preferred to think about murder.

"READY TO MEET Mr. Steadman, the night clerk at the Hotel Piermont?" Alex asked as I quickly closed the car door to avoid getting soaked any more than I already had by the sudden downpour that had rolled into town.

"Ready and willing."

He scanned my body covered in a drenched green t-shirt and white capris. "You know, they have these things called umbrellas."

"I lost mine, so I had to dodge the raindrops. I guess I'm not very good at that," I said with a smile while I wrung out the ends of my shirt.

"There's not even a spare towel in here. I do have an umbrella, though," Alex said with a playful lilt to his voice.

A stream of rainwater ran down my calf with the last squeeze of my t-shirt, and I looked over at him wearing a silly grin on his face like he thought he was amusing. "Funny. Really funny. We can go at any time, or do you have more jokes to tell?"

"None that I can't save for another time," he said as he put the car in drive and headed toward the Hotel Piermont.

"Then let's go talk to that night clerk. I had an idea while I was waiting for you."

Alex arched an eyebrow and glanced toward me. "Anything you want to share?"

"Actually, no not yet. I will if anything comes of it with him."

An expression full of hurt crossed his face as he drove up the hill to the hotel. "We're keeping secrets from each other now? That's not how partners work."

I didn't say anything until he parked the car and turned toward me. That look I'd seen when I told him I didn't want to share my idea about the case had settled into his features, and he frowned at me. I didn't want him to think I was hiding anything, so I tried to lighten what had become a very dark mood between us.

"A girl's got to keep some part of her a mystery," I said sweetly, more joking than anything else and hoping to ease the tension. The frown on his face told me I hadn't succeeded.

"Poppy, don't you trust me?"

The way he said those words like each one was torn from his throat made my heart flutter. If only he knew how much I trusted him. "More than you can possibly know. Don't you trust me, Alex?"

"More than you can possibly know."

I couldn't tell by his answer if he was teasing me or angry with me. The tone of his voice sounded sort of playfully serious, but the face looking at me remained unhappy.

When he looked at me like that—like I'd disappointed him—I hated it. Turning away, I gazed at a tiny stream of rain as it rolled down the window and said quietly, "It's not a big deal, Alex. I just wanted to hear what Steadman had to say before I told you what I came up with since it's a little out in left field."

He said nothing for a long time and then turned the car off. "Okay. Then let's go."

The flatness of his voice told me it was anything but okay. I hated the idea that my desire to not look foolish had caused a rift between us. That wasn't what I'd wanted to happen.

I followed him into the hotel lobby and to the front desk wishing he hadn't reacted like that to my keeping this one thing to myself. True, I'd never kept anything from him before, but it wasn't like I had the solution to our case and I didn't want to share it because I wanted to take all the credit. I just didn't feel like looking silly for the second night in a row.

Joseph Steadman leaned against the front desk looking like he couldn't be more bored if he tried. His stringy brown hair hung in front of his face, obscuring everything above the tip of his nose. Doodling on a piece of paper, he didn't even hear us come in until Alex tapped his hand on the bell at the other end of the desk. I had a hard time believing this guy would have seen every person coming in and out on any given night.

Startled, he looked up, his dark eyes wide as he stared at us. "Officer Montero, how are you?"

"I'm good, but I'm surprised you didn't hear the two of us come in. Makes me wonder if you told me the truth the last time I was here."

Holding up his right hand, he said, "I swear to God I told the truth, sir. I wouldn't lie. I swear."

Alex pulled out a picture of Mary he'd found in the newspaper and placed it on the desk in front of the clerk. "I believe you, Joe. I do. I want you to take a look at this woman and tell me if you've ever seen her here."

He looked down and then up at us. With a smile, he said, "I wouldn't forget a woman this beautiful. I have seen her here. Just this week, in fact."

"Are you sure?" I asked, disappointed to hear the possibility that Mary was even more involved with Canton Walters than I thought. It was getting harder and harder to believe in her innocence.

Nodding quickly, he said, "Yeah, I'm sure. She was here the night before the murder, and she may have been here the night of the murder. That second time I'm not one hundred percent sure, but I know she was here Monday night."

"How do you know that?" Alex asked as he wrote down the words Mary—Hotel Piermont—Monday night in his notepad.

"Because my girlfriend stopped by to say hi that night and saw me check that woman out as she walked out through the lobby. I got an earful from her about not respecting her enough."

"Was she a guest?" Alex asked.

"Nope. I know that."

"Do you know what room she was visiting then?" I asked eagerly as Mary's claim she didn't know our victim slowly became next to impossible.

Joe Steadman shook his head, making his hair swing around like greasy fringes. "No. I'm sorry. We don't stop people as they come in and out. If they don't stop here to ask what room someone's in, we don't know who they're here to see."

Stubborn in my need to still believe in Mary, I asked him, "Were there any visitors for Canton Walters or anyone calling to speak to him while he was a guest?"

The clerk looked at Alex and then back at me. "I told Officer Montero the other night that I didn't see any visitors. I'd have to check if anyone left a message for him. We don't log who calls for guests."

He waited for Alex to look up from his notes and asked, "Do you want me to check?"

Leveling his gaze on him, Alex said flatly, "It sounds like my partner wants you to."

Flustered, the desk clerk scurried away to check the message log as he apologized to me for not knowing he had to listen to someone not in a police uniform. I elbowed Alex when he left and thanked him for backing me up, hoping things weren't still awkward between us, and in return he just smiled.

Maybe we were okay again.

Joe Steadman returned with a tattered black three-ring binder filled with white message forms. Running his finger down the top sheet, he got to the middle of the page and stopped before he looked up at us.

"Room 307 got one phone call the day of the murder, Tuesday. A woman called looking for Mr. Walters and left a message. I remember that. I couldn't understand what she was saying because she sounded like she was crying, so I figured I'd put it down in the log and tell Mr. Walters the next time I saw him. I thought he might know who she was."

"Without a name or number?" I asked before Alex could speak up.

Joe looked at Alex like he hoped he wouldn't arrest him at any moment. "She didn't offer any name or number. As I said, I couldn't understand what she was saying, but I thought he might know since he'd probably know who was calling him at a hotel, you know?"

"It's okay. Thank you, Joe. Is there anything else you remember before we go?"

"I swear, Officer Montero, that's it. I didn't think of the call the last time because you didn't ask if anyone called for him. I'm a pretty literal guy, or so my girlfriend says, so that's why I only focused on whether or not anyone came to see Mr. Walters."

"Thanks, Joe. If we need anything else, we know where to come."

Alex and I left too-literal Joe the desk clerk at his post and walked out to the car. As we got in, he turned to me and said, "How much do you want to make a bet that the woman who called for Canton Walters was Mary?"

"I'll take that bet, partner. I looked into that woman's eyes. She's not a murderer."

"Well, when I get the hotel's phone records, we'll see. How's twenty feel?"

Hoping I wouldn't lose, I upped the ante. "Forget twenty. I say the loser has to buy dinner at Diamanti's. Still feeling so sure of yourself?"

Alex started the car and chuckled. "I'm in the mood for a good steak, so sure, I'll take that bet."

As we drove away from the Hotel Piermont, I had a feeling either way I'd win the bet, but I still wanted Mary to not be our killer. Part of it was I liked her, but mainly I wanted her to be innocent because my gut was riding on it and I wanted to think my instincts were that good.

Chapter Thirteen

ALEX MET ME on the sidewalk outside The Grounds with my morning coffee. Handing it to me, he appeared particularly excited for eight o'clock in the morning. For a second, I had the terrible thought that he had just climbed out of bed after spending the night with Bethany and now he had a newfound lease on life, but no sooner had that crossed my mind, he began to speak and I knew what had made him so eager to get moving this morning.

"Can you take another road trip this morning? I got the LUDs on the Hotel Piermont and found out who our mystery caller for Canton Walters was the night of the murder. The grieving widow wasn't exactly truthful with us, it seems."

I gazed down the block toward *The Eagle* where I was supposed to be sitting behind my desk in just under an hour. My editor had agreed that I could be out of the office more since I'd taken on that new assignment, but I'd been absent a lot lately. Looking back at Alex, I saw the anticipation written all over his face and couldn't deny I wanted to be there when he questioned Rose Walters again.

The hell with it! I'd just tell my boss I couldn't be

there because something juicy was happening in town. I'm sure there was something relatively benign I could use as gossip that he'd enjoy. I didn't think he got out much, so it wouldn't have to be anything really.

"What did you find out? And by the way, as the loser of our bet, you owe me a dinner at Diamanti's."

Alex grinned and nodded. "You'll find no argument from me. You name the night and it's a date."

"I do like a man who can lose as graciously as he can win," I said with a satisfied smile, trying to ignore his use of the word *date*. "Okay, let's go and you can tell me what you found out."

As we walked to his squad car, he explained. "Seems that Mrs. Walters called the hotel that night. What's even more interesting is that she called from a place she claimed not to be."

I took a sip of my morning coffee, and as it slid down my throat, I worked to remember what Rose Walters had told us the last time we spoke to her. Then it dawned on me. "She called from her house, didn't she?"

Alex grinned like someone who'd just found the final piece of a puzzle. "Yep. She told us she was at her mother's house until that morning when her husband was found dead at the Hotel Piermont. She also claimed to not know he wasn't home and didn't even know where he was staying, yet those appear to be lies too."

"Interesting. Now her I can see killing someone by stabbing them in the back. She has that hell hath no fury kind of vibe to her. I saw it right through her sobbing widow act she put on when we met her."

He opened the driver's side door and leaned against the side of the car. "This is just the break we've been looking for in this case. She knew where he was, and I think she decided to pay him a visit to let him know what she thought of what he was up to at that hotel."

Excited from our first real break, I said, "Let's go see how well she can play the grief-stricken widow now."

STOPPING THE CAR in front of the Walters' suburban home, Alex nudged my arm and pointed to the moving van in the driveway. "Looks like she's decided to leave her life with poor Canton behind pretty quickly, don't you think?"

I watched as two young men dressed in jeans and white tank tops walked in and out of the house carrying the Walters' family belongings in their arms and wondered why she would be leaving so soon after her husband's death. I understood wanting to start over, but fresh starts like this usually happened after a nasty breakup, not the death of a spouse.

Alex approached the taller man on one of his trips back to the van and asked, "Where are you going with all this?"

For a moment, the man said nothing, but I saw him scan the full length of Alex's frame standing there in a police uniform and then the sneer that he'd worn at first softened into a tiny smile. "The lady of the house paid us a hundred each to load the van, but we're not driving it, so I don't know where she's off to. I just know all of this stuff has to be out by today."

Alex looked at me and raised his eyebrows. "Someone's in a hurry."

"I'm guessing she's in the house. You know, saying her final goodbyes to the house she shared with our victim."

We walked to the front door and knocked, even though it was wide open. Rose Walters saw us and waved us in. Squeezing past the moving men, we walked into an empty living room devoid of any furniture. Even that portrait of their three children had been taken off the wall above the fireplace. The whole place had a feeling of loss to it.

"Mrs. Walters, are you going somewhere?" Alex asked with no attempt at all at hiding that he considered her behavior suspicious.

"Obviously. They really do teach you guys well at the academy, don't they?" she snapped at him.

Alex took her insult graciously and continued with his planned questioning. "We need to speak to you again about your husband's murder."

A look of rage came over her face, and she threw up her hands. "My wonderful husband! Canton Xavier Walters, the cheating bastard who couldn't even bother to get a real job. My husband who didn't pay the mortgage and now my children have to leave the only house they've ever known because the bank is foreclosing on us."

Her anger surprised both of us, and Alex took a step back toward me as she screamed about her rotten husband. When she was finished, she sagged against the wall and hung her head. The stress of losing the man she'd married and then finding out that he wasn't the man she thought she knew at all looked like it was about to smother her.

"I'm sorry for what has happened, Mrs. Walters."

Rose Walters nodded her thanks for Alex's expression of sympathy and stood up straight. "Thank you, Officer Montero. I appreciate that."

"As much as I understand how much it hurts to lose someone you loved, I need to ask you some questions about the case."

She sighed deeply and pointed toward the chairs still left in the dining room. "We can talk in there. They've taken the table, but we can at least sit down."

The chairs were still in the positions they'd been in around the large mahogany dining table, so we dragged ours toward Mrs. Walters' and Alex took out his notepad and pen.

He didn't waste any time getting to the heart of the matter. "You didn't tell us you called your husband at the Hotel Piermont in Sunset Ridge the night of the murder."

She sighed again and nodded. "Yeah, I did that."

"Why didn't you tell us that the last time we were here?"

"Because I knew you'd think I had something to do with his murder. I didn't. I swear."

Alex leaned forward toward her and rested his elbows on his knees. "You lied about being at your mother's, Rose. You lied about knowing what your husband was up to. You lied about your husband working for Naughty and Spice. You haven't exactly been truthful about anything with us. So let's try this again. Where were you Tuesday night?"

The moving men came into the dining room and looked around in confusion like they didn't know what to do since they couldn't take the chairs next. Alex looked up at the two of them and pointed toward the kitchen. "I'm sure there's something in there you can grab, gentlemen. The chairs here will go when we're done."

They trotted off to grab pots and pans while we waited for Rose Walters to explain where exactly she was on the night of her husband's murder. She hesitated so long I thought she might tell us she wanted her attorney present, but finally she answered his question.

"I was right here. I didn't lie when I told you I'd been at my mother's all week, but I came home earlier than expected because my daughter got sick from too many hot dogs at a cookout we had at my mother's."

Leaning back in his chair, Alex jotted down the details. "What time did you get home?"

Rose looked up toward the ceiling as she thought about his question and then looked back at us. "I think we were home by seven. The kids were in bed before eight, at any rate."

"Did you leave at any time that night?" he asked with that sharpness to his voice that told me he thought she was still lying.

"And who would watch my sick daughter and her brothers, Officer Montero? You're barking up the wrong tree here. I didn't kill my husband."

I noticed how adamant she was when she denied any involvement with her husband's murder. I didn't know if she was innocent, but I had to wonder if what she said was true. Maybe we were on the wrong track with her.

Alex didn't show any uncertainty in what he thought of Rose Walters, though. Pressing her for more answers, he asked, "How did you know your husband was at the Hotel Piermont that night?"

"I found a folded up piece of paper with the hotel's name and number on it in the back of his underwear drawer when I was putting away his wash. I had suspected he was having an affair for a while, and that night after I had a few too many glasses of wine, I called the hotel to see if he was there."

As Alex wrote in his notepad, I jumped in to ask her a few questions. "Mrs. Walters, how long had you suspected he was having an affair?"

"Last year he began to disappear for long stretches of time. He claimed he had to help out some of this students at school. I believed him at first, but then I began to think he was up to no good. Canton always had a wandering eye, but with the birth of our daughter I thought that was all in the past."

"Did you ever find any evidence he'd had any affairs?"

"Yes and no. I found a Naughty and Spice Toy Company flier in his briefcase and when I asked him about it, he said he'd taken on a job selling their products. It was stupid, but I wanted to believe him, so I did. But when I told someone about him working for them, they told me the company didn't hire men to give parties. God, I was so gullible!"

"It happens. I'm sorry. We always want to think the best of the people we love, so we give them the benefit of the doubt. Did you ever confront him about his lies about working for Naughty and Spice?"

"Yeah, and he told me he didn't want to tell the truth about what he was really doing for money to pay our bills. Male dancer. He wasn't exactly Chippendale material, you know? Who was paying him to dance for them? I mean, Canton had an okay body, but even I wouldn't have paid him to see it."

I thought about the man hunched over that desk in Room 307 and had to admit I had a hard time imagining him dancing too, but I hadn't seen him alive so maybe he looked different without that knife sticking out of his back.

"Did you ever find out if he was actually cheating on you with someone? Did you find out a name?"

Rose Walters frowned and looked away, obviously embarrassed at having to answer such personal questions. "No. I never found any evidence, but I knew." She turned back to look at me and continued. "The wife always knows. Even if she doesn't want to admit it, she knows. I gave up thinking about it after a while, though. The bills were being paid and we all were taken care of, so I guess I just accepted the reality of my life."

I knew all too well what she said was the truth. No matter how much a woman wanted to deny it, she knew when the man she loved had strayed.

The movers came into the dining room again to ask her about some items from one of the upstairs bedrooms, and Rose excused herself for a moment to talk to them, leaving Alex and me alone to discuss what we'd heard. He looked up from his notes he'd taken and smiled at me.

"I'm not sure where you're going with all those questions, Poppy. The woman has a penchant for lying, so I'm not really inclined to believe much of what she has to say."

I pointed at the notepad that he held in his left hand. "Then why are you taking such copious notes about her answers?"

He gave me a serious look and I knew the answer before he said anything. "Because I believe in you, even if I don't believe a word that comes out of her mouth."

"Still unhappy with me about that whole thing at the hotel last night, aren't you?"

"I'm sure you'll tell me when you're ready."

Rose returned before I could tell him my idea had been totally wrong. I'd expected to find out that Delilah Roberts had contacted Canton Walters at the hotel. Since it wasn't her but his wife, I really didn't want to admit my foolish theory when Rose was so obviously a better suspect.

"I'm sorry for that, but as I told you before, you're wrong. I didn't kill my husband. I know it seems hard to believe, but I still loved Canton. For all that he'd done, I loved him."

Alex leveled his gaze on her. "You didn't sound like you loved him when we first got here."

"I said I loved him, not that I still love him, Officer Montero. I could handle a lot of things, but losing my home and being forced to move back in with my mother with my three young children is past even my line of things I'll tolerate."

"You certainly sounded like a woman who was mad enough to drive up to that hotel and let him know what you thought of his philandering, not to mention how much you hated losing your house."

She gave him a look of disgust and sighed. "First off, I didn't find out until yesterday that the bank was foreclosing on my house. I can show you the letter they sent postmarked after his death."

"And his cheating? You wouldn't have wanted to kill him for that?" Alex asked.

"Typical man. You can't see the forest for the trees when it comes to love. I would have hated to find out for sure he was cheating on me, but I think I could have forgiven him for that. I had three children with him, so I would have at least tried."

Even though she had shown herself to be a repeated liar, I believed she could have forgiven him. Alex didn't, though. "So you're saying you would have been able to forgive him for sleeping with another woman while you stayed here to take care of the house and kids?"

"You don't know much about women, do you? Your partner knows what I'm talking about, though, don't you? I saw it in your eyes when I was talking about Canton cheating on me. You know what it feels like. Well, when you have kids with the man who's stepping out on you, the choice of just cutting him out of your life isn't there anymore. At least not for me."

Alex glanced over at me for a moment and then returned his attention to Rose. For my part, I had no idea how she saw anything in my eyes when she was talking about her husband cheating on her. It had been a long time since I felt what she was going through, and I'd thought I'd pushed that far enough down that it didn't show anymore.

"Where were you Tuesday night and the early hours of Wednesday?" Alex asked, undeterred by her chastising of him.

Rose shifted in her chair and straightened her back before answering. "I was here, like I told you already."

"Did anyone see you here, other than your children?"

I knew he had to press her for the truth, but the way he sounded it felt like an interrogation of someone who had already been shown to be guilty of a crime. Gently, I nudged his knee with mine as he and Rose stared one another down.

"I'm sure if you asked around the neighborhood someone would be able to tell you when I got home and that I didn't leave all night."

"I'll be sure to ask around. Can you think of anyone else who would be able to show you were here that night?"

Rose glared at him for so long that I had to look away it was so uncomfortable, but Alex continued to stare right back at her as he waited for her answer.

Finally, she gave in and said, "My mother called me at around eleven that night. She wanted to check on her granddaughter."

He handed her a piece of paper and the pen. "I need your mother's name, address, and phone number."

She did as he'd ordered and shoved the paper and pen back at him. "Are we done here or are you planning to haul me off to jail now?"

He stood from his chair and looked down at me before telling her, "We'll be in touch if we need anything else, Mrs. Walters."

Then he turned and walked out without saying another word. Rose Walters glanced over at me and I saw her expression once again was far more pleasant than when she had to deal with Alex. Part of me wanted to apologize for how he acted, but I knew that would be wrong. He hadn't done anything uncalled for. Any cop would have asked her the same type of questions. Maybe it was the way he asked them of a woman who had just lost her husband that made me uneasy. Then again, he didn't see her that way. He saw her as the prime suspect in our victim's murder.

She looked up at me as I stood to leave and said, "I didn't kill my husband. If your partner bothers to actually do his job, he'll find that out."

"I wouldn't worry about Officer Montero doing his

job." Feeling like I needed to defend Alex, I added, "He's good at what he does."

"Then I don't expect to see him again. Now if you don't mind, I need to pack up the last of our things before I leave my house and then I have to plan my husband's funeral."

I sheepishly expressed how sorry I was for everything that she was going through and left as quickly as possible. I found Alex waiting outside in the late morning heat, his arms crossed as he leaned up against the car. As I approached him, I saw he wore a look that made me think he was angry.

The question was why.

"Stay behind for a little chat with the grieving widow?"

"You were pretty hard on her. She did just lose her husband, Alex. I wonder if you could have been a little more sympathetic."

He gave me the same look he'd given her and said, "I know exactly what it feels like to lose someone you love. If she was acting like she actually cared that her husband was dead instead of being unhappy that her meal ticket had gone away, I would have been more sympathetic, Poppy."

What was I supposed to say to that? No matter how I answered, he seemed to be looking for a fight, so I pressed my lips together and said nothing at all.

Alex hung his head and then looked up at me with a smile. "I'm sorry. I shouldn't have snapped at you. I have to do my job, though. I hope you understand that."

I didn't want to fight with him over this. It wasn't worth it. So I accepted his apology and quickly moved to change the subject. "It's getting hot out here and I have to get back to *The Eagle*, so let's get in and get that air conditioning going."

"Sounds good. I talked to her next door neighbor while you were in there and she said everyone but her on this block is still out of town for the Fourth of July holiday. She said she saw Rose and her kids get home around seven but she doesn't know if she left any time after that."

I didn't ask him what he thought about that. I already knew he considered Rose a suspect.

We drove off from Canton Walters' house and headed toward home. I closed my eyes and let the cool air hit me as some song on the country music station played. Figuring it could give me a chance to break the iciness that had settled in between us, I joked, "I never figured you for a country music fan."

"I'm not. Too much sappiness for me. I think Craig was the last one to use this car. Turn it off if you don't like it."

I opened my eyes and chuckled. "I can see Craig liking this kind of music. My wife left me and took my dog, and I miss the dog so much."

Alex looked over and laughed at my indictment of the entire country music genre. "So what was Rose Walters talking about with you back there? She seemed to have your number when it came to how she was feeling about that cheating husband of hers."

"I have no idea," I answered in my best casual voice, truly hoping he didn't pick up on how hard I was trying to be nonchalant. I so didn't want to talk about that with him.

"Really? More secrets, Poppy?" he asked sharply.

Hating that I had to tell him about one of the worst

times of my life, I swallowed my pride and said, "It's nothing really. I just know how she feels because I was with someone I cared for and he cheated on me. It was a long time ago."

"I'm sorry. I didn't know."

He looked at me and I saw his eyes were full of pity. I hated that. I didn't want to be pitied because I'd foolishly believed in someone and they'd turned out to be nothing like I thought they were.

"No need to be sorry. I got over it, and now it's just a bad memory."

We rode along silently for a few miles until I said, "So I guess you're thinking Rose Walters is truly a suspect now, right?"

"Right. She had motive since Canton was cheating on her. She had means as much as anyone else. And she had the opportunity since even if her mother's call does pan out, there's still a few hours she can't account for."

I looked out the window as the trees raced past us and thought about Rose Walters as our killer. She certainly had the whole woman scorned act down pat, but I had a hard time seeing her leaving her kids to drive an hour north just to kill their father.

But as I knew all too well, betrayal brought out things in a person they never knew existed in them before.

Chapter Fourteen

THE CAR SPED over the hot pavement toward home while I daydreamed about what fib I'd tell my boss when I got back to my desk since I had the distinct feeling he'd be waiting for me. I hadn't spent much time in my office at *The Eagle* since this Canton Walters case began, and even though Howard hadn't said anything about it yet, I didn't see that silence on the matter continuing much longer. It was all well and good to claim I was getting details on the local crime scene, but they didn't pay me to hang out with Alex and solve crimes.

I wish they did. I was never happier than when we were trying to tease out the facts of a case, whether it was the minor theft of a few paintings from the Danford house in late May that revealed their son-in-law wasn't who he said he was but an art thief who'd targeted the family or a murder like the one we currently worked on.

That art heist case had been relatively easy compared to the death of Canton Walters. While we had no shortage of suspects, none of them but Elizabeth Freely seemed to have had opportunity to commit the crime. That was really the only thing keeping her as a suspect in my mind. I was nearly one hundred percent sure this case hinged on some kind of rendezvous gone bad, but who had our victim let into his hotel room that night and what went wrong between them?

"You're quiet over there. Everything okay?"

Alex's tone signaled he was still worried he'd upset me by pressing me to tell him why Rose Walters had believed she and I had something in common when it came to cheating men. I wasn't bothered by his desire to know as much as I was by her seeing something in me that said I'd gone through what she was. Granted, I hadn't suffered through a husband cheating on me after years of marriage and three kids, but a cheating fiancé running around with some woman he met one snowy night at the bed and breakfast he was checking out for our honeymoon was almost as bad.

Cringing at the memory of finding out the man I planned to spend the rest of my life had been a cheating bastard, I forced a smile and said, "I'm good. Just daydreaming as I watch the clouds float by."

Alex turned to look at me with concern in his eyes. "I'm not used to you not talking. I thought something might be wrong."

"I thought I'd give the Chatty Cathy routine a break for a little while."

Focusing on the road again, he smiled like my answer had put his mind at ease. "Well, I'm getting pretty bored over here just driving. It's so hot out there I think I'm seeing heat waves coming off the side of the road, or I might be imagining that. I don't know."

"I'm happy to turn the chattiness back on, if that will help," I offered, eager to talk about the case so my head didn't get stuck in the past. That's the last thing I needed.

"Okay. Want to talk about our case? I think we have all the pieces to this puzzle. We now have to find out how they fit together to show us our murderer."

I knew what he was thinking. He'd never trusted Canton Walters' wife, and after that visit today, he saw every reason to believe she had something to do with his death.

"So do you think you know who did it?"

He nodded and said, "Yeah. Do you have your suspect?"

"Yes and no, but I don't think we're going to agree on who did it."

The car turned off the highway onto a less traveled road on the second leg of our trip back to Sunset Ridge. A tree lined road, it was far shadier than the highway from Virginia.

"We don't always agree, Poppy, so that's okay. Talking like this helps us get our ideas straight. It's one of the reasons we work so well together."

I liked when he said things like that. It made me feel like I wasn't the only one in this partnership who enjoyed what we did.

"Okay, you go first. Give me who did it, why, and how. It's like Clue we played when I was a kid. I need to warn you, though. I was always very good at that game."

"Clue, huh? Like Miss Scarlet in the billiard room with the lead pipe? I'm imagining little Poppy McGuire sitting around with her friends and being quite good at that game," he said with a smile as he glanced over at me.

"I was, so you've been warned. So hit me with whodunit."

"The grieving widow. Rose Walters has been on my

radar since the first time we spoke to her. Too much of what she said didn't make sense that day, and the more we learned about her husband, the more I thought she could be our killer."

Just as I suspected. "Well, I respectfully have to disagree. I don't think she's our murderer."

Alex stopped the car at a stop sign and turned to face me. "How can you not think she's involved in this up to her eyes? The woman couldn't find the truth if you handed it to her in a bag."

"She really only lied about being at her mother's the night of the murder. That's the only direct lie she told," I said, surprised by how forceful he'd been in giving his opinion.

Alex's eyes flashed his frustration at my insistence on disagreeing with him. "Poppy, she had motive to kill her husband. The man was cheating on her and she knew. She came right out and told us that."

The car began to move again, so I didn't have to face that angry expression of his, thankfully. I'd never seen Alex so upset with anyone but me, and that was only because he thought I was sneaking around his house and trespassing that night. Even then, he didn't look as angry as he did at that moment driving down the back road to town.

"I admit she did have motive, but I don't think she did it. She had no opportunity, and I'm not even sure she could kill someone she loved like that."

Alex shook his head as his expression morphed to one of complete disbelief. His reaction seemed entirely over the top. Why was he acting like this just because I didn't think Rose Walters had killed her husband?

"Poppy, what makes you think she couldn't drive to

the Hotel Piermont in the hour it takes, find her husband and stab him to death, and then go back home all in the span of a few hours? You think she sat down rationally and thought, 'Gee, I really want to kill that cheating bastard of a husband of mine, but that would mean driving to find him at that hotel and who will watch the kids?' I don't think so."

"Whoa, what's with the attack mode? I just don't think she'd leave her kids like that."

His jaw set, he said in a low voice, "It's not attacking when you believe something."

I didn't know how to answer that. I believed in him and his opinions, and I thought that he believed in me and my opinions too. But as he sat there scowling, I had to wonder.

"Do you think I don't believe what I think is true?"

"That's not what I'm saying, Poppy. You know that. You know I trust your opinions as much as I trust my own."

"It's not that I don't think she's capable of murder, Alex. I think that she knew he was having an affair and may very well have wanted to kill him when she heard he was at a hotel so close to home. I just don't think she got to that point before someone else did."

In a calmer voice, he said, "No one else has motive to the extent that she did. Elizabeth likely didn't even know him. Delilah and her husband may have known him, but so far we have no proof of that. And you can't believe Mary could kill anyone, so who does that leave us with?"

"I get that you're frustrated, Alex. I am too. This case seems to be all leads that go nowhere but dead ends. I'm frustrated too. I just don't know why you can only see Rose as the killer. I think we might be missing something that points to someone else."

He turned toward me, and I saw how discouraged this case had gotten him. "Like who? As far as we know after checking out all the leads, Canton Walters didn't know many people in Sunset Ridge. I called all the people on Delilah's list a second time to ask them if they remembered ever seeing him at one of her parties, and to a person they all said they didn't recall a man ever being present at any of them."

"Alex, those women are all Delilah's friends. Don't you think it's possible they're all lying to you to cover for her?"

"All fifteen women and only Mary seems to remember him? Which seems more likely?"

I almost laughed at his question. The idea of fourteen women lying for their friend seemed perfectly normal to me, a fellow female. It was almost a rite of passage for girls to lie to protect one of their own. I'd done it myself dozens of times, regardless of whether it was parents, school principals, or even cops doing the asking.

"I think you aren't seeing the big picture. Mary said Delilah had probably had him at one of her parties. What if she knew him from that?"

Alex's shoulders sagged. He took a deep breath in and blew it out slowly. "Okay, I'll go with this idea. So that's your theory of the case—that Delilah killed Canton Walters?"

He caught me off guard putting me on the spot like that. I hadn't really formulated a theory of the case involving Delilah Roberts. I had a sneaking suspicion she'd known the victim, but just like with Mary, I couldn't see her killing anyone.

I didn't dare tell Alex that, though. In the mood he was in, I'd likely get an earful about how murders are solved by facts, not feelings.

Hedging my words, I said, "I think it's just as likely she did as his wife. The problem with both women is how did they get into the hotel without that night clerk seeing them and how did they commit the crime?"

Alex shook his head. "I'm thinking Joe Steadman isn't as observant as he claims. He barely heard us come in the other day. Remember?"

"Okay, then if it's possible anyone could have gotten past him without being seen, does that change your opinion on who may have done it?"

"No, it doesn't. The wife still looks good to me," he said setting his jaw defiantly again.

"Not even Mary or Delilah are worth looking at another time if any of them could get in past the desk clerk?" I asked, amazed at how obstinate he was acting.

Without even thinking about what I'd said, he answered, "No."

"And that's it? No?"

I stared at the person sitting beside me and felt like I didn't even know him. He'd never been like this in all the time we'd worked together, so I couldn't understand what had made him change into this pig-headed man who sat obstinately staring back at me, refusing to budge even the tiniest bit.

"We're going to have to agree to disagree on this, Poppy, but I'm going ahead with Rose Walters as the murderer of Canton Walters."

His voice was so flat it clearly signaled he was in no mood for discussion of the point at all. I didn't know how to react to this Alex, but I couldn't simply sit back and let him basically say he didn't think what I believed had any merit at all.

"I thought we were partners. Don't partners take one another's opinions into consideration and leave open the chance that the other person sees something they don't? You've never been like this. You always listen to my ideas because you think I have good instincts. Remember those?"

He turned the car onto the far end of Main Street and drove past the sign welcoming people to Sunset Ridge before he answered me. When he did, I felt like I'd been slapped across the face.

"Poppy, I do value your opinions, but this case calls for a less emotional and reactionary look. Sometimes your jumping to conclusions like Dr. Watson is helpful because it makes me take a look at alternative theories, but this time it's just muddling the case."

I'd never told him how working cases with him made me feel like Dr. Watson, that hapless tagalong to Sherlock Holmes. I'd only told my father that night in the stockroom and Bethany right after Alex and I began working together months ago. Suddenly, I felt like the butt of a private joke between them as I sat there a captive audience in that passenger seat next to him.

Had Bethany told him how inferior I felt working with him? My chest hurt as the thought of them talking about me settled into my brain. Why would she do that? I felt like a foolish girl who'd let herself believe she meant more to the world than she really did.

I opened my mouth to speak, to say something to let him know how much I hated what he just said to me, but nothing came out. All at once, everything I'd ever told her about working with Alex raced through my mind. What else had she shared with him in their time together? I couldn't decide which was worse—thinking about them sleeping together or thinking about them talking about me as they sneered at my inability to do much of anything than follow him around like some eager, clueless idiot who yearned to learn from him.

When my mind stopped spinning from the rage coursing through my body, I tried to speak again, but my mouth had turned as dry as sand. Swallowing hard to create some saliva, I struggled to speak but had to. I may not have been as talented an investigator as he was, but that didn't mean I had to sit there and be insulted.

"I thought my insights helped you, but obviously I was wrong."

"I didn't mean it like that, Poppy. I just meant—"

"I know exactly what you meant. You don't need to explain yourself any further."

"Poppy, please. I didn't mean to upset you. I meant something else, but it came all wrong. Just listen to me, okay?"

With every word that came out of his mouth, I felt like I would burst into tears. I hated how when I got angry to the point that I couldn't even talk that my body resorted to turning on the water works like I was some teenage girl who couldn't handle her emotions. Whenever it happened, the person in front of me always misunderstood, and instead of thinking I wanted to rip them in half, they thought my delicate feelings had been hurt.

Before that happened, I knew I had to escape from that car. "Just stop now so I can get out."

My words shocked him, and he snapped his head

right to look at me. "What are you talking about stop the car? I'm taking you to *The Eagle* so you can go into the office."

The car came to a stop at the red light near Diamanti's, and I flung the door open. "I'm not going to be the reason you use to stop at the newspaper. Find your own excuse for going there."

I shot him a glare and jumped out of the car before slamming the door closed. The last thing I saw was a look of hurt settling into Alex's eyes as I turned away from him in disgust. As if he had any reason to be hurt by anything I'd said!

He lowered the window and called out my name, but I didn't turn around to look at him. I didn't head in the direction of my office either. The sun beating down on me made me break into a sweat before I made it a block away and I didn't know where I was walking to, but if he thought I was going to get back into that car after what he'd said to me, he had lost his mind.

I may have admired him and even idolized him for months, but as of that moment as I turned the corner toward my house, I didn't even want to see his face. I knew if I did I'd just make a fool of myself when my confused tear ducts kicked into overdrive anyway.

Out of the corner of my eye, I watched him follow me all the way home. It was so quintessentially Alex not to say a thing but drive just behind me for blocks. I didn't care that he clearly seemed concerned that I didn't want to be around him. Let him be. He should be. It wasn't that I just didn't want to be anywhere near him at that moment.

I wasn't sure I ever wanted to be around him again.

By the time I closed my kitchen door behind me, my

clothes stuck to me from how much I'd sweat just walking the few blocks home. All I wanted to do was crawl under the covers and forget this day had ever happened, but a shower would have to happen first. After that and a few hours of hiding out from the world, maybe I'd try my hand alone at solving the case of Canton Walters' murder. I may have been reactionary and emotional, but maybe that's what this case called for.

Even if it didn't, that's all I seemed to have to offer, so it would have to do.

Three hours later, I'd all but forgotten what we'd argued about, but the terrible feeling that I'd been the topic of conversation between Alex and Bethany remained, still making my stomach ache. I hated how stupid I felt.

As a late day thunderstorm rolled in, I pulled the covers over my head and closed my eyes as my phone vibrated across my nightstand. Some part of me dreaded what the text would say while another part of me hoped he realized how he'd screwed up. It vibrated two more times before I rolled over and grabbed it, unable to quell my curiosity.

I swiped the screen and saw the first text wasn't from Alex at all. I'd forgotten in all the day's events that I had a job and my boss wanted to know if I ever planned on coming back to the office. As thunder rumbled outside, I quickly shot him a message apologizing profusely and promising to have both my articles for him to read by end of business the next day. He liked when I said things like that. I just hoped I could follow through on my promise.

The second message was The Third National Bank

alerting me to the need to change my password on my account. I had to wonder why I bothered to look at all at these messages.

I deleted the bank text and moved on to see the third message was from Alex. Unsure if I wanted to know what he said, I opened it to find he truly had no idea what had made me so angry.

Typical man. Rose Walters seemed to understand Alex pretty well, after all.

You okay? Let me know. See you tomorrow at The Grounds.

I dropped my phone back onto the nightstand and returned to my place under the covers to hide away my hurt feelings as a crash of thunder rattled the window next to my bed. Out of all that had happened in the past few hours, one thought occupied my mind.

No, you won't.

Chapter Fifteen

AFTER A NIGHT of tossing and turning like a dingy on the high seas, I awoke to clearer skies, if not a clearer head. The rains had passed and the morning sun shined through my bedroom window making me look forward to greeting the day. Well, assuming I didn't think about everything that happened yesterday.

My phone chimed to let me know I'd missed my alarm, and I rolled over to see it was already eight o'clock. The time I usually met Alex at The Grounds. A pang of sadness passed through me as I realized this was the first morning since he and I began working together all those months ago that I didn't want to be across from him enjoying my morning caffeine.

Swiping the screen to turn off the alarm, I saw no more messages had come in since I'd last looked before bed. All the better. There wasn't anything he could say at that moment that I wanted to hear anyway. I couldn't just talk about work after what he'd said, and the truth was we had nothing else to talk about.

We were partners, but it didn't seem like there was much left of that relationship.

By eight-thirty, I knew I had to get out of bed. I couldn't spend any more hours under the covers pretending the world wasn't happening outside my door. I headed downstairs to make myself a cup of coffee, and as I took my first sip, my phone rang.

Alex.

I imagined he'd sat there at our table for the last half hour or so wondering why I hadn't showed up. Or maybe he knew why. I doubted it, though. Neither he nor Bethany would likely understand why what he said comparing me to Watson had upset me so much. To him, it was merely a statement among the thousands he'd made to me, harsher than normal but just another one in his mind. To me, though, it was so much more than him reminding me how differently I looked at things. It was proof that I'd been part of their conversations and none too complimentary a part either.

Like Holmes' sidekick, I was more than likely the butt of a joke. A hapless character they could laugh at. The forgettable tagalong who added nothing of real worth to any investigation.

Five minutes later as I washed my mug and left it to dry in the drainer next to the sink, I heard my phone vibrate across the counter. I looked down to see who messaged, but I knew before I even saw the name pop up on my screen.

I'll be around tonight after my shift. I want to talk about our case.

I didn't answer. I had nothing to say. I didn't want to talk about the case, but that didn't leave us much else to talk about.

That fact had been glaringly apparent since that night at my father's bar as I sat there watching Bethany find out more about Alex than I had in three months. Since then, I'd had to face it. In all that time, he and I had never gotten past being work partners, and after what he'd said in the car yesterday, I couldn't even say we were that either.

What that left was me with all these feelings for someone who barely saw me as an acquaintance, and not even one he respected much. Considering I'd had all those months, I hadn't done much, had I?

I needed to get my head straight or those covers would start to look pretty good for a second day, so I grabbed my laptop and headed to my favorite comfy chair in my living room to get some work done. My editor's message had told me loud and clear his patience was running thin, and if I wanted to stay gainfully employed, I needed to produce some articles or Howard would be handing me my walking papers any day.

For two hours I let my fingers fly over the keyboard as I wrote about the Fourth of July block party the former mayor and First Lady had arranged for the holiday, careful to describe the affair in the most glowing terms or risk having to listen to my boss lecture me on the proper way of treating elected officials and their wives. My intimate knowledge of how crooked the former mayor of Sunset Ridge was and how dreadful his wife truly could be had to be pushed aside in favor of journalistic realism, as my editor liked to call it.

In truth, which played little part in my job, what he wanted me to do was paint pretty pictures of our town with delightful words that told no part of what really went on with the people we wrote about. Not that I hadn't known that fact since they offered me the job. It was just that some days when I felt particularly edgy about things, I didn't want to whitewash the goings on in Sunset Ridge.

On those days, I wanted to spell it all out in vivid terms so everyone could see what we all really were instead of pretending.

However much I wanted to do that, I never did, though, and for one reason. I needed this job. After losing my online investigative work, my role as social reporter and crime beat feature writer was all I had to pay my bills. I didn't want to dip into any more of the money my mother had left me. I'd bought a house, but the rest of the insurance money needed to stay untouched in the bank as long as I had a job.

So knowing that, I put down in words how lovely the Fourth of July block party was and how gracious hosts the former mayor and First Lady were. My readers would get details about how lemony the lemonade tasted and how the baked beans were sweet enough to make even the harshest person smile in happiness when that sugary deliciousness hit their tongue.

Just the way my editor loved it.

I guess I didn't have to wonder why some people in town didn't take me seriously. I mean, how could they when all they knew of me was gossip from the busybodies about my nonexistent love life and my gushing descriptions of small town minutiae?

Stopping to take a break from the world I'd been creating, I heard my phone ring and saw Bethany's name come up on the screen. Now she was calling me too? What did she want? I suddenly felt like the happy couple was everywhere around me, threatening to smother me with their very existence.

Two more calls from her in the next five minutes

told me Bethany was likely unraveling about something. That was her way. Something must have happened at work and she had no one else to turn to, so she was calling me. Unfortunately for her, I didn't want to be a shoulder to cry on today. I knew unlike Alex, she would leave a voicemail, but I didn't intend on listening to that any time soon either.

The calls from both of them made focusing on my job difficult, so I saved my work and figured maybe it was time to get some fresh air. I knew my father would already be at the bar getting ready to open up for the afternoon, so I walked the few short blocks to McGuire's and enjoyed the slightly cooler eighty degree temperatures the late morning offered.

Poking my head in through the open doorway, I found him sweeping the floor like he always did right at the start of his workday, hunched over that old broom of his.

"Hi, Dad!"

He looked up and smiled at me. "Poppy, I'm happy to see you this morning. How are you, honey?"

I walked into the bar toward where he stood, my arms open wide to hug him. "I'm okay. What about you? Another great day as the best bar owner in Sunset Ridge?"

Squeezing me tightly to him, he chuckled low in my ear. "Do you have such low aspirations for your old father?"

I leaned away from him and looked into his faded blue eyes. "You aren't old, Dad. You're a classic."

My father smiled, crinkling the outer edges of his eyes where the crow's feet had become more pronounced in the last few years. "I like that. A classic.

So how is my favorite girl doing today?"

"I'm all right. I've been working all day, so I thought I'd take a little walk to visit you before I get back to the grind."

He propped his broom against the wall and looked at me like he was studying me. "You're not working on your case with Alex today?"

"Not today. I have to make Howard happy with a couple of articles, so it's a writing day for me. What about you? Do anything interesting this morning?"

Thankfully, he didn't seem to pick up on how much I didn't want to talk about anything to do with Alex or my work with him. He pointed down at the floor toward his sneakers and said, "I got my miles in, so that was better than yesterday. Other than that, it's just another day."

He had no idea how much that resonated with me at that moment. Just another day. After months of thinking my life had changed, there I was the same old Poppy doing the same old things like I had for so long.

"How's your case coming?"

I followed him to the bar and sat down on the same stool as Alex had sat on a few nights before. My father slid a glass of root beer toward me as he waited for my answer to his very normal question I didn't want to answer. Whatever I said, he'd see something was bothering me, but if I didn't answer, that would be a dead giveaway too.

Such were the trials of being so close to someone.

I took a sip of soda and pressed a smile onto my lips. "Slow going, to be honest. We're having a hard time with this one."

Lifting the glass to my mouth for a second time, I

watched my father's expression to find out if he saw right through me. I hadn't lied as much as given a summary of the case that didn't include anything about the two people investigating it.

"You two work well together, so I'm sure you'll figure things out between you."

Red flags flew up in my mind at that statement, but I had no interest in talking about anything that was happening between Alex and me. There was too much and too little all at the same time, and I felt like I was the only one in whatever we did together.

"Yeah. You know what I was thinking of the other day? That house you used to rent on the lake every summer and how mom would complain about it being too small every time she saw it that first day. Do you remember that?"

He smiled that way he always did any time I mentioned my mother. It was a smile full of memories and sweetness. A smile of love like I'd never seen in anyone else in the world.

"She secretly loved going there each year. I knew that every time she said it would be too small that she was just teasing me. That's the kind of person your mother was."

"I think it says more about the kind of marriage you two had."

My father took a sip of his ginger ale and smiled again. "I think you're right. We understood each other better than anyone else either of us had ever met. That's how I knew she was the one for me."

"The one for me," I repeated under my breath as I wondered if I'd ever find that person in my life.

"It was nice seeing Bethany the other night. I hadn't

seen her in ages," he said quietly as he pretended to wipe down the bar.

"She's more of a big city club girl," I mumbled.

"I see."

I doubted he truly saw anything but the sweet girl he thought she was, not that he was mistaken about her. I knew she wasn't any different than the good time she'd always been. It was me who was different.

My father leaned on the bar and studied me for a moment before he asked, "Did I ever tell you the story about this guy I knew back in high school that was always so jealous of any guy who paid attention to his girlfriend?"

Sometimes my father was a subtle as a dump truck. I pressed my lips together to stop myself from grinning and shook my head. "No, I don't think you ever did."

"She was gorgeous. Everyone in school wanted to go out with her," he said in a faraway voice.

"More gorgeous than Mom?" I teased, knowing his answer before he said it.

He leveled his gaze on me and twisted his face into a fake grimace. "Nobody was as gorgeous as your mother. No, but Cherie was very pretty and I wasn't the only person who thought so."

Always my mother's biggest fan, even now he wouldn't say there was a more beautiful woman in the world than her.

"Cherie had the prettiest blue eyes. I remember when she'd look at you, I mean really look at you, her eyes got the bluest blue I'd ever seen. She knew she was beautiful too."

"That often means what's on the outside is far nicer than what's on the inside."

"Not with Cherie. Nope, she was as sweet a person as you could ever meet. She had it all. Looks, personality, and brains."

I didn't know where my father was going with this story, but I had a sneaking suspicion he thought it related to me. I loved my father dearly, but sometimes when he tried to slide these lesson stories into my head, I couldn't help but think he saw me as sort of dim. Like in eighth grade how he didn't think I knew he was talking about me and my friend Mandy having problems over a skateboard I got as a birthday gift when he told me a story of how his brother had lost his best friend because he'd been so focused on bragging about some bike he loved.

"But Cherie had one flaw. She loved getting attention from anyone, so often she flirted just to get other guys to flirt with her. This drove her boyfriend crazy, and he became violent one day."

I held my hand up to stop him before he went any further. "Dad, I'm not going to become violent and hurt anyone. I was just feeling sorry for myself the other night."

"You really like him more than just someone you solve crimes with?" he asked in his matter-of-fact way.

I nodded, feeling an odd combination of foolishness and relief. Happy to finally admit the truth of how I felt about Alex to another soul, I still wished I hadn't been so silly to think he might feel the same way about me.

"Then why don't you tell him?"

"I didn't know I liked him that much until I saw him with Bethany and now I can't tell him. It wouldn't be fair to Bethany since she's my friend."

"Jealousy is a difficult beast to keep under wraps,

honey. How are you going to keep working with him if you feel more than you can tell him?"

"I don't know," I admitted as a lump formed in my throat. "Maybe it's better we don't work together anymore."

A sad look crossed his face. "I haven't seen you so dedicated to anything in a long time, Poppy. You and Alex work because you're so different. He appreciates that. I know it."

"Yeah. Sometimes different is too different to work, though."

He squeezed my hand in sympathy and kissed the top of my head. "Maybe you're right. Different can be difficult to deal with."

Desperate for a change of topic, I nudged him to return to his story. "So what happened to this perfect woman who needed to be the center of attention?"

"I don't think anyone ever described Cherie like that, but okay. My friend couldn't understand why she needed to flirt with anyone else since he told her every day how madly in love he was with her. The more he told her he cared, the more she flirted."

"This sounds like it's not going to end well, Dad. Did he hurt her?"

"No, he wasn't like that. What he didn't understand was Cherie loved him, but she loved attention just as much. She wanted all eyes on her all the time."

"Why? She had someone who loved her, so why did she need attention from anyone else?"

"Someone like you would never understand that, honey. For you, all you need is the person you care about to see you the way you want them to, but for others, even having that isn't enough. For the Cheries in the world, love is never enough."

"So she had a perfectly wonderful guy and her need for attention made him feel like he didn't matter. Love sure is grand, isn't it?"

"Sometimes. Other times, it's just not enough."

"What happened to your friend and Cherie?"

My father's frown returned and he shook his head. "I don't know. She moved out of town and I never heard from him again. I sometimes think about them, though. She used to goad him into jealousy so often I wondered how he didn't explode with anger at more people."

"Maybe he did. Did she ever have marks or bruises?"

"No. He would never lay his hands on her. He loved Cherie too much to hurt her."

"He stayed with her knowing she was like that? Seems like a recipe for heartache to me, Dad."

My father squeezed my hand again. "Love is like that, honey. He loved her and I hope he someday learned to accept who she was. I know it hurt him when she flirted with other guys right in front of him."

I wasn't sure why my father had told me this story. I was neither someone who craved attention, like Cherie, nor a long-suffering lover of someone who did. His stories occasionally didn't make sense until I thought about them later, so I filed this one away and told him I needed to get back to my work.

"Will you be coming by tonight? I don't need a bartender, but I always like to see my daughter."

The thought of being there and having to see Alex and Bethany together again was too much to handle. Begging off because of work, I lied and said, "My editor is getting pretty antsy about these articles, Dad. Maybe another night."

He kissed me goodbye without another word about my coming by later, but as I made my way toward the door, he stopped me. "By the way, your partner was in here last night. I think he was looking for you."

"I doubt it, Dad, but thanks."

Smiling, he winked at me. "Okay. I just got the feeling he wanted to see you."

I knew I shouldn't want to know who he was with, but I asked anyway. "Was he alone?"

My father hesitated for just a moment, but it was long enough for me to know the answer to my question before he said a word. With a look full of pity, he said, "He was with your friend Bethany."

As much as I hated to admit it, hearing that made my chest ache, like a vice tightening around my heart. My father must have misunderstood. Alex had no reason to be looking for me.

By the time I made it home, I'd had enough of the world. Climbing under my covers, I pulled them up over my head and tried to forget whatever lesson my father was trying to teach me with his story about jealousy. It didn't apply to my situation.

My problem wasn't being jealous of Bethany. No, my problem was what it had always been. Afraid to take a chance, I'd had the chance taken from me. I couldn't blame her for that. There was only person to blame.

Me.

Chapter Sixteen

FOR THE SECOND day in a row, I woke up to a sunny day, but this one was different. Yesterday, I'd been mired in hurt and anger, but this morning I felt like I had a new lease on life. Maybe it was all the time I'd spent under the covers, or maybe it was just plain old acceptance that had set in, but when I thought about Alex and Bethany together, for the first time it didn't feel like someone was squeezing the air out of me. If they were happy together, then I needed to be happy for them.

My cheery new outlook extended to the case too. As I sat at my kitchen table and sipped on my morning coffee, I thought about the four suspects and what we could have missed because there surely was something neither Alex nor I was seeing about the facts of Canton Walters' murder. I simply needed to re-examine each suspect and every one of the clues to find out what that was.

As much as I had accepted Alex with Bethany, I hadn't forgiven him for making me feel like I couldn't help with the case because I didn't agree with him, so I decided to set off on my own to uncover that missing piece of the puzzle. I hadn't forgiven her either for sharing what I'd told her, but I'd just have to be careful with what I told her from that point on. I had no intention of providing her with any more material for her pillow talk.

I headed over to Elizabeth Freely's neighborhood with fresh eyes and began knocking on doors in the hopes of finding someone who may have remembered even a single detail since Alex and I had been there days earlier. Over and over, people answered their doors only to tell me they'd never seen any males around Elizabeth's apartment. To hear her neighbors talk, she was as single as a nun and had a social life to match.

At the fifth apartment, a middle aged woman with bright red hair we hadn't met the first time we questioned the neighbors answered the door with a look on her face that made me take a step back. Before I could say a word, she pressed her face to the screen and snapped, "If you're here to get that no-good bastard's things, you can forget it. You may be the flavor of the month, but that doesn't mean you have any standing in this house."

I took another step back away from the door and held my hands up to let her know I wasn't there as the flavor of the month or whatever she thought. "I'm not here to get anyone's things, ma'am. I just wanted to ask you some questions about one of your neighbors."

She narrowed her eyes to slits and stared me down. Finally, when she decided I was telling the truth, she said, "As long as you're not here to get Jerry's things."

I smiled, happy to see I'd gotten through to her. "My name is Poppy McGuire. Can I come in, Mrs. –?"

"Connie. I'm nobody's Mrs. anymore."

"I promise I won't take much of your time, Connie. I

only have a few questions."

She swung open the screen door and stepped out to join me on the concrete slab of a porch. "I've got a few minutes. Which of my delightful neighbors do you want the dirt on?"

"Elizabeth Freely. She lives in the building next door," I answered, pointing to the house to the left.

With a sneer, she asked, "Which one is she? Is she one of the biddies who loves to threaten to call the cops every time a couple has an argument? Like two people can't disagree from time to time."

"No, she's young. Dark haired girl in her twenties. She lives in the upstairs apartment."

Connie looked up toward the second floor of the building and nodded. "I think I know her. She has parties sometimes. I bet she gets threatened to have the cops called on her too. Old people don't remember what it's like to be young and have fun."

"Do you remember anything about these parties? Anything about who came to them?"

"No. They got loud a couple times, but it was just a bunch of girls having a makeup party. No harm there. I say let them have their fun. Some of that stuff they sell at those things is pretty nice."

"Did you see any men at the parties?" I asked, wishing I had a picture of Canton Walters other than the one *The Eagle* had run.

"Not that I remember."

I took the picture of the victim out of my bag and handed it to her. "Are you sure you never saw this man around Elizabeth's apartment, either at a party or any time?"

Connie took a long look at the newspaper clipping

and shook her head before she handed the picture back to me. "Nope. I've never seen this guy in my life, and I'd put money on the fact he's never been here."

"How can you be so sure?"

She took another look at the picture and smiled. "I'd remember a guy who looks like this coming around. Nope, he's never been here and I'm home all the time."

"Thanks, Connie. I appreciate your help. A policeman might come around asking some of the same questions. Do me a favor and don't mention I was here."

She gave me a wink and a sly smile that made her look far less frightening than when she was serious. "Any chance he'll be as cute as the guy in the pic?"

I chuckled at the thought of Alex talking to Connie. He wouldn't have to turn on any of that charm of his with her.

"Even better."

Her dark eyes lit up with interest. "Then I'll be sure to keep my eyes open for him too."

I left Connie as she turned to walk back into her house and moved on to the house next door. Two no-answers later, I knocked on a door on the main floor of a house directly behind Elizabeth's apartment. Alex and I hadn't checked out any of the neighbors back there, so I hoped to find something we may have missed.

The name on the mailbox said Schultz. The door opened and there standing in front of me was my fifth grade teacher, Mrs. Anne Schultz. I recognized her jet black hair pulled up in that same tight bun she'd worn every day of the thirty-five years she worked at Sunset Ridge Elementary. Back then, she always had something stuck in her bun, like the pencils that stood in the rice on the counter at the one Chinese restaurant we had in town.

"Yes? Can I help you?" she asked in that same insistent tone she used as a teacher.

"Mrs. Schultz, I don't know if you remember me. I'm Poppy McGuire. You were my fifth grade teacher a long time ago."

I peered through the screen at her to see if she recognized me, and after a few seconds, she smiled. "Poppy McGuire. I would have thought you left Sunset Ridge years ago. What are you doing on my doorstep on this hot July day?"

Why was it whenever someone from my childhood saw me they always made that same comment about thinking I would have left town long ago? I'd never really fit in, but why did that automatically mean leaving my hometown?

"No, I'm still here," I admitted as I wished I could ask her why she thought I'd have left. I didn't have time for that discussion, though. "I was wondering if you could answer some questions for me."

"About what?"

"About one of your neighbors."

Mrs. Schultz scowled like she did when a student did poorly on a test. "I try to keep out of my neighbors' business. Are you with the police or something?"

I didn't want to lie, but since Alex wasn't with me, I technically wasn't working with the police at that moment. She didn't need to know that, though, so I smiled big and nodded. "Yes, I am. They don't let me carry a gun, but I get to ask questions."

She arched one eyebrow at my attempt at being cute and opened her screen door. "I can see them doing that. You have a way about you that always made me feel comfortable. If I remember correctly, you were writing the society column for that local rag, weren't you?"

I walked into her house as she insulted my one and only paying job and stood just inside the door enjoying the air conditioned splendor of her living room. "I still do, Mrs. Schultz."

She waved for me to follow her, so I walked with her into the kitchen and sat down in the chair she offered me. Smoothing back the stray hairs from her bun, she sneered at me. "Your editor is an idiot. You know that, right? I had him in class before your time, and he couldn't find the right place for a damn comma then either. You were a good writer, Poppy. What led you to that cesspool of journalistic talent?"

Ouch. Another all-too-truthful indictment of *The Eagle*.

"I needed a job when I came back to town to be with my father after my mother died."

I generally didn't like trotting out that kind of sentimentality, but if it got people to shut up and let me ask what I needed to, I wasn't above doing it.

Her expression softened and then settled into the frown that looked most at home on her face. "I know. I was sorry to hear about your mother's death, Poppy. She was a delightful woman. Like you and I suspect your father too, she didn't belong in this town. She was too big for minds so small."

I'd heard people say things like that about my mother for years, but it never got old. Hearing it from someone like Mrs. Schultz, a woman who never pulled any punches, felt better than when I heard it from most people because I knew she meant it.

"Thank you. I hope every day that I can follow in

her footsteps." I handed her the picture of Canton Walters from the paper she so detested and said, "That's part of the reason why I'm helping the police. Do you remember ever seeing this man around your neighborhood?"

She examined his face and shook her head. "Is this the man who got stabbed at the Hotel Piermont? I heard he was married with children."

"Three young children."

Shaking her head, she knitted her brows at the details of Canton's children. "What on earth was he doing at that place then? Three children at home and he's at that den of inequity."

Old school teachers always had the greatest names for things. The Hotel Piermont certainly had the makings of a den of inequity. Smiling at her apt description of it, I said, "He seems to have been there for almost a week. Are you sure you never saw him around here, say at your neighbor Elizabeth Freely's house?"

A rare smile brightened up her face. "The girl who likes to have the parties? I don't think so."

"Did you ever see any man at those parties?" I asked, sure if anyone had seen a man coming or going during them it would have been Mrs. Schultz. She said she liked to keep out of her neighbors' business, but I knew she was too curious to live up to that.

"No. I even went over there one night to tell her to keep the music down since it was nearly eleven o'clock, but I saw it was just a lingerie party of some sort and figured I wouldn't bother."

"So you're sure you never saw a man at any of the parties?"

"No. If that young man was at any of them, he must

have found a different way to get in since I didn't see him."

I stood from the table and extended my hand to shake hers. "Thank you, Mrs. Schultz. I appreciate your help."

She gave me another smile and then like we were both back in her classroom at Sunset Ridge Elementary, she pulled out a tiny pencil hidden in her bun and grabbed a napkin from the holder on the counter. She scribbled some words on it and handed me it.

"Give that to your editor and tell him I'm watching to see if it helps him."

Looking down, I silently read the words she'd written and barely stifled my chuckle.

You're in desperate need of Strunk and White. Get yourself a copy and do us all a favor.

"Thank you. I'll make sure he gets it."

"Take care of yourself, Poppy. Asking questions can be a dangerous avocation. Maybe the police should accompany you when you go out for them."

I smiled but didn't answer her before I left and moved on to my next idea to solve the case. A quick look up toward Elizabeth's house told me she had the day off, so this was a perfect time to speak to her manager at the hotel. If she and Canton Walters knew each other, someone had to see them together at some point, and he was the only person left to ask.

I found him behind the desk checking a couple in just before eleven o'clock. As the happy couple left to go upstairs to one of the rooms, I was greeted with the cheery smile of Andrew Rime, the manager of the Hotel Piermont. A nondescript man, he had brown hair, brown eyes, and wore a brown suit coat. Everything about him said bland. That he worked in a place that traded on sex and infidelity seemed odd since I had a hard time imagining him with anyone that way, but this was Sunset Ridge. That we had a den of inequity at all struck me as strange.

"Hi, Mr. Rime. I got your name from your night clerk, Joe Steadman. I was wondering if I could ask you a couple questions."

His smile disappeared, and he grumbled, "You're that woman who's always with the cop, aren't you? I want you to know our business has suffered because of your investigation."

"Neither Officer Montero nor I stabbed that poor man in the back in Room 307, Mr. Rime. We're just trying to solve a murder case." I took a quick glance behind him and saw nearly half the cubbies had no keys in them. "By the look of how many keys are out, you aren't hurting for business."

He spun around to look at the cubbies and then turned back around to glare at me. "What do you want?"

"Just a few answers about Elizabeth Freely and that's it."

"My desk clerk? What does she have to do with this?"

"Can you tell me if she has ever had any men visiting her at work?"

"I watch those tapes every day, and I can tell you unequivocally that she has never had any male visitors at work. What she does on her time off is her business, but what she does here is mine and she's never entertained any men while she's working."

For a man who managed a hotel with its interesting

reputation, he certainly seemed to be offended quite easily. Sure I wouldn't get much more out of him before he stormed away, I snuck in one more question.

"Before I go, can you tell me if you believe Elizabeth knew the victim, Canton Walters?"

He must have expected me to ask something else because he opened his mouth to give me his answer and then said nothing. I waited and then he finally spoke his answer. "I don't believe she did. Is that all?"

"Yes, thank you."

I turned away to leave and one thing was clear. If Elizabeth Freely knew Canton Walters, there wasn't a shred of evidence to prove it. I had to face the fact that whoever our killer was, it wasn't her.

So it was time to look at the other suspects. I headed downtown to my father's bar for a quick soda and to regroup before I went to see Mary again. As I walked in to find my usual barstool, I saw in the back of the room a pretty blond woman sitting alone and realized it was Delilah Roberts. She shyly waved for me to come back to her, so I made my way to the dark corner of the bar as I wondered what she was doing there.

"Hi, Delilah. How are you?"

She pressed her lips together and took a deep breath. "I wanted to talk to you, so I figured I'd see if you came here."

I took a seat at the tiny bar table. "Is everything okay?"

"I wanted to talk to you about that man who was murdered at the Hotel Piermont."

"Canton Walters. Did you know him?"

Delilah's eyes filled with tears, but she wouldn't let herself cry. Straightening in her seat, she cleared her throat and said, "I never met Canton Walters."

"We've heard he danced at one of your parties, Delilah. Is that not true?"

Her eyes opened wide and she shook her head violently. "No! You can ask any one of my friends. He's never been at any of my parties."

"We have asked your friends and they did say the same thing. The fact remains that it's been mentioned. So if you aren't here to tell me you knew him, why did you come looking for me?"

She took another deep breath and slowly let it out. "I wanted to explain about my husband. I'm worried you got the wrong idea about him when you and the officer came to the house. He's not a bad man. He just doesn't like me having my parties."

The story my father told me about his friend and Cherie echoed in my head. Was Delilah like her and needed attention so much she'd risk her marriage to have an affair with Canton?

"Sometimes men don't understand it's the little things in life. Like sometimes it's nice to have a little attention paid to what you're doing, isn't it? I get the feeling Alan doesn't understand that."

Delilah's shoulders sagged and she nodded as I spoke. "He doesn't understand that those parties aren't all about sex. They're about my friends and me having a good time. But all he sees is sex and he's sure I'm out using the products when he's not home."

"He's not home a lot, though, is he?"

For the first time, the tears that had been waiting finally spilled down onto her cheeks. Sobbing into her hands, she said, "It's not his fault. He has to work that much. I know that. I just…I just wanted to know I was still desirable."

The hair on the back of my neck stood up straight. Had she confessed to having an affair with the victim?

Struggling to keep my voice even, I asked, "Did you sleep with Canton Walters? Is that what happened?"

She dropped her hands, and I saw the shock on her face as she exclaimed, "That's not what I said! You're twisting everything I'm saying into these horrible things!"

I moved to calm her, but she jumped up from her seat and ran out before I could say another word. Looking around to see if anyone had noticed, I saw only a few men sitting at the bar engrossed in some baseball game. Even my father seemed to have missed all the action. All the better since I couldn't really explain what had happened quite yet anyway.

As I walked toward the door to leave, he saw me and called out, "Poppy, when did you come in?"

"This heat is making you guys slow, Dad. I've been here for about ten minutes. You didn't see me come in?"

Albert, my father's barber, chucked my father on the shoulder and joked, "We were deep into the game, Poppy. We didn't get to watch it last week, so we figured we'd watch the replay today."

"Sorry, honey. I guess I don't notice you coming and going so much anymore since you're here so often. You're a regular like these guys now."

The three men with my father raised their glasses of beer to welcome me to the club of regulars, and I thanked them as I walked out the door to head home. My time with Delilah had left me a bit rattled, and at that moment, I really didn't feel like hanging out at my father's bar with a bunch of old guys. I had a case to solve, even if I didn't seem to be making as much headway as I'd hoped.

I arrived home to find a note slipped under my kitchen door from Alex saying he had found out something about the case he wanted to tell me. Why he couldn't have merely texted me the same thing I had no idea, but it didn't matter. I wasn't ready to talk to him yet.

A knock at my door startled me out of my thoughts about Alex, and I turned around to see Mary Jessick on my porch. She looked eager to speak to me, so I invited her in and hoped she could shed some light on what had just become a more muddled case.

"I'm sorry for coming to your house, but I wanted to speak to you without having to say this in front of the cop," she said quietly as she took her seat at the kitchen table.

"No need to worry. He and I aren't working together today, so it's just the two of us."

"Good. I had a feeling he didn't quite understand the kind of person I am, but I think you do."

Alex had acted a little provincial when we visited her, so I could understand her desire to speak when he wasn't around. I offered her a drink of iced tea, and once we were seated again, she began to explain the real reason she was there.

"I'm not like people think, Poppy. They think I'm the town slut, but it's not like that. I just like having fun."

I understood exactly how she felt. "Sunset Ridge isn't the most progressive place, is it? A woman dates more than one man and all of a sudden she's a floozy."

Mary's mouth spread into a big smile. "I knew you'd understand. I bet you experience the same thing. The gossipy people in this town just can't understand that a young woman would want to enjoy life before settling down to an existence of block parties and boring small town events."

I took a sip of my tea and considered how to steer her toward talking about the case. Maybe a direct approach would do the trick. "Mary, was Canton Walters someone you had fun with?"

"I have seen the guy who died at the Piermont the other night. He and I met one night at Diamanti's and he came back to my house. But I swear that he was alive the next morning and I didn't kill him."

"What night was that?"

"Monday. Poppy, I swear he was fine when he left my place. It was just one night and we had fun. That was it."

I leaned forward and tried to tamp down my excitement at hearing what I'd suspected had happened. "Did you see him again before he died?"

"No." She shook her head and frowned. "I didn't want to lie, but I knew it looked bad. I couldn't keep it in anymore, though. But I promise you he was fine when he left that morning."

Uneasy about the next question I had to ask, I said, "I'm sorry if this sounds indelicate, but do you know if he was seeing anyone else in town while he was here?"

Mary thought about it for a second. "I wouldn't doubt it. He was a good time. Lots of laughs. It wasn't all about sex. Delilah came over that night and hung out with us and we all had a good time. Then after she left, he and I had our own good time."

"You know, I just saw Delilah over at my father's bar. It seemed odd since I've never seen her there before."

Rolling her eyes, she clucked her tongue. "I'm surprised Alan let her out at all. He's so difficult with her. That man won't let her have a second of fun without making her regret it. She had to sneak out Monday night just to come to my house. If he ever found out a man was there at the same time she was, he'd lose his mind. My brother-in-law is awful."

I looked closely at Mary's ears. They weren't pierced. Then her comment about meeting him one night recently made me remember how she'd said he'd danced at one of Delilah's parties.

"I'm confused. I thought you said Canton Walters was a dancer at one of your sister-in-law's Naughty and Spice parties?"

Mary lowered her gaze to the table and quietly admitted the truth. "I said that because I didn't want you to think I killed him."

"So he didn't dance at any party?"

She looked up at me and shook her head. "No. I'm sorry. I know it was wrong, but I didn't want you to think I was the murderer. I'm not. He was fine when I saw him Tuesday morning. You believe me, don't you?"

I did. I knew it may have seemed that she might be the best suspect so far, but something didn't feel right when I thought about her killing Canton. She didn't exhibit any anger toward him when she spoke about their time together, and I still didn't think she could kill anyone.

"I do believe you. Now I just have to find who really killed him."

Mary stood and took a last sip of her iced tea. "I hope you do, Poppy. He wasn't a bad person. I think he just got himself into a life he never wanted. He told me right before he left my house that morning that he was married and he planned to ask his wife for a divorce. I don't know if that was true or his way of absolving his guilt for what we'd done together, though."

Left alone with my morning's work to think about, I had to admit maybe Alex was right about Rose Walters. Maybe she had snapped that night and decided her husband had cheated one too many times.

My gut still said she wasn't the murderer, but there didn't seem to be anyone left but her on the list of suspects.

Chapter Seventeen

M Y EYES FLEW open as my brain tried to process what the hell was making all that banging noise downstairs. Within seconds, terror raced through my body. Was I being robbed? I grabbed my phone to dial 911, but then a familiar sound reached my ears.

No one had broken into my house. Someone was banging on my kitchen door.

Unsure who would be making a noise like that at the crack of dawn, I grabbed the baseball bat I kept in my closet and started down the stairs. What time was it? I focused my bleary eyes on my phone and saw it was just after five. Why would someone be banging on my door at so early in the morning?

My house was still dark, so I crept into the kitchen to stand next to the door and said, "Who is it? Who's there?"

"Poppy, it's Bethany. I need to talk to you. Please let me in."

It was Bethany and she sounded like she'd been crying. I switched on the lights and opened the door to see her standing on my porch still dressed like she'd never gone to bed last night after going out. But why was she there at all if she'd been out all night, probably at

Alex's?

"What's wrong?" I asked as my brain quickly switched from defense mode to confused.

"I need to talk to you. Can I come in?"

Stepping back, I opened the door to let her pass. "Sure. Come in."

She walked in, and for the first time, I saw how horrible she looked. Her mascara had settled into the lines beneath her eyes like she'd cried it off her lashes, and her makeup looked stale on some parts of her face and was missing entirely on others.

What had happened to make her look like this?

I offered her a seat at my kitchen table and headed to the coffee maker. If I was going to be entertaining someone at this time of the day, caffeine would be needed. Stat.

"Do you want something to drink?" I asked, feeling rather impotent from my offer as she sadly shook her head no.

"I didn't know who else to talk to, Poppy. I need your help."

"Of course. Just let me wake up a little so I'm not entirely useless here."

In truth, I didn't know how much I could help her with whatever the problem was that brought her to my door before sunrise. My back turned to her as I got the coffee maker what it needed to make my much needed morning drink, I tried to imagine what had happened. Had she and Alex had a fight? It seemed a little early in the relationship for them to be having fights that left her looking like she did at the moment. Bethany did have a tendency to be more emotional than most women, but even she wouldn't have fallen into the crying act after just a few dates.

Had she been out at a club and been attacked? I turned around and spied a look to see if there was any evidence of that. She was in a cute pale blue sundress that said she had probably been on a date or at a bar, but she didn't have bruises or cuts, so someone attacking her seemed unlikely.

By the time the last drop of coffee had fallen into my mug, I'd run through half a dozen possibilities about what may have happened and discounted them all. She'd tell me in a few seconds anyway, so I took a deep breath to prepare for what she had to say and sat down across from her at the table.

"I'm sorry that took so long. I'm really a wreck without my morning coffee."

She sniffled and tried to smile. "I know. Alex said that a few times. He says you're addicted to your dark roast." As the last words left her mouth, she began to sob. "Two sugars and extra cream."

I looked down into the dark brown liquid in my mug and mumbled, "Yeah, usually, but I'm doing black this morning. I figured I needed it straight up so I could wake up faster."

My feeble attempt at a joke didn't register with her, and she sniffled and sobbed more. "I know you don't like us together, do you? Did you tell him that?"

The plaintive sound of her voice made my heart contract for a moment. I didn't know what had happened, but it did involve Alex. She didn't have to worry about what I thought, although it was clear she did. My epiphany from the day before now had the chance to be more than just helpful to me.

"I'm fine with you two together. You're a good

friend of mine, and Alex is my work partner. Two good people deserve to have fun, and if it's with one another, then that's even better."

I may not have believed every word of that one hundred percent. Maybe sixty or seventy percent. That was a vast improvement from just a few days before, though, so I was making good progress. I just wished my words could help Bethany, but as she covered her face and began to cry behind her hands, I knew they hadn't.

Reaching over, I gently touched her arm and quietly asked the question I wasn't sure I wanted the answer to. "What happened?"

She dropped her hands to reveal her mascara had once again lost its fight against her tears and was running down her cheeks. I quickly grabbed a napkin from the holder at the edge of the table and handed it to her.

"Don't cry. I'm sure whatever happened will be okay."

"I thought we were having a good time. I thought…I thought he liked me, Poppy. I really like him."

Her words became harder to understand as the tears returned and syllables got lost in her sobs. Part of me hated seeing her crying there in front of me, but another part of me—and not a part I was particularly proud of— that part wanted to know the details of what happened to make her cry over Alex.

Thankfully, the good part of me kept the evil part at bay so I didn't blurt out half a dozen questions to satisfy my curiosity. "It's okay, honey. Let it out."

I'd always found that advice helped at least give me a reason to think crying my eyes out was okay. I hoped it would help her too. I wasn't entirely evil.

She looked at me with her bloodshot eyes rimmed with defeated mascara and shook her head. "I don't know what happened. We were having a good time. At least I thought we were. We had dinner a few times and I thought we'd sleep together tonight, but then he told me right out of the blue after we got to my apartment tonight that he thought we should slow things down."

Some tiny area of me deep inside where the parts I'm not particularly proud of hung out rejoiced at hearing they hadn't slept together yet. I knew I shouldn't have cared, especially after my recent epiphany, but I did. It was petty and sort of sad, but I did.

And then Bethany spoke the words that made me ashamed.

"Why would he do that? What's wrong with me, Poppy?"

The last remnants of jealousy I'd felt over her with Alex disappeared with that one question. Every woman in the world has thought that or asked that out loud to her friends at least one time in her life. What's wrong with me? It cut to the heart of every fear a woman secretly carried with her every day of her life.

What's wrong with me? I hated hearing that coming out of Bethany's mouth as she sat there after a night of crying over that very question because that's what it was. She may have seemed to be crying over Alex, but it was bigger than that.

She'd spent hours crying because she thought there was something wrong with her. I may have been a pretty rotten friend to her in the past, but I had a chance to be someone much better and I wanted to be that.

"Bethany, listen to me. There's nothing wrong with you. You're beautiful, smart, fun. Any man who has any sense would see you're great."

She wiped the tears from beneath her eyes and smeared her makeup past her eyes to her hairline. "Then why doesn't Alex see that?"

I had no idea why he didn't. I reached for a napkin and wiped the mascara and eyeliner from the sides of her face as I tried to find the words I knew she needed to hear. "I don't know, honey, but he's crazy if he can't."

Fighting back more tears, she said in a tiny voice, "I really liked him, Poppy. He's not like any other guy I've ever dated. He's smart and strong, and I knew we were complete opposites since he's so quiet and I'm so outgoing, but I thought he liked that about me."

Opposites. More and more it seemed everyone was the opposite of Alex. I knew how Bethany felt, even though I'd never dated him. She admired how different he was from her and liked being around someone who complimented who she was with who he was. Now, though, his apparent rejection of her felt like a rejection of everything she was.

Like those differences had suddenly become something bad she wished wasn't so much of who she was. I understood all too well.

"I'm sure he did, Bethany. He only said he wanted to slow things down, though. That doesn't mean he doesn't want to see you anymore."

She hung her head and sighed. "I know what slow things down means. I've heard it before. We'll go out a couple times a month and each time we'll seem to have a good time, but he'll always seem to be happy with just hanging out or having sex and never want more. I've been here before."

I hated the idea that Alex would be one of those guys

like she described. He was better than that, wasn't he? I wanted to believe he was the man I'd built up in my mind.

"Maybe it will be different this time. Alex is a good guy. I don't think he'll be that way with you."

Honestly, I didn't know what he'd be like. I hadn't expected him to be like this with her and move into slow down mode so early in their relationship. I knew I had been seeing things through that ugly green haze of jealousy, but I thought they'd begin dating and he'd fall head over heels in love with her.

Why wouldn't he? She had everything men loved, and as she'd said, she was his opposite and that usually attracted a man to a woman.

Bethany blew her nose in a napkin and looked at me with a pleading stare. "Would you talk to him for me? I know he thinks the world of you. I can't tell you how much we talked about you when we were together. He raves about how much he values your insight with the cases you guys work on and I know he would listen to you. He said he's never had a partner who knew so much about him."

Valued my insight. That should have made me feel great, but it didn't. I hated that he described me in all work terms. Just as I'd feared, he only saw me as his work partner. Nothing else.

And he'd never had a partner who knew so much about him? I had to wonder who he'd worked with in the past since I barely knew anything about him.

"Please, Poppy. I really want to try to make a go with things with him. You know him so much better than I do, so will you talk to him for me?"

Why did anyone think I knew Alex better than they

did? My father knew about as much about him as I did, and compared to Bethany, I was practically a stranger in his life. His mailman probably knew more about him than I did.

As much as I dreaded the idea of talking to him about her, I couldn't say no with her looking at me like I was her one and only chance for happiness with him. I pushed down the demons inside me plotting her romantic demise and did the only thing the good parts of me could.

I said I'd help.

"Okay, but I think you might be overstating how close we are. Really. When he says I know a lot about him, I think he means he knows a ton about me, not the other way around."

Tears filled her eyes again, and she grabbed my hands to squeeze them tightly. "Thank you so much, Poppy."

I smiled and told her it was my pleasure to help a friend as the good and evil parts of me began their latest war inside my brain. It was their favorite battlefield, especially when it came to moral issues. On the one hand, good me wanted to help Bethany get together with someone I knew she liked a lot. On the other hand, though, evil me knew if Alex already had gone to the slow down place in the relationship, it wouldn't take much to make him want to end it completely. A few well-chosen words on my part and Alex and Bethany would be no more.

I knew what I'd do when the time came, but those evil parts of me sure did sound like they had the better idea.

Pushing all that aside for the moment, I did what I

could to cheer her up and on her way. "You better get going. You have work in a little while, and you don't want to walk into *The Eagle* looking like that. You know how tongues wag in this town."

She wiped under her eyes again and nodded. "You're right. I'm going to go home and take a nice hot shower before I go to work. Thank you so much for being such a good friend, Poppy. I was worried when I came here that you wouldn't even talk to me since you haven't answered any of my texts or phone calls in the last few days. I thought you were mad at me because Alex and I had decided to go out."

Instantly, I felt ashamed for how I'd acted. "No, it wasn't that at all," I lied. "Howard has been on my back about getting more work to him lately, so I had to hunker down and get it done so I don't lose my job."

A look of relief washed over her, and she stood from the table to leave, smiling for the first time. "I should have known that. Alex asked me what I thought could be wrong last night at dinner and I told him I thought you might not be happy about us together. When he didn't tell me I was wrong, I thought for sure you'd said something to him about it."

I stood and brought her into my arms in a genuine hug. "I would never do that, Bethany. You're my friend, and I'm sorry I wasn't around the last couple days. I'm just glad I could be here for you this morning."

"Thank you so much, Poppy." Leaning away from me, she wiped the last of her mascara from her cheeks and smiled. "I'll talk to you later, okay?"

"Okay. I don't know when I'll get to talk to Alex since I still have to focus more on my articles for my editor, but I promise I'll speak to him. Don't worry.

Things will be okay."

She hugged me again and thanked me before leaving. As I closed the door behind her, I felt a twinge of guilt about hedging when I'd get to talk to Alex about them and lying outright about having to focus on my newspaper work first.

To make myself feel better, I messaged Alex for the first time in days and hoped he wasn't as stubborn as I was.

Hey, I've been in the writing cave but I'm ready to come out now that I've finished my work for my editor. The Grounds at 8 this morning?

Less than ten seconds later, his text back to me made my phone vibrate in my hand. I looked down to see he was already up and raring to go.

I was beginning to get worried about you. I have news about the case I want to talk about. See you at 8.

The difference between him at six in the morning and Bethany couldn't have been starker.

TWO HOURS LATER, I walked into The Grounds for the first time in days and felt like a changed person. I didn't know why since the coffee shop hadn't changed in the least, but I was different. Nothing a little change in perspective can't fix.

Two women sat at our usual table, so Alex was at the one next to it. Yet another small but notable change. I saw two coffee cups sitting on our new table in front of him, so I walked directly to where he was and sat down.

"Good morning. I'm happy to see you back," he said in a way that made me look twice at him. I wasn't sure I liked what I saw.

He didn't look tired like he'd been up for hours parsing the words of someone he cared about or wondering what was wrong with him. There were no dark circles or bags under his eyes, and he didn't look like he'd quickly gotten a shower before running out of the house to meet me.

In fact, Alex looked rather refreshed this morning. I didn't know exactly why, but that bothered me. Was I angry he had gone out with Bethany at all? Angry that he didn't seem to want her as much as she wanted him? I wasn't sure I had a valid reason to be angry at anything other than what he'd said to me before I jumped out of the car, but as I stared at him looking far too rested and enjoying his morning coffee, all I knew was I was angry at Alex.

"Looks like you had a good night's sleep," I remarked, instantly hating how snarky I sounded.

Clearly confused why I'd snapped at him about how well he'd slept, he opened his mouth to speak but said nothing. Shrugging, he finally said, "I guess. Are you okay? The last I saw of you was that nasty look you threw at me just before you jumped out of the car, slammed the door, and stormed away."

Now seemed as good a time as any to get my cards on the table, even if I'd decided not to put them all out there for him to see, so I took a sip of my coffee made exactly like I loved it and said, "I didn't like what you said, so I left. Nothing more than that."

Not exactly a friendly way to tell someone what was wrong, but it was the best I could muster without having all the misplaced resentment I was feeling over how well he'd slept last night spill out in some bizarre rambling diatribe that would do no one any good.

Alex studied my face long enough that I grew uncomfortable, so I turned away and pretended to watch a couple on the other side of the restaurant who were obviously having a similar morning to ours, except the woman had decided not to hold a thing back. In hushed tones that only made what she was saying more interesting to those around her, she reamed out the man across from her as her hands spoke volumes with their jerky flailing.

As I witnessed the disintegration of their relationship right there in The Grounds, I heard Alex say something and turned back to see a hopeful look in his eyes. Curious to know what had brought that about, I asked, "What did you say? I missed it. Sorry."

"This morning must be the time for apologies. I said I was sorry for what I said to you in the car the other day. It wasn't what I ever felt about you and our working together, and I don't know why I said it. Sometimes I hear things and they filter into my thinking, but I don't think of you like that."

"Like some hapless tagalong Dr. Watson to your Sherlock Holmes?"

I hadn't planned to be so honest about how he'd made me feel when he said those things, but now as I sat there across from him as another couple waged their own relationship war, I suddenly felt like I wanted to throw more cards on our table. If he didn't feel that way about working with me and had obviously just picked it up from what I'd told Bethany, then how did he feel?

It was about time for him to come clean too.

Uneasy because I'd put him on the spot, he gave me a forced smile and said, "You are not that, Poppy."

Now it was time to go for broke, so I asked the question that had rolled around my head for far too long. "Then what am I?"

He didn't answer, so I continued with even more questions. "You didn't seem to think much of my helping you when you said those things, so what is it, Alex? We aren't anything but work partners. That's clear. But what am I in this partnership?"

For a moment, Alex looked more uncomfortable than I'd ever seen him before. He winced like he was in pain and shifted in his seat before he opened his mouth to speak and nothing came out. Clearly my questions weren't easy for him to answer either.

Finally, he cleared his throat and said, "I think of you as far more than just someone I work cases with. I've never had a partner who knew as much about me as you do. There's something about you that makes me open up, even though it's not my nature at all. I lived alone in that house not really talking to anyone for years, and then one night you showed up to ask my help and I didn't want to live like that anymore."

"So we're friends in your mind too?" I asked, stunned by what he'd said so far.

"I thought so. Didn't you?"

I shook my head and told him as much of my truth as I could without admitting how much I cared for him. "I know next to nothing about you, Alex. You say you've never had a partner who knows as much as I do. How is that possible? All I know is you used to be a Baltimore cop and you moved here after your wife died. After all these months, I still don't know much else about you."

"That's not true. You know how I take my coffee and that I only drink it in the morning. You know I drink scotch neat. You know I don't like country music."

"These aren't really big things to know about someone, Alex."

"I can't think of anyone else who knows them."

"I'm willing to bet Bethany knows a lot more than that about you."

I didn't mean to say that, but it slipped out and then once the words had left my mouth, I couldn't take them back. In just a few misspoken words, I'd shown him what had been at the root of my anger with him.

I looked away feeling more exposed than I could deal with. I didn't want to look into his eyes when he realized all I'd been was jealous. That's all it had been, and now as I avoided his piercing gaze, I wished I hadn't said those words.

"Bethany knows what she wants to know, Poppy. She's nice to spend a little time with every so often. You know, to break up the time alone. She wants more than I can give, though. But she doesn't know me better than you do. Nobody does."

I didn't know if that was the best thing he could tell me or the saddest admission I'd ever heard since I still didn't feel like I knew more than the surface of Alex Montero. If I knew him better than anyone else, I couldn't help but see now that he kept the world at arm's length, letting no one in. He hadn't changed from that sullen guy I first met in Derek's office or that angry soul who'd threatened to shoot me for trespassing on his property.

"Well, I still don't think I know much about you compared to what you know about me, but what's most important to me is that you respect me for what I bring to this partnership because if you don't, then there's no point in us working together anymore."

My mouth suddenly became devoid of all traces of moisture as I waited for him to answer. I hadn't meant for it to sound like an ultimatum, but it had come out a bit more stridently than I intended and I'd basically told him it was time for him to put his cards on the table.

I wasn't sure our little table at The Grounds was big enough for all these cards we'd been holding so close to our chests.

"I do respect you, Poppy. I wanted to apologize as soon as I said all that. And if I didn't feel bad enough after that, the next two days without you made it abundantly clear. All the joy felt like it had been sucked out of my work, and the only thing different about it was you weren't around to talk to."

For a guy I barely knew anything about and who said very little, he really had a way of saying just the right things sometimes.

"Oh." Every so often another human surprised me into silence. This was one of those times.

"I found out some things about the case in the past couple days, but I don't want to talk about them here. What do you say we go to your house?"

He stood from his chair before I could answer, so I assumed he wanted to leave immediately. "Okay. It must be something big, right?"

"I think you'll be pleasantly surprised by what I have to say. Let's go."

Chapter Eighteen

ALEX SAT DOWN at my kitchen table and waited for me to adjust the air conditioning to cool the place off. Houses like his may have had the luxury of central air, but old houses like mine had air conditioners scattered around to keep the summer heat at bay. I'd forgotten to turn the air on this morning after being startled out of a sound sleep, so my house currently hovered at a temperature somewhere between excessively balmy and downright overbearing. A few degrees more and I would have walked into a house with the wallpaper peeling off and unlit candles melting into puddles of wax.

Wiping my hairline of the beads of sweat that had already begun to form there, I sat down across from him and joked, "We should have stayed at The Grounds. Sorry about this. I guess I was distracted this morning and forgot to fix the daytime temperature."

He got a strange look on his face like I'd said something wrong and asked, "Distracted? What's that mean?"

On the off chance Bethany had been able to keep from calling him and spilling her guts about her feelings after she left me this morning, I chose a white lie over the truth. "Oh, nothing. Just got a call from my father before I left. So what did you find out?"

"You were right."

"About what?" I asked, thrilled to hear I'd been right about something in this case.

"Rose Walters isn't our killer."

"And what brought you to this conclusion?" I didn't want to appear to gloat, but inside, I was giving myself a nice pat on the back.

Without even a hint of sheepishness, he said, "I checked out her story front and back, and she never drove to the Hotel Piermont that night. You were right about her."

"I think that's very big of you to admit that, Alex," I teased, enjoying that his feet were made of clay after all. "Thank you for telling me. In all fairness, I guess I should admit I was only going on my gut feeling about her."

He smiled. "I know, but your instincts were right and I was wrong."

Pleased with his mea culpa, I figured it was time to tell him all that I had learned in our time apart. "Well, I have something for you. Two somethings, actually."

Alex's eyes lit up with interest. "I like how this sounds. What did you find out?"

"I had a couple people visit me yesterday. It was definitely a day for confession."

He waited for me to continue, and when I didn't, he leaned forward slightly and impatiently asked, "And?"

"And I think you're going to find what I learned interesting."

I enjoyed stringing him along like this, and he knew it. "Poppy, I know you think I deserve this whole piecemeal thing because of what I said, but can you give me the information so we can see if it helps or not?"

Rolling my eyes, I gave in and explained about my two visitors. "Okay. You don't have to get testy just because it's nearly a hundred degrees in here. You really do know how to take the fun out of things."

He winked at me. "Someday, I'll show you how much fun I can be. For now, we have work to do."

The way he looked at me with those dark eyes that seemed to see directly into my soul and said things that sounded too sexy to be coming from someone I worked with made me lose my train of thought. Fumbling for the right words to say, I knew I needed to get my head straightened out. I was sitting too close to him for that to happen any time soon, so I jumped up out of my chair and turned away toward the refrigerator.

"I think I need a drink. Want some iced tea? I think I'm going to grab a glass for myself."

"Yeah, sure. About those two somethings, Poppy?"

I took my time pouring out two glasses of tea so my brain could remember what we were supposed to be doing. I'd had that wonderful epiphany and truly believed I had found a place for whatever I felt for Alex somewhere deep inside where only I knew about it. The problem was if he kept acting like he was, it wouldn't be my secret for very long. I didn't want him to know the effect he had on me.

"Okay, now at least we have some drinks to deal with the heat in here."

I turned around to see him waiting for me and completely confused about what had happened. Good. Maybe that meant he didn't know what was going on with me.

"All right. I won't make you suffer anymore," I said as I placed his glass in front of him. "I just thought a little theatrical pause might be good."

Alex took a sip of his drink and chuckled. "I promise I'll take whatever theatrical pause you want to give me after we solve this case. For now, I'm hoping you're going to tell me something we can use."

Moving my chair so I sat across the table from him, I sat down and said, "What about both Mary and Delilah coming to see me about the case?"

"I like how this sounds already. Mary first. What did she have to say?"

"Good choice. Mary confessed that she did know Canton Walters. They had a one night stand on Monday night and when he left her house on Tuesday, she says he was fine."

"Interesting. Do you believe her?"

I thought about how forthright Mary had been. "I do. I know I've said from the very beginning that I couldn't see her killing anyone, but I believe her. She said Delilah came over that night to hang out with them too before they…"

My sentence trailed off, and I smiled. Alex caught on immediately and nodded, but then he asked, "Didn't Delilah know our victim because he danced at one of her parties? Not that we have anyone but Mary who says it happened."

"She told me she lied about that. From what she said, she met Canton at Diamanti's that night."

Alex folded his arms across his chest and leaned back in his chair. His body language told me Mary's confession had produced more questions than answers for him.

"So what was our victim doing in Sunset Ridge if he wasn't here for a job as a dancer and didn't have a long-term affair going on with Mary?"

I hadn't thought about that, but now that he mentioned it, I didn't know.

"Are you thinking Mary lied again?"

He sighed and nodded his head. "Something's not right. Every time one of these women says something, it makes the reason we thought he was in town disappear. First, he was a Naughty and Spice salesman. Then we found out that wasn't the case. Next, we hear he was a dancer at one of Delilah's parties. Now that's not true either. So what the hell was this guy from Virginia with a wife and kids doing at the one place in Sunset Ridge where cheaters spend their time? Who was this guy sharing his extracurricular time with?"

I was beginning to share Alex's frustration. Not only hadn't my surprise helped us, but now it felt like we'd taken two steps back without even getting that first step forward.

"Maybe his staying at the Hotel Piermont was just a coincidence. He might not have been there because he was having an affair."

The look Alex gave me was the definition of skeptical. "So instead of staying at any of the major chain hotels just a few miles down the road, this guy chose to stay at some hotel people stay at for hours instead of days. It still leaves us with the question of why he was in Sunset Ridge at all."

"He loves quaint small towns?" I said in a feeble attempt to lighten the mood.

"I guess he came to the right place then," Alex said with a frown.

"Don't worry. We'll figure this out."

"Yeah, but we're no better off than we were before Mary decided to confess, and to be honest, I'm not exactly sure whatever she told you could be used to build the case since no officer was there."

"Well, I guess you better stick close to me then from now on since these people love to talk to me."

And then, as if he'd just heard the best news ever, he smiled in that way that made it all the way up to his eyes and he was happy again.

"What was the second something you wanted to tell me?"

"Delilah found me at my father's bar to talk to me about how her husband wasn't as bad as he may have seemed when we talked to them the other day."

With a sneer, Alex discounted Delilah's claim. "Dr. Alan Roberts is a piece of work. Something tells me in private he's even worse to her if he didn't mind acting that way in front of two strangers."

"I asked her directly if she'd ever met our victim, and she got very flustered and told me repeatedly that she hadn't. Then she bolted out of the bar and our visit was over."

"I'm not even going to ask if you believe her. I can see by the look on your face that you don't, which is good because I don't either since we know she met him that Monday night with her sister-in-law. I think she knew Canton Walters, though. I don't know how, but I'd bet a week's pay on it."

This was all very interesting, but it wasn't something he couldn't have whispered to me at the coffee shop. "So what's your news about the case since mine has just made things more confusing. Was it that you figured out

Rose Walters isn't our killer?"

Shaking his head, he pulled his cell phone out and swiped the screen. "No. I just thought I'd say that first. What I didn't want to talk about in front of all those people at The Grounds was the coroner's report that just came in this morning. Donny sent me a copy during the night, and I wanted you to see it."

I scooted my chair closer to his to see the report on his phone. Excited, I asked, "Did you look at it already? Is there something in it that points us to one of our suspects?"

Scrolling through documents on his phone, he got to Donny's report and answered, "No, I wanted to wait for my partner, although to be honest, if you had still refused to answer my texts and phone calls this morning, I was going to look at it without you."

I turned to look at him and saw that way-too-sexy grin he sometimes wore when he said something cute and he knew it. I didn't know what other people thought of that smile, but it had a way of making me melt in ways I wasn't sure he should ever know about.

"Then I guess it's a good thing I texted you," I said with a smile in response to his.

We read through the report noting the angle of the knife when it was inserted into Canton Walters' back. Donny found it interesting that there were no drugs in his system and no alcohol either. After the report, he'd included a note about the knife wound, which Alex read out loud.

"The length of the knife and the angle in which it was driven into the victim's back indicates the killer is right-handed. It also indicates he or she is at least five feet eight inches tall."

Quickly, I looked at Alex and saw he was doing the same thing I was—mentally running through our list of suspects to figure out who was that tall. Elizabeth Freely was nowhere close to being that tall, so she couldn't have done it.

"I think we can safely say our favorite hotel desk clerk can be ruled out," Alex said with a chuckle.

"I was just thinking the same thing, although I think she might be your favorite desk clerk. I'm a much bigger fan of the strange but nice Joe, the night desk clerk."

He took his notepad out of his pocket and flipped to a new page. Writing Elizabeth's name, he noted next to it she was too short. "Who's next?"

"Rose Walters isn't tall enough either, so I think that seals it with her."

After Rose's name, he wrote Poppy was right. Looking up at me, he gave me that sweet smile again and returned his attention to his list to write Mary Jessick's name.

"Mary's definitely too short. I know you had a soft spot for her, so I'm happy to say she's off the list now too."

"Who does that leave? Are we saying Delilah Roberts did it?" I asked, still unable to believe she could kill anyone. Delilah wasn't violent. She was needy, but those kind of people didn't kill others, not as long as they got the attention they craved.

"She's definitely tall enough," he said as I remembered her towering over me and looking nearly the same height as her husband, who had to go at least six foot. She was wearing high heels, so maybe she was tall enough like Alex thought.

He scrolled back through his documents as I tried to

imagine Delilah Roberts ever being angry enough to kill someone. Finally, after a minute, he read off his phone.

Turning to look at me, he asked, "Do you remember that single diamond earring we found in Canton's suit pocket hanging in the closet?"

"I do. I'd wondered if we were ever going to find out about that."

"I sent it to be dusted for prints and they found a thumbprint on the post. Guess whose it was?"

Alex held his phone up for me to read what was written in the report. There in black and white was the name Delilah Roberts.

"How did you get hers to compare it to? I doubt she has a criminal record."

He slid his phone back into his pocket and wrote Delilah's name in his notepad. "You think too highly of the doctor's wife. We did have her prints in the system."

Was it possible I'd completely misread her innocence and had been fooled by an act? Curious, I asked, "What did she do?"

He chuckled at how serious I'd become. "It wasn't anything terrible. Your faith in her is still warranted, at least until we find out she's Canton's killer. She was arrested in an underage drinking party incident back when she was seventeen. That's why we had her prints on file."

"Wow. Talk about a permanent record. So the earring was hers. What's the theory on why she did it?"

Alex sat back and looked up at my kitchen ceiling. "I don't know." He lowered his head and continued, "Maybe she was having an affair with Canton and wanted more but he wouldn't leave his wife. Maybe he was blackmailing her and threatened to tell her husband, so she killed him. Either way, if he knew her because they were sleeping together, he would have happily let her into his hotel room."

"That still doesn't account for how she got past the night desk clerk, Alex. Unless we're wholly discounting his ability to see anyone that night, we have a problem with that."

"Then she found a way."

"And what about how someone her size drove that knife into a grown man's back? From what the coroner's report said, Canton Walters was standing up when he was stabbed. So we're to believe she stabbed him with enough force to drive that knife far enough in to kill him and then moved his body to the chair? He wasn't a huge man, but he would have been dead weight."

Alex thought about these contradictions and shrugged. "I can't explain it yet, but crazier things have happened. People have been known to lift cars off their children and after it's over, all experts can say is the adrenaline was pumping through them so they could do impossible feats. Maybe he enraged her to the point that she had the same feeling and with the adrenaline pumping, she killed him."

"That report said the only blood found in the room was like ten feet away from the desk. That's pretty far for her to carry a dead man. She'd have to still be under the influence of that adrenaline to do that, don't you think?"

He took a deep breath in. Letting it out slowly, he nodded. "I admit the theory has some holes. I think I know someone who might be able to help us plug up some of those holes, though."

I was intrigued. Was there someone in town who had some knowledge of dead bodies other than Donny?

"Someone here in Sunset Ridge?"

Grabbing his phone, he slid his finger down the screen and tapped on Contacts. "No, it's someone from back in Baltimore. His name is Ken Bryer. He's a pathologist and an expert on knives and knife wounds. I guess you'd call it his specialty. More like an obsession."

"Interesting fixation to have."

"I think we should give him a call and see if he can shine some light on these problems we're having."

I waited as Alex called his friend and hoped he'd be able to help us finally get a real break in this case. He seemed to believe in him, so it couldn't hurt.

"Ken? It's Alex Montero. Do you have a few minutes for me to pick your brain?"

The man said something to make Alex smile and he answered, "Let me put you on speakerphone. I want my partner to hear what you have to say."

He set the phone in the middle of the table and said, "Ken, let me introduce you to my partner, Poppy McGuire. Poppy, Ken Bryer."

A deep voice came through the phone, and I instantly understood this person wasn't just some old colleague of Alex's. "Poppy McGuire? That's an Irish girl's name if I've ever heard one. I'm happy to finally hear that my friend there has jumped back into the dating pool."

I looked over at Alex and shook my head. Together, we both protested, "No, no. It's not like that."

"You sound like twin souls there answering together," Ken said with a chuckle, making me blush.

"Sorry to disappoint, but I'm not the girlfriend. Just the partner," I said in an attempt to clear things up.

"So I wasn't wrong. I knew I heard something

different in your voice, Alex. You sound like a man who's finally let himself love again."

I watched Alex roll his eyes at all of Ken's talk of romance, and my chest contracted for a second at the mention of him loving again. Loving Bethany? Epiphany or not, I hated the sound of that.

It didn't make Alex happy either, if the way he was cringing was any indication. Shaking his head, he leaned down toward the phone and said, "Enough about me. Do you have a few minutes to talk about your favorite topic, Ken?"

The phone went silent for a few moments and then Ken Bryer made a noise that reminded me of how children sounded when they gorged themselves on chocolate. He certainly must have loved knives.

"You know how to get me off a topic you clearly don't want to talk about, Alex. I'll agree to let you pick my brain about whatever you want if you agree to tell me about what you're up to these days with such a sweet Irish girl."

I mumbled about not exactly being a sweet Irish girl while Alex agreed to Ken's terms. "Okay, but there's not much to tell. I'm back to police work up here in Sunset Ridge. Poppy's my partner, and she's definitely easier to work with than Gary. Remember him?"

Ken laughed and started to tell a story about this Gary person Alex had been partners with back in Baltimore. This pathologist certainly loved to talk. I tried to imagine how the man I knew ever spent much time with Ken Bryer since they were like night and day.

"Okay, okay, enough about Gary. I did my time with him, but now I need your help. Quid pro quo, my friend. Time to let me ask some questions of you."

"Shoot. What do you want to know?"

Alex flipped through his notebook to the first page of his notes on the Canton Walters' murder investigation. "I remember you telling me once that killing someone with a knife wasn't as easy as everyone thinks. I've got a murder victim who was stabbed in the back with a kitchen knife."

Ken whistled into the phone. "A kitchen knife? That's a hard way to kill someone."

Curious, I asked, "Why? It's a knife into skin. Wouldn't it just cut through some artery and kill the person?"

"Not as easily as you'd think. TV and movies make it seem like it's as easy as jabbing a knife into a loaf of bread, but the human body isn't like that. Skin, tissue, muscle, bone…they'd all fight against a kitchen knife."

Alex and I looked at each other as Ken explained how our murder was even more difficult than we'd thought. "Ken, our coroner says the wound is consistent with someone being right handed and at least five foot eight. We're wondering if a female that tall could kill like this."

After he thought about it, Ken answered, "I can't say, but I will say this. She'd have to be a very strong woman to stab a man in the back and kill him."

Thinking aloud, I said, "I don't think Delilah fits that description. She's tall enough, but I'd call her frail, if anything."

Alex nodded toward me. "I think you're right."

"The problem is that anyone aiming to kill someone by stabbing them in the back has to be even more than strong. They have to be lucky. Most of the time, even if they get the knife in deep enough, they won't hit anything that will kill the person. It's why most knife attacks don't end up as murders."

Flipping through his notepad until he reached the last page of our investigation, Alex showed me what he'd written and said into the phone, "Ken, my coroner tells us the knife hit the pulmonary artery, and that's why our victim died."

"Wow. That's either incredibly lucky or your murderer knew where to slice into your victim. The odds of an average person hitting the artery would be astronomical, especially if it was a crime of passion. I'd say you're looking for someone who knows a thing or two about the human body."

Alex and I looked at each other and I knew he was thinking the same thing I was. As he promised Ken he'd come back to visit him soon, I wondered if he'd take Bethany along for that visit. That could wait for later, though. Right now, we finally knew who killed Canton Walters. Now we just had to prove it.

Chapter Nineteen

I SAT IN the passenger seat of the cruiser beside Alex as we waited for Judge Harlow to return from his lunch. We'd been outside his office for nearly an hour hoping to catch him so we could get him to sign a search warrant for the Roberts' house, and I saw the sluggish pace of Sunset Ridge's small town justice had begun to wear on Alex's patience.

He shifted in the driver's seat for the fifth time in as many minutes and sighed. "I should have gone to a county judge. This guy spends more time lost in the bottle than doing his job."

Judge Reginald Harlow was really more a local magistrate than a real judge, but he was a friend to the police, so when they could, they always used him to get search warrants. The problem with that plan, though, was depending on him to be sober enough to issue said warrants.

"It's going to be okay. We'll have more than enough time once Harlow comes back from his liquid lunch to get over to the Roberts' house."

Alex leaned back against his seat and pinched the bridge of his nose. "I don't know if I'll ever get used to the pace things happen around here. Back in Baltimore,

I'd already be in that house looking for evidence. As it is, I'm stuck sitting here waiting for Judge Lush for going on an hour. Ridiculous!"

Seeing some distraction was desperately needed, I asked, "So that Ken guy, how long have you known him? He seems like he knows you pretty well, if that conversation was any indication."

Staring straight ahead with his eyes peeled for the judge, Alex answered, "I know what you're saying, but he doesn't know me that well. He and I worked together on a lot of cases back in Baltimore. That's it."

"So he doesn't know how you take your coffee or what your favorite drink is?" I asked with a smile. Something about the way Ken had been so interested in Alex's love life told me he knew far more about him than I did, no matter what my partner claimed.

Alex tore his gaze from the judge's office door to look over at me. Knitting his brows, he said, "He probably knows the drink answer."

I playfully tapped his shoulder as he scowled. "I'm serious. Who is this guy, other than some coroner with an obsession with knives? You never talk about your friends, so I was surprised to hear him be so familiar with you."

"Ken's always like that with me. We both worked the same cases a lot of times and he's that kind of guy. I used to tease him that he tried too hard with the living because he spent too much time with the dead."

This Ken Bryer person intrigued me. I couldn't imagine Alex being that comfortable with anyone, but he'd obviously let Ken in.

"So you guys became friends over death. Sort of creepy but I like knowing there's the possibility we may be like that someday."

He turned away and went back to watching the judge's door as he said in a flat voice, "I don't think that's possible. He and I got close when we were chasing the same woman. I won, but we stayed friends."

The same woman? I'd never heard Alex talk about any women from his past. My curiosity piqued, I pressed for more information. "Really? Well, the plot thickens. He must be an okay guy to accept defeat like that. Most men don't give up so graciously."

"I think her saying I do pretty much sealed it for him."

And with that, Alex mentioned his wife for the first time in all the months we'd worked together. That he hadn't even said her name seemed odd. I wasn't sure I should continue, but my need for some details about her won out over decorum.

"What was her name?"

He swallowed hard, making his Adam's apple bob, and said in a low voice, "Helena."

The hollow sound when he said her name made me regret asking anything. His expression never changed, but I knew from the way he answered that her death still haunted him. "I'm sorry, Alex. I shouldn't have pried."

"You didn't ask anything wrong. Talking to Ken made everything come back anyway. He was a good friend through all of it. The good times and the bad. He even helped me try to find out who killed her, and when all the leads went cold, it was Ken who sat me down and made me realize I had to let it go or it would make me crazy forever."

For one of the few times in my life, I didn't know the right words to say. I thought back to when my mother died and remembered all those kind sentiments everyone expressed never changing the simple fact that ruled every minute of my days and nights then. Someone I loved dearly was gone. Death was something that took over those left behind, and nothing anyone said or did could change that.

The only remedy for that pain so acute sometimes I didn't know if I could on to the next day was time. I saw that same pain on Alex's face now and knew time hadn't finished its job with him yet.

"I'm sorry for bringing it up."

He turned his head to look at me and smiled, but in those dark brown eyes I saw it. The look that lingered in the survivors' eyes even when they thought they'd moved past all the sadness. It was a look of grief so complete it made my breath catch in my chest. Of all the times I'd stared into his eyes looking for some clue as to what he was thinking, I'd never so clearly seen his emotions telegraphed like I did at that moment.

Then he somehow switched off what he was feeling and became the man I'd known for months. Quiet and thoughtful but nearly emotionless.

Out of the corner of my eye, I saw Judge Harlow stumble along the sidewalk to his office. Thankful for something to break the tension in the car, I pointed toward him. "There he is!"

Alex's head snapped forward, and in a flash, he was out of the car and practically accosting the judge as he opened the office door. The shocked look on his face faded as Alex made his case for the warrant, and when I saw him turn around to let the judge use his back to sign the paper, I knew he'd gotten what he wanted.

He climbed into the car and handed me the warrant.

"I'm going to have Craig meet us there. Delilah isn't going to be a problem, but if that husband of hers comes home to find us searching his house, he might lose it. I'm not sure you should be there, though. Things sometimes go bad in cases like this."

I knew what was going on. His memory of losing his wife had made him think twice about putting me in danger, but he was overreacting. Delilah Roberts and her husband, no matter how difficult he was, weren't going to try anything that would get me hurt.

In an attempt to make Alex realize that and lighten his mood, I chucked him in the shoulder as he started the car. "This is Sunset Ridge, partner. We're talking about a housewife who has sex toy parties. What's the worst that could happen? Is she going to throw a vibrator at me?"

He didn't want to smile, but he couldn't help it. Throwing his arm across the back of my seat, he rolled his eyes at me as he looked behind the car before backing up. "Let's hope that's the worst she does."

As we sped away toward the Roberts' house, he radioed for Craig to meet us there and I joked, "You better warn your buddy there, though. Craig's pretty innocent, so getting a sex toy thrown at him might freak him out."

Again, he rolled his eyes at one of my comments, but he also smiled, which was the whole reason for me making a joke of this. I knew the danger involved in working with him on cases like this one. I also knew I didn't like seeing him so sad about the past. I'd been there at that place he still lived in and remembered how hard it was to find anything to smile about when the pain of missing my mother settled into my heart.

Anything that got me out of that place, even for a brief moment, was priceless. That's what I wanted to give Alex, and if joking about sex toys did the trick, then I wasn't above that.

Craig met us at the Roberts' house, and as we walked up to the front door, Alex explained that if we didn't find what we were looking for there, the warrant also gave him the right to search Dr. Roberts' chiropractic office too. He knocked on the door as I let my imagination wander to that possibility. Dealing with Delilah was one thing, but Alan Roberts had a nasty temper.

"What's wrong, Poppy?" he asked as we waited for her to answer.

"I was just thinking about Dr. Roberts unraveling like a cheap suit if you have to search his office."

Alex thought about it for a moment and nodded his head toward Craig. "That's why he's with us. There's still time to change your mind and go back to the car."

"No way. We're partners, so where you go, I go."

The door opened and Delilah's genteel smile she often wore dropped into a frown as Alex explained our reason for being on her doorstep. Holding up the warrant for her to see, he said, "Please move aside so we can search your house, Mrs. Roberts."

We walked past her and put on our crime scene searching gloves, as I affectionately called them, as she pelted us not with sex toys but with questions about why we were doing this and what we could be looking for. The heartbreak in her voice signaled to all of us she was frightened, but I couldn't decide if it was because she was guilty or if it was just the mere presence of two policeman and myself preparing to rummage through her house.

Craig took off upstairs to check the bedrooms for any items of clothing with blood on them while Alex and I checked the downstairs. In addition to clothes that would put her or her husband at the scene of the crime, we were looking for any evidence that would tie her or the doctor to Canton Walters.

Delilah sat on the couch with her head in her hands as we looked through the desk near the French doors in the living room. Thankfully, both she and Alan were obsessively neat, so the papers we found were organized into tidy piles inside the drawers. I noted a stack of what looked like receipts and sat down in a chair opposite her as Alex grabbed them before continuing to search the desk.

After a few long minutes, Delilah asked, "What are you looking for? I told you I didn't kill that man. Why would you do this?"

I looked at her and didn't know what to say. Her life was coming apart in front of her eyes, and there was nothing she could do to stop it. I couldn't imagine how it felt to be in that position.

"I'm sorry, but we have to do this," I answered, hating how lacking my words were.

I returned to where Alex stood rummaging through the bottom drawer of old bills. "Find anything? This stack just looks like old utility receipts."

He shook his head and frowned. "No, not yet. Don't stop looking. We need something to connect them to that hotel and that room."

Just then, I looked over and saw Delilah's earrings. Gold hoop earrings. Turning to Alex, I said, "I'll be right back. I want to see something upstairs."

I tore up to the second floor and ran to the master bedroom to find Delilah's jewelry box. On her dresser, I saw a teakwood box and called for Craig to open it. All she kept in it were necklaces and bracelets, but no diamond earrings. Looking around the room, I saw nothing else that would hold an earring, so I instructed him to open the drawers to search through her bras and panties. If what we'd been doing downstairs felt intrusive, it was nothing compared to what rifling her undergarments felt like.

But my hunch told me that diamond earring was hers and it was still in the house. "Run your hand along the bottom of the drawer, Craig," I said.

He did as I told him to, and in just a few seconds his eyes lit up. "I feel something like a bump."

Moving aside the clothes, he showed me the back of the center drawer and I saw a piece of masking tape covering a small portion of the wood. Craig peeled it off to reveal a single sparkling diamond earring that looked like the match to the one Alex had found in Canton Walters' suit pocket.

Craig bagged it, and I ran down the stairs to the main floor to find Alex holding a single piece of paper that had written on it Room 307 in the same handwriting as the note we'd found in that very room. Interestingly, it wasn't in the same handwriting as the list Delilah had written out for Alex. Showing it to her, he asked, "Been to the Hotel Piermont lately?"

"Look what we found!" I said breathlessly. I held up the bag with the diamond earring and said proudly, "I'm willing to bet this has a match waiting for it at the station."

"So we have a note that corresponds to where the

victim was murdered and a diamond earring that matches one we found there."

Delilah jumped up from the couch. "No! It's not like that! You don't understand."

I turned toward her and asked, "Then why did I find this earring taped to the back of one of your drawers in your bedroom dresser. You were hiding it."

"No! It's not what you think. My grandmother always taped her most expensive jewelry to the back of the drawer. She didn't want to misplace an earring like that. I learned that from her. I wasn't hiding it. I swear."

"Where's the other one then?" Alex asked in that forceful policeman voice he used when he thought suspects were lying to him.

"I don't know," she sobbed. "Mary wore them one night and she only gave me one back. She told me she'd look in her car for the other one."

Delilah's explanation sounded iffy at best. As we stood there waiting for her to continue, Craig walked into the living room holding a pair of gloves. "Found these in the bottom of the closet behind some shoe boxes. They look like they have blood on them."

Terror filled Delilah's eyes as she stared at the gloves. "I've never seen those gloves before in my life. I have no idea where they came from. You have to believe me!"

Craig brought over the gloves to be bagged, and just then Alan Roberts stepped into the room and bellowed, "What the hell is going on here?"

Everyone in the room turned to look at him, and for a moment, it felt like we were all frozen to the floor. Then Delilah ran over to him sobbing and explaining how we were accusing her of killing a man, and he wrapped his arms around her shoulders like he wanted to comfort her.

"You'll never prove my wife killed that man," he said in a cocky way so different from the way he'd spoken to us the last time we were there.

Alex casually pushed me behind him and took a step toward them. "I don't intend on trying to prove she killed Canton Walters. You killed him."

I watched as Delilah's face fell at Alex's accusation, and she turned to look at her husband with an expression of shock. "Alan, tell them it's all a mistake. Tell them you wouldn't do that to anyone."

Cradling her face, he quietly said to her, "Oh, Delilah, did you think I'd let you get away with it forever? How long did you think I should allow you to play me the fool before I did something about it?"

"What are you saying?" she asked with pure fear in her voice. "Tell them you wouldn't do that!"

In one swift movement, he went from cradling her face to holding her to him, his forearm pressing on her neck. Alex pulled his gun from his right hip, but it was too late. Alan Roberts already had a gun pointed at his wife's head.

"I can't tell them that, Delilah. I can't tell them I wouldn't kill a man for sleeping with my wife. I told you when I married you I didn't abide by that kind of behavior from any wife of mine."

"You don't have to do this, Dr. Roberts. Put the gun down and let your wife go," Alex said calmly, but I had the sense that the time for calm had ended for Alan Roberts long ago.

"I do have to do this. She was sleeping with that man. She has a husband who's a doctor and she wants some damn gigolo dancer."

As he spoke, his voice grew louder and louder, echoing off the walls of the beautifully decorated living room. It didn't seem to matter to him that two officers had their guns pointed at him and would shoot if he made a move to hurt Delilah. He seemed unreachable, lost to his misery.

"Just put the gun down, Alan," Alex repeated to no avail.

Delilah sobbed, but her husband's face turned icy, as if all emotion had left him. "Everyone thinks I'm just some bore married to a beautiful woman. Her friends come over and laugh about those damn toys she sells and make her feel like she didn't get a good husband. They told her lies about her life, and she believed them. My own sister-in-law even helped. They took her out and she met men. She met him."

"No, I didn't do anything," Delilah cried. "It was all harmless fun. I swear."

Pulling her tighter to him, he silenced her and looked at Alex. "That bag with the earring there contains the proof I needed to know she was sleeping with him. There he was at Diamanti's bragging that night about the hot piece who'd lost her earring as he was…"

He stopped talking and cleared his throat. "I bought her those earrings. Diamond earrings she picked out herself and said she had to have them. See how she cared for them? I couldn't let him treat them like that. Treat us like that."

"I get it, Dr. Roberts. I wouldn't be able to deal with my wife running around on me. I get it," Alex said in that same calm voice that hadn't worked before.

Now, though, it seemed to make Alan Roberts want to get what he'd done off his chest. He sighed loudly and said, "I listened to him brag about what he'd done and heard he was staying at the Hotel Piermont. Just the thought of my wife being at that place made my stomach turn. I struck up a conversation with him and told him I was staying at the same hotel. I listened to him talk about how he had hooked up with some woman in the next town for months but wanted some new blood."

Alan cringed and stopped talking for a moment before he said, "That's what he called the woman I loved. New blood. For hours I listened to his stories until I offered him a ride back to the hotel and when he took it, I knew what I had to do. He was sober, so I knew I'd have only one chance. I walked him up to his room and told him goodnight. Then I waited. I gave him long enough to get changed out of his suit and then returned to his room. He was surprised to see me, but he let me in. Why not, right? It's not like he couldn't take me, if he had to."

"And then you stabbed him in the exact place where you knew he'd bleed to death."

Dr. Roberts nodded, affirming what Alex had said, and added, "He never saw it coming. He was just standing there in the middle of the room watching something on the TV and still talking about the woman he'd had the night before, so I grabbed a knife that was sitting on the dresser and plunged it into him as hard as I could. He fell back against me, so I put him down on the desk chair and left him there to rot like the scum he was."

The whole room fell deathly silent as the reality of what Dr. Roberts had just confessed to settled into all our brains. Now that he'd explained how and why he did it, the bigger problem was his belief his wife had slept with the victim and his desire to kill her for it. I didn't know how Alex planned to get the gun away from him, but I worried if he didn't do it quickly, Delilah wouldn't be long for this world.

"I'm sure the DA will take into consideration all the extenuating circumstances," Alex said. "I just need you to let your wife go. You love her, so no matter what happened, you couldn't live with yourself if you killed her. Put the gun down and let her go."

Alan Roberts listened to what Alex said and tears filled his eyes. "I wish I didn't love her, but I do. Still."

He looked down at his wife as she cried and then pushed her toward the couch before turning the gun on himself. In a second, my fear for her evaporated as I watch him pull the trigger and collapse on the floor.

"Poppy, get her! Craig, get an ambulance here now!" Alex barked as he ran over to where Dr. Roberts lay on the rug surrounded by a pool of blood from his wound.

I raced to help Delilah onto the couch and held her close as she cried out for Alex to tell her if the man she loved was dead. We sat there waiting for him to answer for so long I was sure Alan was dead, but Alex turned to look at me and nodded.

"He shot himself in the shoulder. I don't think it'll be fatal."

As he attended to his murderer and I rocked Delilah back and forth while she cried about how all she wanted to do was have a little fun and never meant to hurt anyone, the ambulance siren wailed outside announcing its arrival. My heart went out to her. I didn't think she ever wanted to do anything more than just have some fun and laughs with friends. Her husband's jealousy had made it out to be something more, something sinister. Jealousy did that once it wormed its way into the brain.

Chapter Twenty

Alex's text had told me to meet him at my father's bar, but the crowd at McGuire's made finding anyone difficult. It looked like everyone in Sunset Ridge had piled into the main room to watch the All-Star game. I stood on my toes to try to see over the crowd, but all I saw were men's necks.

A male voice called out, "Poppy, we're back here!" and I followed the sound to the very back table where I'd sat with Delilah just days earlier to find Alex, Derek, and Craig sitting there.

"Is this a boy's club thing or can a girl join in?" I joked as I dragged a chair over to make a fourth.

"Alex here tells me you were key to solving this murder case," Derek said in his most serious way. "I'm thinking I might have to deputize you, Poppy."

Excited by the idea, I asked, "Can you?"

Derek shook his head and chuckled. "I was just kidding, but he did say you were invaluable."

I couldn't help but feel crestfallen and sighed. "Well, I guess there's that."

Alex lifted his glass to make a toast and we all followed his lead, lifting our glasses above the center of the table. "To Poppy, the only person out of all of us who can get anyone in this town to spill their secrets."

"To Poppy!" Derek and Craig cheered as we clanked our glasses together.

"That's why you keep me around. I know how it is," I said, half-joking but wishing I wasn't.

Derek stood from his chair and patted me on the shoulder. "My bad judgment that I didn't figure that out earlier. Duty calls, so I'll leave you guys to celebrate."

I knew by the look in his eyes he thought there was something going on between Alex and me. If I thought it would make a difference, I'd have told him how wrong he was. But it didn't matter. I knew that.

"I have to go too, but thanks for bringing some excitement into my day," Craig said as he downed the last of his beer.

"Are you drinking before going back to work?" I asked in surprise, sure he wouldn't do something like that being the straight arrow he was.

Grinning, he shook his head. "You know me, Poppy. No, I have a date tonight. This pretty girl who works at the Hotel Piermont heard me talking last night at Diamanti's about how we got the murderer and came right up to me to ask me out. So I'll see you two later."

Craig left for his date, and turning to look at Alex, I wondered aloud, "I hope he's ready for her. I think Elizabeth Freely has some tricks up her sleeve he might not be old enough for."

"Naughty and Spice tricks?" Alex said with that sexy smile I both hated and adored.

"Yeah. I'm not sure he's up for them."

"I wouldn't worry. He's young. He'll recover, and at least he'll have a good memory for his trouble."

The crowd cheered a homerun, drowning out any

conversation between us for a few minutes. When they calmed down, Alex had finished his drink and stood from the table to get another.

"Want one? My treat," he offered.

I drank my beer quickly, giving me a head rush, and handed him the glass. "Your treat? What's the occasion, Officer Montero?"

"The best reason to celebrate. Another case solved with my partner."

I liked how that sounded. Loving the idea of celebrating with him, I stared up into his relaxed face and said, "Well, since it's a big day, I'll have what you're having."

Surprised at my choice of drink, he winked at me. "Two scotches it is. I'll be right back."

Knowing I had a few minutes at least for my beer rush to dissipate, I sat back and watched him disappear into the crowd. We did have reason to celebrate. We'd solved another murder case, and even though things had been rocky between us for a while there, we came through it as partners in the end.

"I hear congratulations are in order."

I turned to see my father sitting down where Derek had sat. He wore an expression that told me he wanted to say more, so I leaned over and kissed his cheek. "I thought you were up behind the bar tonight, Dad. Is something up that you're back here with me?"

"Nope. I have a bartender tonight, so I thought I'd come back and steal some time with my daughter before her partner comes back."

The bar wasn't that dark that I couldn't see his eyes, and in them I knew I saw concern. "What's wrong, Dad? You look worried."

He hesitated for a moment and then nodded, as if he'd resigned himself to say what was on his mind, regardless of how much he wished he didn't have to. "I was just wondering how you're going to be if your friend stops in tonight to join you and Alex."

Leave it to my father to know that it would bother me if Bethany stopped in during our celebration. While that was true, I was seeing things differently after the past few days.

"I'll be fine. No need to worry about me camping out in the stockroom tonight."

"Okay. I just wanted to make sure. I don't like seeing you like that, Poppy."

"Like what?" I asked, trying to brush off how upset I was that night, even though I knew he knew full well how much it bothered me to see Alex and Bethany together.

"Jealous."

I'd seen more jealousy than I liked in this case, so there was no way I wanted to have it in my own life too. But his mention of it did remind me to ask about his story, which had been on my mind since he'd told me about his friend and Cherie.

"I can't stop thinking about what you told me, Dad. I wonder whatever happened to your friend. I hope it ended up better than it did for Delilah and Dr. Roberts."

He gave me one of his broad Irish smiles and took my hand in his to give it a gentle squeeze. "It did. He ended up marrying the most wonderful woman in the world and having a beautiful baby girl. The only thing that worries him is his daughter is a little too much like him when it comes to being jealous."

My father's words confused me for a moment, and

then it all dawned on me. "You're the friend? You told me that story because you were worried that I was going to do something out of jealousy. I knew it!"

"I worry about you, Poppy, and I know you care for Alex more than you admit."

"Oh, Dad, you don't have to worry about me with that. He's in love with a ghost, and no Bethany or Poppy is going to change that any time soon. Save your worrying for my investigating crimes."

Alex returned with our drinks and sat down in his chair. Handing me my scotch, he said, "Should I leave? You two look like you're having a private conversation."

I shook my head. "No, it's okay. I was just telling my father if he's going to worry about me, he should save his concern for my solving cases with you. I really worried Alan Roberts was going to shoot the place up at some point. He definitely didn't seem like he was thinking straight."

My father's expression turned to one of horror. "I don't want to hear that, Poppy. You know I worry about that too."

Alex jumped in immediately to calm him. "You don't have to worry, Joe. I wouldn't let anyone hurt Poppy. I made sure to shield her as soon as he pulled the gun. Her safety means the world to me."

I saw my father relax and he thanked Alex for keeping me safe and sound. As he stood from the table to leave, he kissed my cheek and whispered, "I think those ghosts are on their way out, honey."

Whatever my father thought he was seeing, it wasn't there. I didn't know what Alex planned to do about Bethany, but I had promised her I'd speak to him. Now seemed like as good a time as any, so I took a big gulp of my drink and as it warmed my insides on its way down to my stomach, I tried to find the words to begin, even if I didn't want to hear the answer.

"I know it's none of my business and I don't mean to pry into your personal life again like I did when we were in the car waiting for the judge, but I was wondering what's happening with Bethany."

The words tumbled out of my mouth like when I didn't like the taste of something I'd eaten and I spit it out. I'd hoped to be smoother than that, but maybe my father was right.

For his part, Alex looked like he'd almost expected me to ask about her. There was no surprise in his eyes. If anything, they looked sad.

"You're not prying, Poppy. It's just that I wish I had a good answer for you."

He took a sip of his drink and carefully placed his glass down on the table before he continued. "I thought I was ready to get into a relationship again, but I was wrong. I'm not."

Once again, that part of me that was nothing less than pure evil rejoiced at hearing him say he wasn't ready to be serious with Bethany. It was wrong and I knew it, but it didn't change how I felt deep inside where that jealous demon lived in me.

"Oh. Okay. It's okay if you don't want to say anything more about it."

He took another sip and sighed. "It's been a long time since Helena died. Everyone said I'd be able to move on, but when I didn't, they didn't understand. So I left Baltimore and came here. I've spent years living alone and thought I'd be content with that. Then you came along and all that got upended."

I couldn't help but smile every time he described that night he founded me skulking around his house like some cat burglar in a way that made it seem like I'd gone there specifically to change his life. "That's my thing. Upending lives one at a time."

"It's what you did, Poppy. You walked into my life and I couldn't stop thinking about what you said after you left."

I chuckled at his delicate description of that night. "You mean after you ran me off with a gun."

He missed my attempt at a joke and remained serious. "I don't think I realized how much I'd closed myself off from the rest of the world until you showed up. I owe you more than you can ever know for that."

"I didn't do anything, Alex. That was all you. I just trespassed on a guy's property because I wanted his help to solve a murder. You did everything else with you."

Alex shook his head. "Not true. I'm not sure anyone else in the world could have roused me from that life of living but not living. You gave me purpose for my life again, something I hadn't had in a long time, and it's because of you that I don't spend every hour of my day alone in that house."

His words made my heart clench. I had no idea when I met him that he'd been through such sadness and loss. If I had, I might have stayed away because I knew what it was like to suffer through losing someone like that.

"I'm just happy you didn't shoot me and you wanted to work with me. Don't forget that I'm not a cop like you."

He raised his nearly empty glass for another toast. "To my partner, who helped bring me back to the job I love."

I touched my glass to his and gave my own toast in honor of him. "To my partner, the best in the world."

We drank our scotch and stayed silent as the bar erupted into cheers at another homerun. When it returned to a noise level that didn't require us to scream over their voices, he placed his empty glass on the table and answered my original question.

"I don't know if it's fair to her, but I'm going to keep seeing her even though I'm not ready for what she wants. I've told her I don't want anything serious, though."

I didn't have anything to say to that. I understood not wanting to be alone. I did. I just wished he didn't want to be alone with me instead of her.

"I'm sure she'll understand," I said quietly, grasping for anything to say so he wouldn't think I was bothered by what he'd just told me.

"What about you?"

"What about me what?" I asked in return, sure he'd seen how much I hated the idea of him with her written all over my face, despite my attempt at hiding it.

"Our police chief couldn't have a bigger crush on you. Why haven't you ever gotten together with him?"

Every memory of Derek from school ran through my mind, making me smile and probably look like I loved the idea of being with him. "Derek and me? He's not my type."

"Why?" Alex asked, more interested in my private life than ever before. It must have been the effect of the alcohol.

I shrugged and tried to find the words that would let me keep my secret while telling the truth. Finally, I said,

"I like a man who's my opposite. Derek isn't. He's very much like me."

Alex's eyes lit up and with that grin that never failed to make me feel like my insides were melting, he said, "Opposite, huh? Interesting."

I felt my cheeks warm into a blush at his comment and feared I hadn't been very successful at keeping my feelings for him a secret. He looked into my eyes like he was searching for some answer to a question only he knew, and even though I wanted to look away, I couldn't. A few more talks like this, just the two of us together over a few drinks, and nothing I felt would stay hidden for much longer.

Part of me wished that day would come soon, but another part of me was more frightened of that day than any gun waved at me because that day might be the last we spent together as partners.

For now, though, we were Alex and Poppy, partners in crime. And he owed me dinner at Diamanti's.

"So about that bet. Ready to pay up?" I asked with a chuckle.

Alex smiled and finished his drink. "I can't think of anything I'd rather do tonight than enjoy a great dinner with my partner. Let's see if we can get a table at Diamanti's. I'm in the mood for steak."

Poppy and Alex return in Top of The Hour:
A Poppy McGuire Mystery
(Poppy McGuire Mysteries #3)

About The Author

Anina Collins has always loved a good mystery. From Agatha Christie's Hercule Poirot to Sir Arthur Conan Doyle's famous detective Sherlock Holmes to Dan Brown's intrepid Professor Robert Langdon, she's spent some of her favorite reading times with mystery novels. When she's not writing her favorite mystery couple, she can be found watching entirely too much Supernatural and dreaming about the beach.

Visit Anina's Facebook page at facebook.com/Anina-Collins-429334270597293 for news about her books, along with giveaways and other fun stuff!

And sign up for her newsletter today for exclusive news first! Visit her website at aninacollins.com for more details.

Books by Anina Collins:
The Eleventh Hour (Poppy McGuire Mysteries #1)
After Hours (Poppy McGuire Mysteries #2)
Top of the Hour (Poppy McGuire Mysteries #3)

And look for the next book in the series, **The Darkest Hour (Poppy McGuire Mysteries #4)**, coming JULY 2016!